A SW

TO THE THORAX

A SWIFT KICK TO THE THORAX
Copyright © 2022 Mara Lynn Johnstone

Contact Info: www.MaraLynnJohnstone.com

Cover Design by: Mara Lynn Johnstone
Author Photo by: Mara Lynn Johnstone

ISBN: 979-8-218-08807-1 (paperback)
979-8-218-08810-1 (ebook)

First Edition: 2022
Reality Collision Publishing

A SWIFT KICK
TO THE THORAX

Reality Collision Publishing

ALSO BY
MARA LYNN JOHNSTONE

Spectacular Silver Earthling
(science fiction novel)

We're the Weird Aliens
(science fiction anthology)
(edited and contributed)

Sweeping Changes
(fantasy novel)

Dedicated to the child I was, who wanted to be a veterinarian, but also to meet fantastical creatures and visit other worlds. This adventure's for you.

Chapter 1
(Robin)

Of all the things I expected to find under a hedge on an alien world, a rabbit didn't even make the list. Rabbits weren't allowed. Cats and dogs were barely allowed, and that was with all the screening, breeding, and training that Earth could muster. Nothing from our planet was going to cause problems for our new trade partners.

Nothing except for this rabbit, doing its best to hide among the greenery as if it didn't stick out like a cotton ball in a salad. It was even a fluffy Angora breed, all wispy white fur with a dark face and feet, like it was wearing a sweater. This was a high-maintenance pet. It did not belong here. Judging by the fast breathing and the whites showing around its eyes, it knew that as well as I did.

"Can you catch it?" asked one of the turtledillo children behind me. The two of them were watching from a distance, worried that it was dangerous. They had flagged me down on my way to lunch, reasoning that the best person to deal with an alien on the loose was another alien.

"I should be able to," I said, keeping my voice gentle. "These little guys are fast, and this one looks scared. It won't hurt you." I shifted position to reach farther into the cool shade. No smell of rabbit pee yet, just good clean dirt. "It might bite *me* since I'm the one going after it, but that wouldn't even get through your armor."

The turtledillos (properly called Rockbacks, though Earthlings agree they resemble an armadillo-turtle cross) shifted uneasily on scaly feet, each clutching their four hands together into anxious bundles. Their turtley beaks were shut tightly on the many other questions I'm sure they had. These two were probably siblings, given the identical size, mannerisms, and similar whorls of lavender paint on their shells. I would have liked to ask their names and introduce myself properly ("Robin Bennett, human extraordinaire and Earth animal expert; what can I do for you?"), but there was a higher priority right now.

"Hey there, bunny bunny," I cooed in English. "Let's go somewhere safe, yeah?"

It kicked up its heels and was gone in a spray of leaves.

"Argh." I crawled backwards out of the hedge, ducking low to keep my braid from getting stuck on the rough twigs. "Or you could make me chase you. Just what I wanted to do." Switching back to Rockback as I stood to my full height, I asked the kids, "Can you stand by the gate and make sure it doesn't get out?"

They vowed to guard it well, making a four-handed salute and standing as tall as they could (not even waist height on me) before scampering off toward the gate.

I wished them luck and began cheating at the hedge maze. The rectangular shrubbery reminded me of a boxwood from my grandma's neighborhood, just trimmed for a shorter species who didn't want to get completely lost. And something low enough for a turtledillo to see over is easy for a six-foot-tall human woman to step over.

Not entirely dignified, mind you, but easy. I made a series of long-legged hops in the direction the rabbit had gone, eyes searching for flashes of white. Nothing. I changed tactics and dashed for the low stone wall at the edge of the maze. With a vault I was proud of, I landed on top of it to survey the maze.

Exclamations of surprise came from the turtledillo pedestrians on the other side. They'd just seen one of the tall aliens appear out of nowhere, which had to be startling. With my pale skin, brown hair, and greeny-beige work clothes, I was a normal enough sight back home but the strangest of beings here. Especially crouching on top of a wall like this.

"Sorry," I said. "Don't mind me. Just needed to get a

better view. Have a good day!" With a cheery wave, I stood up and made a show of peering out over the hedge maze that passed for a public park. Hovercars puttered by. Distant honks echoed from further out in the city, more lower-pitched than the ones back home. Warm sunlight and a gentle breeze were more Earthlike than they had any right to be, right down to the faint smell of seaweed drifting in from the bay. This capital city was a lovely place. Except for one troublesome rabbit.

There, a tuft of white. Way the heck over on the other side already.

I took off jogging along the wall, which prompted more surprised chatter from the pedestrians, then when I reached a connecting pathway, I jumped down. The rabbit heard me coming, and thus began a merry chase.

It was fast, like only a terrified prey animal can be: skittering across paving stones and twisting to dive through thin spots in the hedge. It left bits of silky fur on some of the twigs. I hated to scare it like this, but if I waited for it to calm down, I might never find it. And I was so sure I could grab it. I kept being wrong.

The lunge that got the closest was near the sidewall of the maze, which was wooden instead of the stone that lined the street. It was a strange kind of wood, as so many things here were, looking like enormous brown blades of grass that had been transmogrified into wooden planks. They overlapped instead of fitting perfectly side-by-side. There was a gap at the bottom just the size for a rabbit to fit through.

"No, no, no — Dang it, come back here and let me rescue you!" I stopped, winded. The rabbit ignored me.

Well, fine. This wall was higher than the other one, but nothing I couldn't handle. I considered jogging back toward the street and trying to enter from there, but I liked my odds with this crooked tree better. It was right up against the fence, along with others providing shade, and its trunk tilted at the perfect angle for running up.

Never one to turn down an opportunity for parkour

on a workday, I went for it and was among the branches in seconds. The view on the other side of the fence held an open courtyard with scattered tables, chairs, and surprised turtledillos eating lunch. I waved again.

"Hi there. Did a small fluffy animal just run by here?"

Many three-fingered hands pointed away from the fence. Several voices asked if it was dangerous.

"Nope, just scared and fast. Excuse me." I got my feet over the fence and dropped to land carefully, collapsing like an accordion and slapping the ground to disperse momentum away from my joints. I hadn't injured myself, and I hadn't stepped in anyone's food. Full marks.

And it gave the locals an exciting story to tell, which was always a plus.

I sprang up, rubbing my stinging palms, and trotted in the direction they'd indicated. This led to another branch of the outdoor eatery, where the air was spicy with the smell of foods made for people who ate a lot of bugs. A familiar scent by now. The turtledillos here were eager to direct me further.

I repeated my assurance that they didn't need to fear for their safety. I privately hoped that this was the only mysterious animal around, and that I wasn't lying to them. What *was* the rabbit doing here?

Answers would have to wait. Capture first. I followed the pointing claws toward the closest thing to a dark corner: behind a pair of trash cans. I approached quietly, crouching to look for the white fur. Yep, there it was, holding perfectly still and hyperventilating something fierce, with its face pressed into a corner as if that would hide it better. Poor thing. The cans smelled like rotten spicy-bug-food too, which surely made the experience worse. I gently leaned a knee against the trash can on the left, so the rabbit couldn't wriggle past, then dove between the cans to get a double fistful of wild fur.

The rabbit bucked and kicked in my hands, but I managed to wrap it in my shirt and hold it close. It huddled against my chest with its heart beating wildly.

I spoke the traditional soothing words of my people. "There, there, you're okay. Good bunny. Please don't pee on me. Let's get you home."

When I got to my feet, the air filled with hearty applause (which sounds different coming from scaly hands). I bobbed my head in body language that was close enough to a bow for either culture, and I reminded them that they were safe. "I'd better get this guy some rest after all the excitement. Enjoy your meals!"

They thanked me, and I left feeling like a hero. The rabbit cooperated, despite flinching at a loud hovertruck engine on the road. I took the sidewalk back instead of trying to climb the fence with my arms full. It was a short enough walk; I'd swing by the front entrance of the maze to tell the kids that I'd caught it, then cross the street and leg it back to base.

The kids saw me coming. They ran up all excited like I'd expected, but instead of asking to see the exotic Earth animal, they said something else.

"More of them!" they said, pointing back into the maze. "Lots more!"

Chapter 2
(Robin)

"Show me," I said, with my grip firm on the rabbit. The alien kids hurried back in the other direction, and I followed on my long human legs. The rabbit pressed its head into the crook of my arm like that could shut out the world. I tried to walk gently.

The kids led the way into the park, past the entrance to the maze portion, and farther on to a wide meadow. The grass was sky blue and smelled faintly of cinnamon, but otherwise, it was a familiar kind of lovely.

And it was full of rabbits. The kids tried to whisper, but the rabbits heard them anyway. Ears popped up across the meadow, even in places that I didn't think they could have reached, and in an instant, the quiet scene transformed into a stampeding herd of hind feet and fluffy tails. Then they were gone into the underbrush.

"Hooboy," I muttered, sniffing the cinnamon-scented breeze. Could the rabbits eat alien grass safely? Had they already tried?

The kids apologized for startling the herd, rattling the claws of their lower hands against leg scales in agitation and spreading their upper hands in a placating gesture.

"It's okay," I said in their language. "Thank you for telling me about this. I'll go get some people to catch them all. If you want to help more, you can stay and try to keep them from going out into the maze."

The kids jumped at the chance, insisting that they had nowhere else important to be. I wondered about that, given their age, but I'll admit I had bigger worries on my mind. Their next assertion helped.

"The rest of the family is meeting us here soon. They can help too!"

"Excellent," I told them. "Fantastic. Remember that they won't bite you unless they feel like they're trapped in a corner, and they run *very* fast. I'll be back as soon as I can."

I made my exit, the first rabbit still held close, and I spent a moment being glad the meadow was near to where I worked.

Then I spent a longer moment being worried, because it would look suspicious enough to have a swarm of escaped Earth animals somewhere on the planet, much less within hopping distance of the Earth embassy.

We didn't have any rabbits to lose. Where had they come from, and was it designed to make us look bad? Because it definitely would.

And what are we gonna do if we can't catch them all? I thought as I speed-walked. I knew full well what kind of havoc a bunch of rabbits could wreak on an ecosystem, especially if they were capable of making more baby rabbits. Every animal brought here through the official channels had been sterilized and screened for all possible ailments. I went down the list of potential problems, and did NOT like the outlook.

The part of the Embassy compound that held the vet office loomed in front of me in all its gray-blue, human-sized glory, and not a moment too soon. The rabbit in my arms had started to squirm. It was all I could do to keep it under wraps as I hip-checked my way through the front doors into cooler sanitized air.

"Crisis!" I called out to the receptionist. "Inexplicable swarm of bunnies in the park! All hands on deck, cuz this is a *problem!*"

Jasmeet straightened up in alarm. "No kidding!" he agreed, grabbing the phone and stabbing buttons with slim brown fingers. "Go on through. Does it look alien at all? No chance it's some bizarre coincidence?"

I shook my head, walking quickly. "Pretty sure it's a Jersey Wooly."

He waved me through the doors, already talking into the phone. I took the appropriate hallway, glad that most of the doors here were easy to open without a free hand.

Shoulder the swinging door, elbow the handle — get a better grip on the rabbit — then kick this one until somebody opens it. I tried to kick politely.

"Hello! I have an armful of rabbit for you, with more on the way!"

Karina swung the door wide, her blonde hair tied back and her eyes wide. "Jasmeet just called," she said as I walked past with the agitated rabbit. "Where the hell did rabbits come from? We didn't bring any!"

"I know. Weird, right?" I grunted, struggling. "Where do you want this guy?"

She shut the door and unlatched a wall cage for me just in time. The rabbit was kicking free by the time I made it over, and the fuzzball managed to jump into the cage. I slammed the door with a little more force than necessary.

"Sorry," I apologized to both of them for the clang. "Anyways," I said, straightening up and checking my shirt for pee. All was dry, but a couple of raisin-sized poop pellets tumbled to the floor. "Great."

"I'll clean it up," Karina said. "Sounds like you have more to catch?"

"Yeah, there's over a dozen hopping around the park," I said with a vague wave. "I don't know yet if the problem is big, huge, or catastrophic."

"Well, keep your phone handy," she suggested. "I'll call you if this one tests positive for any problems you should know about."

"Sounds good. Here's hoping it's not pregnant or carrying a plague. Or fleas. We've been so careful about fleas!"

Karina agreed wholeheartedly, gathering supplies for her inspection. I bid her goodbye and left the room. Outside, I paused only to get a good palmful of hand sanitizer from the dispenser on the wall.

I followed checkerboard linoleum to the launch bay

where we kept everything from catch-poles to cage trucks. With a detour toward the vending machine that would have to substitute for lunch, I strode in with several energy bars and a juice bottle in hand.

Three coworkers had beaten me there.

"Hello!" said Reed the turtledillo. "Tell us about these rabbits." He was tall for his species, but only chest height to the two humans he stood with. His shell paint favored pale greens and browns in a pattern that was the equivalent of classy businesswear. Paul and Anne wore the human version.

"They are fast and numerous," I replied. "You know what a rabbit looks like, right?" I didn't think the subject came up much in Reed's experience as the lead person in charge of matching Earth pets with prospective owners.

Reed nodded. "Yes, I just brushed up on that section of the handbook. I assume we'll want the nets to catch them."

Anne snorted. "And some caffeine, and luck. Guess my lunch will have to wait." She rested fists on wide hips with an expression that said she was ready to tackle the challenge. Anne enjoyed challenges. Her brown hair was shorter than mine, like the rest of her, and her skin was the sort of pale that wanted to be darker with just a bit more sun. She spent all her time indoors, solving problems.

"I will happily put off the sedated tooth-cleaning I was about to do," Paul said, tugging on his favorite red baseball cap and going for the supplies. He had tan skin, dark hair, and a great love of complaining. I could tell that this crisis would get the appropriate amount of sass with these two around. "We'll want nets and gloves so we don't lose a finger. You said they're in the park? Is that the one just down the road?"

"Yeah, which feels suspicious," I said. "Like somebody's trying to smear our reputation."

"They'd better not," Anne said. She stomped toward the net-poles in a way that said she wanted to threaten some hypothetical troublemaker with one.

"We can address that possibility once we've captured the animals," Reed declared. "Let's get as many cages into the big truck as we have on hand."

A fine idea. After a few hurried minutes of packing, we all clambered into the hovertruck and hit the road. Anne drove while Reed sat on a booster seat and gave directions. Paul looked for rabbits. I shoved food into my mouth, fully aware of how short the drive was. The fact that my fingers smelled like hand sanitizer didn't bother me the way it once would have. This was simply the reassuring scent of professional cleanliness now.

I had mostly finished by the time Anne found a parking space near the far entrance to the park. Several hovercars were settled into the neighboring spots with a handful of turtledillos there to watch as we piled out of the truck. Our clothes had the same logo as the enormous human-scale vehicle did, as if there was any doubt what our job was. The majority of the humans on the planet lived in this capital city, and the majority of those worked with the sanctioned Earth animals.

We were here now for the unsanctioned ones. I lost no time in explaining that to the onlookers, to prepare them in case a little alien beastie rocketed across their path soon.

"If you see a small animal that doesn't belong, will you kindly let us know?" I asked the assembled strangers. "There are some lost in the park. They won't bite unless you try to grab them, and that's our job."

The bystanders agreed. They kept their distance, though several watched as we entered the park with nets and cages. I carried one of each. The cage bumped my leg, and the net-pole was a tripping hazard if I didn't watch the end of it — if only that was my biggest concern for the day.

This part of the maze must have been designed by a different person than the other: soft hedge walls with green, heart-shaped leaves rose high enough that I could barely see over them, and they made a barrier all the way to the ground. Smooth paving stones lined a path that turned corners repeatedly as if designed to make people lost. I hadn't been here before. Maybe this entrance was the hard mode.

My thoughts were interrupted by the sound of claws scrabbling on the pathway ahead of me. I shoved the cage into a hedge, wielding the net like a broadsword.

"Incoming!" I said as three speedy furballs rocketed around the corner.

I actually managed to net two at once, purely because they ran into each other in their panic. The third one flashed past, and Paul and Anne exclaimed about it behind me. I focused on the thrashing rabbits in my net — they were liable to hurt each other if I wasn't careful. Keeping them above the ground, I twisted the net so they had less space to kick each other. Then I wrestled the cage out of the bush.

Both in the same cage, or go back for another?

As I thought it, Reed appeared with a spare cage. I thanked him, and the pair of us wrangled the rabbits into separate cages without losing either. It was a near thing. The big brown one was merely fidgety, while the smaller gray one grunted urgently at us. Not a happy sound from a rabbit. I let Reed grab that one, since his hands were tougher than mine, even with the gloves.

Anne and Paul had managed their one capture by the time I turned to look: the feisty little white one spun in the cage, searching for an exit.

We exchanged a collective *whew*. Reed and Paul took the three cages back to the truck while Anne and I followed the path toward the meadow. A warm cinnamon-scented breeze blew. It was a lovely sunny day full of problems.

By the time we exited the maze to see the field of waving blue grass, multiple voices ahead of us chattered with concern. I was too worried about what might be happening to make any jokes for Anne about bluegrass music, which I'd planned on.

We stepped out to behold a handful of turtledillos, all trying vainly to herd the rabbits toward the center of the field. A couple of them held fabric that looked like picnic tablecloths. Probably the kids' family, come to meet them as promised, and taking it upon themselves to catch the wayward Earth animals.

The rabbits were having none of it. In that moment, while we watched, a good half-dozen scattered past the tablecloths and into the nearest bush. Judging by the number of other bounding shapes, there were more in this meadow than I'd thought.

"The humans are here!" shouted a young voice from across the field. Every head turned to greet us as all-knowing saviors. A camera drone with a newscaster's logo floated above.

No pressure.

We did our best, striding forward with confidence and net-poles to coordinate the tumult. Reed directed our willing volunteers out into a wider ring to hopefully drive the rabbits back into a central area without stranding them in the open just yet. Other curious locals drifted in, and their assistance was most welcome.

"This one's not running!" someone called.

I hurried over to find a large turtledillo woman hovering near a small black rabbit, which was indeed sprawled on the grass, panting. The white of its eyes stood out against its dark coat.

"It just fell down!" the woman was saying, "I didn't even touch it! Is it okay?"

"Let me see," I said, putting down my net and approaching carefully. The rabbit barely flinched at my touch. I held it down gently, prodding for injuries and finding none. It let me pick it up. "I think it's just tired," I said, tucking it into my shirt like its predecessor. "And probably thirsty. I'd better get it back to the truck. Will you make sure nothing happens to this?" I asked with a nod at my net-pole.

"Of course!" the woman said, taking up a position beside it with the alert posture of a security guard.

I thanked her and whipped through more cinnamon grass on my way back to the street. Halfway there, I passed

Anne waiting like a lacrosse goalie with her net-pole while some of the locals tromped around on the other side of a bush. She nodded at me as I left the field.

Back at the truck, I deposited the rabbit into a nice cool cage equipped with a water bottle. To my relief, the rabbit started drinking right away. I grabbed two portable cages and jogged back. There were a lot more where that one came from, and dehydrated or not, these rabbits were fast little bastards.

But we caught them. One at a time, slowly, and with great difficulty, we caught them.

Under bushes. In tall grass. Behind benches, trying to climb low trees, and pressed vainly into corners with the hope that we wouldn't see them. They were everywhere, and they were fast, but we kept at it.

By the time the sun was low in the sky, the wild chase had devolved into a quiet hunt through dark corners for stubborn holdouts. The black ones were the hardest to spot, though most of those had already succumbed to heat exhaustion and been picked up. The white ones were most eye-catching, and the brown ones didn't quite blend in the way they would among Earth plants. That left the gray ones the color of shadows as the most successful players of hide-and-seek.

"Too bad we don't have any good-smelling food to put out for them," I remarked to Anne in passing. "I haven't seen any bites taken out of the smelly grass, and I have no idea if they can eat the local fruit."

She grunted in agreement, looking tired.

I pulled a squashed energy bar from my pocket and threw it at her. "Catch."

Anne fumbled it a little, then laughed when she saw what it was. "Thanks." She didn't argue, tearing open the package and biting off a mouthful. "Mmf. I needed that. Do you want some?" She offered me the bar.

I shook my head. "I had one in the truck. And it looks like we may be done soon."

"I sure hope so," Anne said, taking another bite. "Let's

check that back wall again. We never did figure out where they came from, and there are plenty of bushes that could hide a hole."

I agreed with this logic. We headed over, pausing to say goodbye to the first two kids and their family. I thanked them for staying as long as they did. The parents insisted it was their pleasure, something the children would remember for the rest of their lives. All four were there, a standard family unit in turtledillo society: four children, hatched from four eggs, each named in the order that they were hatched (Primus, Secunda, etc.). What with that and the four arms, the number four was a popular one around here.

"Have a great day!" I said as the family left. "Come by the facility for a tour sometime after things settle down!"

"We will! Thank you!" They waved and disappeared into the maze. That left the field feeling very empty since not many other volunteers had stuck around. But most of the work was done.

Anne and I strolled through the quiet shade along the back wall. Trees on the other side were tall enough to cast diagonal shadows from the setting sun, which I appreciated, sweaty as I was after all the running and shouting. We inspected the wall — more of those same huge-blades-of-grass wooden planks, though in multiple tight layers this time, with no holes that I could see. But Anne was right about the bushes: they covered a lot of the wall. More than enough places for a hole to be hiding. We kept looking.

Anne jerked back in surprise as something orange flashed past. I reached for it, but it dodged and sprinted down the path to run improbably *up the wall* before disappearing behind a tall shrub.

We stared.

"That didn't move like a rabbit," Anne said first.

"You're right," I said. "I have the sneaking suspicion that was a cat."

"Where did it go?"

The answer, we found when we pulled back the shrub, was "through that hole we couldn't find." The planks of the wall were broken here. By the looks of things, a tree had fallen on the other side and gone unnoticed, thanks to the bush. A stub of branch as thick as my ribcage stuck out into the greenery, smelling of cut wood instead of cinnamon. This was high enough for hungry rabbits to jump down from. But only a cat could make it back up and out.

"Can you see what's on the other side?" Anne asked. I fought the bush, finally managing to push in to where I could stick my head through the hole. Twigs jabbed me in the ribs.

"It's a forest," I told her, "Or somebody's private park. It looks pretty wild." I'd learned early on that turtledillo cities were more Swiss-cheese-patterned than the ones I was used to, with roads that wound between patches of private land. Regular folks lived in the equivalent of suburbs and single-story apartment blocks, but the wealthy Rockbacks had little walled-off territories. Some not so little. This one looked huge.

"Are there any roads?" Anne wanted to know.

"Not that I can see," I told her. "It's all dark and bushy, without much that would appeal to a rabbit. Our side must glow like an oasis from over there. Wait—" I edged forward as my eyes adjusted to the dimness. "Okay, there's the cat. It is indeed a housecat. No collar. Orange tabby, probably came from wherever all these rabbits did. It's walking down the other end of the fallen tree. Here, kitty kitty!" I raised my voice in hopes of coaxing it back.

Heads popped up from several directions.

"Ohh crap."

"What? More cats?"

"You want the bad news or the bad news?" I asked, staring.

"What is it?"

"It's cats. And more rabbits. And a dog. And something with stripes in the distance that I want to say is a zebra."

"What the *hell?*"

"Yeah. And here I thought we'd get to go home soon."

Chapter 3
(Robin)

As it turned out, we did get to go home, but not for the reason I'd hoped. When I called back to report this latest wrinkle, I was told in no uncertain terms that the forest was Off Limits. No stepping foot past the wall for any reason.

"Why?" I asked. Beside me, Anne gestured for me to explain the one-sided conversation. I held up a hand for her to wait. "Is it dangerous?"

"Only in the legal sense," Jasmeet told me. "Property law here is vicious. Without permission, it would be like starting a war."

I really should have known that. "So let's get permission!"

"Working on it," he said. "Come on back if you're done. We just got reports about two other loose animals, and we've sent a team out. This isn't looking good. People think it's our fault."

"I was afraid of that," I said. I ended the call and told Anne the further bad news. She complained while I did my best to wedge the broken fence bits back into place. Still going strong on the way back to the truck, she only paused to say goodbye to the remaining locals as we passed. Reed and Paul didn't have to ask before Anne brought them into the loop.

"...I can't believe they think this is our fault. I mean, I can, but c'mon, *really?*" Anne griped as we all buckled in, getting blue cinnamon grass stains on the seats. "I hope we find the person responsible soon, cuz I have *words* for them."

She finished ranting so she could drive with the proper

amount of attention for a vehicle full of traumatized rabbits. I spent the ride watching out the windows for any signs of animals that shouldn't be there. Didn't spot any, but I did see a new mural going up that I'd missed earlier: a glorious galaxy-scape along the cobblestoned side of a bookstore. A pair of artists were sketching out spaceships with a distinctly Earthling design, soaring between octagonal windows and the low roof. That painting would be spectacular when it was done.

I hoped they didn't regret their choice of subjects.

When we rolled in to park, multiple assistants were waiting to help unload. More than a few people had been called in for extra shifts, so this wouldn't be all on the regular crew's overtime. It was a lot of cages and a lot of checkups. I was intensely grateful that we four didn't need to do all of it.

"Keep an eye on this one," I said, handing over the little black rabbit. "It might have been just heat exhaustion, but this guy collapsed like a cake in the sun." It seemed alert enough now. I crossed my fingers about germs and parasites.

Once the truck was empty, I went to check in with the boss before heading home. The next shift could handle the cleanup without me. They did it every day, whether or not there were umpteen strange animals to quarantine. I made sure to scrub my shoes on the antibacterial mud mat and grab more hand sanitizer as I left.

Chelle was in her office, just wrapping up a video call on the large wall screen. She had a body type that was more turtledillo-like than I would ever say out loud, the complexion of someone who lived indoors, steely gray hair and, currently, a matching expression.

"Thanks for checking," she said to the screen, waving me in. "Goodbye."

"Good luck!" replied a female voice. Before the screen went blank, it held the improbable image of a human with waves of black hair drifting like she was underwater. A pencil floated past the camera. As she moved to grab it, someone behind her clung upside down to the back wall, digging into an open panel of high-tech controls. The screen blinked off.

I stared. "Was that the space station?" I asked. "What's up with their gravity?"

"Some glitch in that sector," Chelle said with a sigh. "They're apparently having trouble with hooligans fighting the cops and breaking things, which sounds like all kinds of fun, but they aren't missing any animals. I expected as much. But I had to check when I got the chance to reach a colleague. Now, how did it go catching bunnies?"

I gave her a rundown that she accepted with her usual calm, barely wrinkling her nose at the way I was probably making her office smell like incense. She thanked me for my hard work and said that all the relevant authorities were being contacted. Soon enough, she waved me out the door to go home. I didn't have to be told twice.

Tired though I was, I smiled when I reached the single-story parking garage that held my chosen mode of transportation: a turtledillo hoverchair, in the biggest size I could find without commissioning something special. It sat between regular cars like a prank. More than one coworker had asked if I wanted something more practical, but no, I did not.

I'd wanted a hoverchair since I'd first arrived and seen the locals zipping around on them like seated scooters. The things were designed for the short-legged turtledillos to sit while comfortably reaching the handlebars. But child-sized or not, the hoverchairs were great fun, so I made it work.

Specifically, I sat cross-legged on the beanbag seat and leaned back so my elbows didn't stick out sideways. Even exhausted and covered in scratches, it made me grin.

Dignified, no. But effective, yes. I sped out of the parking garage past slower cars, fully aware of the looks I was getting. I'm pretty sure that it was about the same level of absurdity as if a giraffe on Earth had taken to riding scooters. Or maybe one of those tiny fuel-efficient cars, with its head stuck out the roof. Yeah, it was probably about that silly.

But only if giraffes were normally thought of as solemn diplomats, I thought as I drove. *Giraffes are already a little bit silly. Every other local I talk to comments on how I'm not as serious as they expected. I guess if all they have to go on is the official videos, that does make sense.*

The trade agreement between our worlds was still a new thing. There was more interaction now than ever, but every human visitor went through rigorous screening and training, to make sure nobody screwed things up. We thought before we spoke, we were well-versed in local customs, and we made sure none of the Rockbacks would be insulted by the comparison to random fauna before any of us ever said "turtledillo" to them. A certain level of dignity just came with the territory.

But there's dignity, and then there's dignity, I thought as I took a corner at high speed, freeing a hand to make a cocky salute toward several young adults who were likely to appreciate the sight.

They did. I heard the exclamations as I drove away.

Surely that looked cooler than a giraffe, I thought. *Possibly approaching Gangly Dragon On A Motorcycle.*

As fun as this was, my thoughts danced around worries about the way our reputation could suffer from this bizarre animal situation. A new alliance was a fragile one. It was all I could do to stay upbeat while I drove.

Preoccupied, I navigated the roads toward the housing complex on the far side of the massive Earth Embassy. I could have taken internal roads to get there, but this was actually faster, not to mention more interesting. My first couple of weeks had been spent cooped up in buildings designed to be as human-friendly as possible. While they were that -- no short doorways to be found -- they were also deadly boring when there was a whole alien world outside to explore. I'd jumped at the chance to venture out as soon as I'd been allowed.

Now, I had full permission to go where I would. And I loved it. Seeing the sights and interacting with the locals was an endless joy, without fail.

I stopped at an intersection behind a pair of single-person hovercars, both painted a dark salmon pink. Everything here was familiar but different in the details, from the popular car colors (no white), to the traffic lights (symbols instead of colors), to the well-tended plantlife everywhere. A gardening crew was pruning a public fruit tree across the street, making sure those bushy green branches remained in easy reach when the next batch of redfruits grew in. The tiny fence around it — barely a handspan tall — made sure no fruits rolled into the road.

Other trees peeked over the low buildings farther ahead, planted just for the aesthetic. Looking upward around here gave me an excellent view of the sky, with just enough greenery to accent any cloud structures we had going. There were no canyons of skyscrapers here. If turtledillos needed extra space, they dug down instead of building up. And their structures weren't very tall to begin with.

Another car pulled in behind me, this one with the windows open and peppy music playing. I smiled at the tune. The driver immediately changed it to talk radio, and my smile was gone.

"Drone footage has caught sight of Earth animals that we don't know the name of yet," declared the radio. "Was this an exciting new shipment that they were about to announce to the public? Or something more sinister?"

It went downhill from there.

What is going ON? I thought. *Who could have even brought the animals here — a zebra, of all things! They must have some quality stasis chambers to keep that kind of finicky beast healthy.*

I knew that the spaceways were open to anyone, though we really were out in the boonies here. Only Terminus Space Station was a reasonable distance away. It was the nearest human habitation, our closest link to home.

And it was apparently plagued with gravity problems and riots against the cops. That wasn't normal either.

Is there a connection? I wondered as the light changed

from a diamond to a crescent, and the cars in front of me hummed away. *I hate not knowing. There's nothing I can do to fix this.*

I drove my scooter across the intersection with professional posture, not turning my head or giving a hint that I'd overheard the extremely loud radio. The air was full of flowers and distant music. This really was a lovely drive home. I wanted to keep doing this instead of getting sent back to Earth in disgrace as the whole alliance crumbled.

If only I knew what's happening at the space station, I thought. *Surely that would help.*

Chapter 4
(Jacinta)

Broken gravity controls weren't the worst thing I'd had to deal with in my time as a mechanic, but it did take a little extra brainpower to make sure I didn't lose a tool by forgetting to strap it down. This sector really shouldn't have its own separate gravity. It was just an office block, but some dingus had decided to repurpose a zero-g sports center to make it. The old place went out of business, got sold to someone fond of cubicles and money, and voila: offices where there was a chance of pencils drifting toward the ceiling. I'd actually been called in to fix this same problem before. Maybe the owners would pay for a proper overhaul soon, and I wouldn't have to come save the workday again.

No, it wasn't a difficult fix, but it was tiring on top of the work I'd already put in. There had been a scooter with a stuck seatbelt *and* a malfunctioning hover height (that's a winning combo right there), a faulty moisture adjustor in the private quarters of an amphibious resident, and several jimmied locks on the doors leading to the central ventilation controls. That last was the most worrying. Bored young troublemakers were always looking to get places they shouldn't, just for the thrill, but they could do real damage there. Security promised me that they would be on top of it.

As for me, my time was finally (finally) my own now that the gravity box appeared to be functional. I righted myself and told the other human in the room to prepare to be heavy again. She shut off the video screen she'd been using while I worked, then set her feet against the floor.

I flipped the switch. Gravity eased back into the room, much to my satisfaction. I settled downward with only a slight adjustment to my mech-pack full of tools and cybernetics. My hair didn't take any kind of corralling, being the short and bushy variety, unlike the hazard that the office worker kept on her head. She was obviously not used to spending time in zero-g.

Pretty, though. I might have asked for her number if I wasn't on the clock and wearing an unflattering uniform.

"Thank you!" she said, offering a handshake. "You do good work. I'll be sure to give you a glowing review."

"My pleasure," I said. I returned the handshake *without* caressing her knuckles. Maybe I'd stop by on my day off and try my luck then. At closing time, of course. I wasn't about to pester her while she was at work either.

After a polite farewell, I exited into a maze of hallways full of quiet chatter and the hum of ventilation. Other office workers gave me space as I followed well-lit corridors toward the elevators. Even moving calmly, a space station mechanic was someone who might be on their way to fix something important. When I'd first started the job years ago, the instant respect took a while to get used to. Nowadays, I appreciated it. I'd had more than one actual emergency that I'd only reached in time because people made way for me.

I was technically off duty now, but it wasn't obvious. Until I could take off my big cybernetic backpack and change out of my uniform, the average station-goer was going to look at me and see an Important Being who should be allowed to go first on the elevators. Later, I'd be out in civilian clothes, just another human: a Latina who was stocky and on the short side but unremarkable. But for now, I got to skip the line. I thanked the handful of people who let me.

Elevators on this station came in as much of a range of styles as the other architecture, depending on which species had been consulted for it. This one was a Frillian design: cylindrical with glass doors, lined in holographic underwater scenes, and *full* of office workers sneaking out early. Several humans and three big Waterwills, the blobby columns of goo that were somehow intelligent. I didn't pretend to understand the biology there. All I knew was that getting squashed up against one wouldn't leave snot on my clothes, but it would sure feel like it was going to. And it would smell like algae.

This was an unpleasant elevator ride.

Three levels up, the food court awaited, with much better smells. I slid out of the elevator in a rush. A pair of Hard Skins waiting outside stepped back with a rattle of their exoskeleton plates. I nodded as I passed. I'd go home and change clothes later. Now, I had friends to meet.

As I crossed the open walkway, I ignored the long drop to lower levels and searched among the rainbow of colored food signs on metal walls, artificial plants from multiple planets, and glossy white floors. The tables were pretty full today. A familiar figure was nevertheless easy to spot, sitting alone at the edge. I leaned against the railing to scoot past a cluster of Hard Skins who hadn't noticed me, then headed toward where a single arm waved in greeting. Just the one, because that was all she had.

I waved back at Roka, the purple alien with unilateral symmetry and infinite patience. She had one leg, one arm, one eye, and a clear breathing mask that made the air moist enough for her lungs. It was her people who needed moisture adjustors in their quarters. You might think that this kind of setup would make a person timid and cautious, worried about tripping and knocking their mask askew.

You would be wrong. Roka could do a standing backflip on a railing, and she was an excellent shot with a light grenade. The name for her species translated as "Solos," and she definitely was a singular specimen.

I hoped that she'd get to show off her skills today. Our group of friends was fond of a good stress-relieving lightball game, and we should all have time. I could certainly use it. And knowing Roka's job in the ambassadorial sector, she probably could too.

I was right.

"Guess what the biggest topic of complaint today

25

was!" she greeted me, leaning her single elbow on the table, palm up.

I took a seat. "Unruly delinquents on the roadways?"

"Close!" she said, pointing a gloved finger at me. "Unruly delinquents on the spaceways! Apparently the route to this station is, and I quote, 'full of lowlifes and sewage eaters unfit for a civilized galaxy.'"

"Well, aren't those complainers so high and mighty?" I asked as I settled my pack beside the seat. "They're lucky they didn't get stranded by raiders themselves, see how they do in the Crud Cloud." The nebula of trash and ungoverned ships was an ongoing problem. It had started as a dumping ground for travelers who didn't want to pay recycling fees, then blossomed into a maze of hiding places for a whole range of people. Space pirates. Salvagers. Even those who'd been kicked off the station and couldn't afford fuel to go anywhere else.

Plans and protests and budget proposals for how to Fix The Problem came and went. The Crud Cloud stayed.

"Are the complainers going to front any money for the cause?" I asked with mock sincerity. I knew the answer.

"Oh, of course not," Roka said with a wave of her hand. "Ranking nobility here to visit their minor king? Fixing problems is for lesser beings. And honestly, they've been here for a few days and are only now making a stink about it because they ran out of other things to complain about. It feels like a hobby."

"I've seen that before. They figure you'll just make it happen somehow, right?"

Roka made a rude noise behind her mask. "I told them I would speak with the most important officer I could get ahold of today, and left it at that."

I smiled. "And he'll be joining us soon, right?"

Roka nodded. "I didn't even lie."

Right on cue, the other two of our group appeared from the direction of the taxi lot. The mass of blue-gray tentacles wearing a police hat was Conderu, our good friend and low ranking cop, who kept forgetting to remove his hat when he was off duty. It looked silly without his uniform vest to go with it.

Before he reached earshot, he had the hat swatted off his head by Vittr, who'd just realized he was still wearing it. We couldn't make out the words that Vittr berated him with, but knowing Vittr, they were colorful and Russian-accented.

This was endlessly hilarious to me since Vittr was what you might call a bug alien, looking more like a praying mantis than like any Russian I'd ever met. But he'd learned the language on a spaceship run by Russian humans, and the accent had stuck, with some variations. It suited him.

I'm told the species name "Mesmer" is short for "mesmerizing," a reference to the many colors that some of them sported. Vittr was a simple enough green — though with knee joints painted a sparkly silver for fashion — and he was fascinating in his own way. The accent helped.

Con was a different flavor of eye-catching. His people had named themselves the Strongarms in pride of having walked out of the sea in eons past, on tentacles alone. He was personally more proud of the ability to get places he shouldn't and to imitate other body types at a glance. Truly the most dignified of lawkeepers.

The guys approached with Con holding his hat rolled up in one tentacle rather than taking it back to the cruiser that he'd parked among the taxis. Vittr had opinions about all of that.

"If you are getting foodstuffs on your hat of officialness, it will not being Vittr's fault," he said, clicking his mandibles. "And your car is all of the obvious in taxi area. Easy target for passing idiots, or any of your buttnugget colleagues who happen to be in the area. At least you are not parking it next to Vittr's taxi."

Con lifted a tentacle in an easy shrug. "Buttnuggets are a risk anywhere I park," he said. "At least this way, it's close. Hi, everybody! Ordered any food yet?"

Roka and I made space at the table. The conversation fell into the familiar pattern of discussing food and workday

27

details. Con's less upstanding coworkers were a concern, since now of all times the police personnel were needed at their best. And they were rarely that. Honestly, the rest of us had suggested more than once that Con should quit and find a job that was less rife with corruption.

"I actually got a tip that there's supposed to be another showdown," Con told us while he scrolled the table's digital menu with a tentacle. "Not a very reliable tip, since the guy was just hoping I'd give him drugs in exchange for the info, but we're looking into it. Never seen Armorlites hold a grudge like this before."

"Did they say when and where this showdown is supposed to happen?" I asked, somewhat concerned. The big scuffle with the police two days ago had triggered the station-wide lockdown that we were still suffering under, with no one allowed in or out. According to Con, it had started with a small gang facing off against a big one, then the police got involved, and everyone started shooting each other. The loss of life had made other fights more likely, not less. If another battle was actually planned instead of spontaneous, how much would it escalate?

Roka had other concerns. "Did you give him the drugs?" she asked with a disapproving tilt to her single eyebrow.

Con snorted. "No. I did give him something readily available at any store if he just figures out what section to look under. It'll make his species drunk, but it's not illegal."

Vittr tapped a wrist claw on the tabletop. "Terrible role model," he said.

"Better than some," Con was quick to point out. "And no, he didn't have much in the way of specifics. But I have people connecting dots right now, trying to puzzle out the details of this theoretical brouhaha." He pulled a communicator from somewhere among all his tentacles — a pocket that had always seemed questionably sanitary to me — and checked his messages.

He froze, then shut off the menu in a cloud of the burbling noises that passed for swear words. He stood on his chair to look around quickly.

"What?" I asked as the rest of us caught on.

Con spoke quickly. "It might be nearby and hereby."
He looked around, then stopped and burbled, flailing
briefly in a motion that almost slapped all of us. Then he
jumped down. "Forget the food," he said. "If the
troublesome types coming this way are the kind of trouble I
expect, then we'll be hearing sirens to clear the area any
second now." He unrolled his hat and put it on.

"You're off duty," I reminded him, "And don't have a
weapon."

"Yup," he said, waving tentacles at us to stand.
"People are coming to handle that part."

We all stood and looked around. Sirens started
whooping. An amplified voice directed civilians to vacate
the area, while a different voice shouted from down the
walkway for them to cower under the tables like the
weaklings they were. It sounded like an Armorlite: the
vaguely dinosaurian, toothy types from a culture that prized
physical strength and domination over just about everything
else. This usually meant that they got into fistfights and
such, petty thievery and assaulting strangers, not the
current mess.

I stood on tiptoes to see past a crowd of running
civilians. All I could make out was a row of police hats
facing the other way. It looked like they were defending the
food court, but would the Armorlites even be attacking if
the cops weren't there? Civilians hadn't shot their
compatriots. That had been the cops. And also the other
gang, the one called the Hive, which was mostly Mesmer.
Luckily for all of us, those guys didn't seem to be part of
today's unfolding disaster.

"This way," Con said, speeding off toward the cars in
a tornado of tentacles. We raced after him with Vittr in the
lead, me holding my backpack straps and considering using
my jets, and Roka leaping along faster on one leg than I ran
with two. People panicked, scattering in all directions.
Officers in full uniforms appeared behind us to direct the

crowds, their vest lights cycling through red, blue, and yellow.

Someone down the walkway fired an electricity weapon. I scowled over my shoulder as I ran, knowing there was a good chance I'd have to fix some of the damage from that later. Inconsiderate. Even if these ruffians had good reason to be mad, they were making it everyone else's problem. I could already smell the scorch marks on the air.

"I'll give you all a ride," Con said, pointing out his cruiser. It was indeed very conspicuous, hovering there in the parking space as the only non-taxi, all primary colors and a good head or two higher than the other vehicles, which glittered to various degrees. Taxis were iridescent, as a general rule, to make them easy to spot for multiple vision systems. Police cars did the same thing by looking like they were colored by a child with the most basic set of crayons.

Just as Vittr was complaining about leaving his taxi behind, Con discovered the sabotage to the engine. A screwdriver was jammed through the side of the fuel compartment, left there as an obvious insult, leaking all over the floor.

Con burbled and flailed some more. Vittr darted away. A rumble sounded, and his taxi zoomed over to stop inches from Con, in all its rainbowy prismatic glory. Yes, all taxis were iridescent, but nobody did flashy like a Mesmer. In Vittr's own culture, this glitterbomb marked him as a stylish badass. In mine, it made him a pretty-pretty princess, but I wasn't about to tell him.

"Getting in," Vittr commanded. He reached out through his window to place a police light on the roof. He pressed a button, and it whooped to noisemaking life.

"Why do you have that?" Con asked, scrambling through the passenger window. Roka and I crowded into the back.

"Vittr have many things." He put on sunglasses. "Buckle yourselves."

"What—"

"Vittr be driving the irresponsible speeds, and you will

not be arresting me because YOU IN THE CAR!"

I strapped my harness on tight, pack wedged between my shins, and braced for irresponsible speeds while Con admitted that Vittr's logic was sound.

"Just don't run over anybody unless they're actively shooting at civilians," he said.

"Vittr will reserve injuries for pooplings who deserve them."

The engine whined, and we shot across the parking lot. Vittr dodged cars, pillars, and people with great skill and small margins. One Armorlite tried to tailwhip the hood, to no luck. Vittr complained as he drove about the criminal element that was such a problem on this space station, and a thorn in the backside of this particular taxi driver.

"Always, they are ramming peoples on roads! And driving in front of car, nearly hitting! And blocking other cars at intersection so their fleet of twenty vehicles can parade through, making everyone else late for very important things! And now they are shooting the place! Probably shooting the cops, but also shooting the walls and potentially peoples. If one gets in front of Vittr's taxi, one had better move fast!"

None did, thankfully for all involved, and soon enough, we were zooming down a tunnel with a metal ceiling above, underwater murals on either side, and utter pandemonium behind us. I twisted in my seat to look, spotting more police cars entering the scene. The civilians seemed to have cleared the area. Angry Armorlites and electronic damage were visible even from here.

I sat back to exchange looks with Roka. Even with one eye and a breathing mask, her "I can't believe this" expression mirrored the one I was probably wearing. This was not what any of us had signed up for today.

As we zipped down an offramp and passed the office where I'd fixed the gravity earlier, I thought briefly of the video call with someone on a nearby planet.

Surely life was easier there.

Chapter 5
(Robin)

When I came in to work early, I was greeted by Paul walking past with his arms full of empty cages. The air smelled of more hand sanitizer than usual.

"Good morning!" he said. "All of the politicians hate us, and three of the cats are pregnant."

"Seriously?" I asked his retreating back. "This is getting ludicrous."

"Welcome to today," Anne said sourly, trailing after him. "Today sucks."

"I see that," I said. "So now what?"

"We're watching the news in the break room," Anne told me. "At least no one's spotted a Citizen Animal running around lost."

"Small mercies!" I said, falling in behind her. "The authorities would be *really* upset about that." I hadn't spent much time with any of the more intelligent nonhuman Earthlings, the ones who had been granted galactic citizenship alongside us, but I knew the protocols. And the history books about the uproar caused by that decision made for good reading.

Hopefully we can avoid a brouhaha now, I thought grimly, *But it's not looking good.*

The break room was full of people who had arrived even earlier than I did. Well, to be fair, some were on the overlapping night shift and hadn't gone home yet. The room held more employees than it was meant to, human and turtledillo both, with chairs pushed aside so we could all stand.

I took a position at the back. I'm tall, even for a Tall

Alien. This meant I was treated to the sight of Emiko and Fala making eyes at each other, which I would rather not have noticed. One of them was wearing deeply unfortunate perfume, too. Stale flowers.

There was a strict "No dating the coworkers" policy here. Couldn't risk a lover's spat making our species look bad. And as someone who had grown up completely uninterested in all of that, I just couldn't see what made it a tempting rule to defy.

The news program popped up on the wall screen, and everyone quieted. "Breaking news," declared the newscaster. "Human irresponsibility!"

Everything about the situation sounded dire. In a nutshell, yes, the law-keepers and policy-makers all had a much dimmer view of the Earth representatives. We'd given a statement that we weren't responsible, but the rumor mill was more powerful. The short clip of a top diplomat explaining our many levels of animal screening was followed up by a group of "experts" who all tried to outdo each other in their skepticism.

Then came the footage from that drone I'd noticed. It showed in clear detail how many rabbits had been scampering around the field and how easily they evaded capture. The experts had a lot to say about that too.

Only when the point had been beaten into the ground that this was a disaster and we were incompetent did the reporters move on to a related segment. Apparently, the drone that had been watching the rabbit misadventure had spotted a mysterious area of fallen trees in the forest, only visible when it rose to max height. Other drones had come later to get as good a view as they could from this side of the property line.

No one was turning the TV off, though they talked over it, so I kept watching — surely this was related to the animal situation. It looked like a bunch of trees had been gently pushed aside. The muddy patch of grass in the middle was sunken, but it wasn't much of a crater. The reporters didn't know what to make of it and treated the thing like a bit of celebrity gossip: weird gardening practices on private land.

Which just made it stranger since it *had* to be related.

"Ohhh," said a shocked voice at my shoulder. "It's a smuggler ship."

I turned to see Reed standing on a table to see over the crowd, with a poleaxed expression on his turtley face. "What smugglers?" I asked as Emiko and Fala edged past to leave.

"Did they not tell you?" Reed clicked his beak in surprise. "I suppose they like to sanitize any reports of illegal goings-on. The local criminal element has been coming up with things that were clearly acquired offworld. No one has been able to pin down the details, and it's relatively recent from what I've heard, but that—" He pointed at the depression in the trees. "That looks to me like something fell from the sky and landed there."

"Yeah, but why isn't there a real crater?" I asked. "If a ship crashed from even tree height, there would be more of a hole than that."

Anne joined the conversation, leaning around someone else who was leaving to go work. "Inertial dampeners!" she said. "I'll bet cleaning duty on it."

"Inertial— Oh!" I remembered now. "Yeah, it probably is!"

When Reed asked what we offworlders were talking about, I explained the bit of tech that some high-end ships had, basically space bumpers.

"I think it's based on the same stuff that led to gravity control," I said, "Though that's everywhere, and this is super expensive."

"Nah, it's a different tech base," Anne said. "I heard that a species with incompatible machinery invented it, and it's expensive because the materials to make it work on other ships are hard to come by."

"Makes sense," I agreed.

"So the people smuggling contraband are well-funded," Reed said bitterly. "Or they stole it from someone else. Either way, I don't like the odds of trying to catch them."

Anne looked speculatively at the screen. "Even worse if that ship's invisible. They've probably got visual shielding."

"So there *are* invisible spaceships?" Reed asked. "I thought that was an exaggeration."

"Well yeah, they exist," I told him. "But I doubt any of the ones coming here from Earth have visual shielding. Pretty much all the friendly species agree it's underhanded and dangerous to use."

"Space trash," Anne declared. "Exactly the kind who'd make connections with local smuggling rings."

I gestured at the screen, glancing at Reed. "I can't believe the reporters aren't talking about this. Our higher-ups know ships exist that can take a bump without being seen, and of course they would have told yours. It's hardly a secret. Is the *smuggling* a secret?"

Reed shook his head as more people filtered out of the room; the program was over. "Everyone knows," he said. "Though the officials try not to talk about it."

"Oh, that's annoying," I said. "They'd better start talking about it! And what about whoever owns that forest? Are they part of this smuggling ring, but too rich and powerful to piss off? We should already have people in there searching for the animals!"

"I couldn't say whether the property owner is involved or not," Reed said. "But if permission to enter has not been granted, then the authorities can only breach the boundaries with proof of significant crimes."

"What about harboring illegal animals from offworld?" I asked, pointing again at the screen. "Which could easily bring disease, parasites, and environmental destruction with them. All that stuff the reporters are pinning on us. Is that not significant enough?"

Reed shrugged helplessly. "Not if it's accidental. I'm sure someone's working on a workaround."

"Not quickly enough!" Anne said. "Not if the news

didn't even say so!" She stomped toward the door with her hands in the air. "Everybody's going to keep blaming us. I'm not looking forward to any of this."

I had to agree. Reed and I exchanged unhappy expressions before leaving the room to join the rest of the crew in tackling the workload that awaited us. The night crew had been busy, but there was still more to do than usual. Animals to care for, clean up after, triple-check for fleas, and shuffle about in search of a better place to keep them all. Plus, helping Jasmeet fend off reporters and phone calls.

When I stepped outside later, bringing a bag of trash to the dumpsters (which were just like the ones back on Earth, only half the height), I got a brief respite from all the rushing about. I took a deep breath, trash-scented though it was, and appreciated the calm of the back lot.

A familiar song drifted through the air. It was a recording with multiple voices and music coming from somewhere around the corner of the building. Sidewalks and a tree-lined sitting area lay in that direction. Someone out there had good taste. I tossed the trash and sang along with one of my favorite space shanties.

"What do we do with a stabby Roomba, in the void between stars? Give him the best knife and some respect..."

The volume turned down, as if whoever was listening to it had just realized that one of the voices wasn't from the recording.

I kept singing as I walked toward the street. "Way hey, and hit the warp drive, in the void between stars!" When I rounded the corner, I found a trio of young adult turtledillos with a music player and some very surprised expressions. "Good choice of songs!" I told them.

They thanked me, embarrassed, and one asked if I could tell them what the words meant. The recording had been in English.

"Sure! It's an old song for space travel, about a cleaning robot that ... has knives taped to it." I paused. "Actually, I'm surprised this made it past the censors.

Where did you get it?"

Shifty looks. "A friend."

"I see. And do you know where this friend got it?"

"Another friend. We should be going, actually. Thank you! You have a good singing voice!"

I said my own polite goodbyes as they scrambled away with the music player turned off.

I should have asked more questions, I thought. *There's no way an official channel gave them a song about shanking the captain in the ankles.* With a sigh, I turned back to the building. This was something new to discuss with my coworkers.

Chapter 6
(Robin)

"It's in there," declared the store owner as we walked up. His shell was painted red, his expression was sour, and he pointed at the doorway, clearly uninterested in the greeting that Reed had just launched into. "It destroyed my plants and left this foul mess!"

Hmm, yeah, that was some diarrhea. I guess those potted plants didn't agree with a rabbit's digestive system, leafy and green though they were. I reflected that we were lucky the blue grass at the park hadn't proved to be similarly toxic. Catching the speedy buggers was hard enough without dodging nasty piles of poo.

"I apologize," Reed said. "Thank you for calling us. My associates here will catch it right away. You said it's just the one?"

Anne and I quick-stepped toward the door while the guy went into detail about how he'd seen the terrifying creature (rabbit) bare its teeth at him and dash inside to lay claim to the building (hide). Since the man had only just unlocked the front door of his furniture store, he'd let the rabbit have the place.

He was still complaining outside when Anne and I ducked through the Rockback standard sized door to find a dark interior that we could just barely stand up in. Anne turned the lights on. I was instantly glad the guy hadn't followed on our heels.

"Ooh," I said. "Let's find it quick." Rabbit pee and shreds of paper were everywhere among the furniture. One of the tabletop lamps didn't come on, even when I checked it for a separate switch. Didn't find one. Did find a cord that had been chewed through.

O-kay, moving on; we don't need that to see anyway. Where's the bunny?

In the far corner of the room, of course, under a couch that it did NOT want to leave. We had to shove furniture to surround it, covering all exits but one, which I stood over with my net-pole while Anne nudged the rabbit with hers.

This bunny wasn't as fast as the others, and I caught it with relative ease. And more diarrhea. Lots of that.

"Oh, man," Anne said as she held the cage out at arm's length. "We're gonna have to quarantine this one."

"Absolutely," I agreed. "I feel equally bad for it and for whoever has to clean this place." *And whoever has to clean the bunny,* I thought. *Better not be me.* The rabbit was a lop-eared gray that would have been charming if not for the color of its hindquarters.

We picked our way through the mess, only to find the owner at the doorway discovering the chewed-through cord. He was, as expected, not pleased.

"Look at this! That *thing* did this! What kind of abomination eats wires?" He waved the lamp in Anne's face.

"It doesn't eat them," Anne said, holding the cage away from the guy. "It was just chewing to wear down its teeth."

Surprise, surprise, that didn't help. The turtledillo said some very unkind things as Anne and I scooted outside. Reed made an effort to calm him, with middling success. We secured the cage in the truck while Reed said his goodbyes to a slammed door. He scuttled over to join us with unprofessional haste.

"Let's go," he said as he jumped in. The owner shouted anew from inside the building. I guess he was just now exploring the damage.

Anne didn't have to be told twice. She sped off toward base while I hoped the guy stayed inside instead of coming out to throw stuff at us. He sounded that mad.

The drive was short and aromatic, with the windows down and the occasional passerby looking up in revulsion. Glad to see my professional assessment was holding up: diarrhea smells bad on any planet.

When we rolled in and handed off the rabbit (which would be quarantined in that cage, set in a stockroom since we were out of space), Chelle met us in the hallway and sent us right back out again.

"It's a cat this time," she said, sending the info to our phones. "Climbing fences in a residential district, frightening locals and terrorizing the small animal population." She put her own phone away. "Look for it near the remains of the rodenty thing it picked apart in the back yard. They'll leave the gate open for you, but don't expect anyone to venture near it."

"Can't fault 'em for that," I said.

"I'll get the dry food to shake," Anne volunteered.

That proved to be just the thing. Fifteen minutes later, the three of us stood on a deserted suburban street near an open gate, with a dead pile of fur visible in the backyard and neighbors watching from every window.

I shook a bag of treats. "Here, kitty kitty!"

"Mrrow?" A head popped up from behind a decorative black rock. "Mow mow mow!" The gray tabby trotted up eagerly and leapt into my arms.

"Oh, what a good kitty you are," I said to the cuddlebug nuzzling my face. "Let's get you some snacks and water. And all the scritches, yes." It was certainly as friendly as one of ours, but more overweight than any cat at the vet center or at the Earth section of the zoo. I kept up the encouraging babble all the way to the truck. Reed held the door, and Anne put away her net-pole. I gave the good kitty a handful of treats and more attention.

Thankfully the cat was thirsty and didn't object to going into a cage as long as it found water there. I'd been expecting to have to convince myself not to let it ride on my lap for the drive back.

Reed disappeared, then returned with a plastic bag of

furry leftovers. "In case it gets sick from eating this," he explained.

"Ah, good thinking," I said. While I'd memorized the list of local prey animals that an escaped cat was likely to bite into, I couldn't tell what that one used to be. We'd need to be sure what we were treating for if symptoms cropped up.

Reed stored the airtight bag of dead animal, and we hit the road. None of the locals so much as waved as we drove away. Super eerie.

We didn't even make it back before a call came in for somewhere close to us. This one was urgent. And weird.

"They swear it's a human ghost," Jasmeet said on my phone. "Voices in the back room of a restaurant."

"That's new," I said. "Did you tell them that there are other animals on our planet that can mimic a human voice?"

"Yes. Too rattled to listen to me. Good luck. Here's the address." The notification chimed in my ear.

"Thanks," I said drily. "We'll let you know how the ghost-hunting goes."

When I relayed the directions to Anne, she changed course with a laugh. It really was close by.

"So," Reed said from the back seat, all four hands clasped in his lap. "Which of your animals can talk?"

I twisted in my seat. "You haven't heard about parrots?? And mynah birds, and lyrebirds, and — actually, it's a lot of birds."

"I have not! Do tell me."

I did. With great enthusiasm and glee, going off on a tangent about the history of Gorilla Sign Language that got interrupted when Anne parked.

"We're here," she said. "I'll take the net again."

"Right. Sure. Anyways, it's all very cool," I said to Reed, who was already getting out.

"I will do my best to convince the people inside that the alarming apparition is, in fact, marvelous."

"Yes. Good luck."

The restaurant workers were waiting at the door, desperate for reassurance. Much better than the angry guy. Reed asked them for details while ushering us through another low doorway and a low-ceilinged kitchen full of fish-scented steam to the private dining hall beyond.

This place had fancy vaulted ceilings with bare beams and shadowy corners. The aesthetic seemed a little creepy compared to what I'd seen so far, but there was still a lot I didn't know about turtledillo history. It could have been local medieval style or something that only the richest patrons would enjoy.

Anyways, there was a huddled form up in the rafters, muttering to itself in English. Didn't look like a ghost to me.

Anne made as if to poke it with her net pole. "Hm. Should I…?"

"Wait," I said, setting my carrying cage on a table. I pitched my voice to its most friendly. "Pretty bird!"

The shadow perked up. "Pretty bird!" it replied, fluttering and shuffling closer. "Who's a pretty bird?"

Taking a wild guess, I called back, "*You're* a pretty bird! Come give kisses!"

With happy cooing sounds and a shower of dust, a red parrot glided down to land heavily on my outstretched forearm. (Hooray for sturdy work sleeves; no scratches.) I stroked the bird's dusty plumage — an adult Scarlet Macaw, with no signs of injury. Not to be denied, the bird dodged my hand and nuzzled my cheek, muttering happily about kisses. I told it that it was a very good bird, and a pretty bird, and all manner of other things.

Anne looked around. "Less of a mess than the rabbit; that's good. Though, it's probably a biohazard to have in a restaurant."

I sighed. "Yeah."

"I wonder if it's one of those swearing parrots."

I shook my head in disapproval and stroked the red feathers. "You're a lovely little biohazard. What's your name?"

"Can you say 'dickbutt'?" Anne tried at the same time.

The parrot stood up straight to proclaim, "Sunny is a pretty bird!" followed immediately by, "Jasper is a dickbutt!"

Anne burst into helpless guffaws.

"Good bird, Sunny," I said. "We'll take good care of you and see if we can get you back to somebody who knows Jasper."

"Dickbutt!"

"Bahahaha!"

"Yes," I said to the air, "This is the representation that Earth needs. This right here."

"Ah, nobody out there can understand him," Anne said, looking at the cage. "Do you think he'll go for this?"

We tried. He didn't. Sunny insisted on riding on my shoulder, which I finally allowed when we figured out how to make a leg leash out of several hair ties I'd had in my pocket.

It would be a short walk. Just Reed and a few restaurant workers in the next room, then our truck right outside. Theoretically.

The first part went fine, with the workers relaxing when they saw the very-much-not-a-ghost with pretty red feathers. I introduced them, and one small female even worked up the nerve to touch Sunny's wing. Sunny didn't mind. I could tell Reed was itching to do the same, though he maintained the image of a knowledgeable expert on all things Earth. It was convincing enough.

In short order, everyone was charmed by the Earth bird and not as stressed as I would have expected about the idea of closing for a thorough cleaning.

"We do a deep clean often," said the hefty male who seemed to be in charge. "Our highest-paying customers demand it. Thank you for catching the animal."

"Our pleasure," I told him in Rockback.

"Hey, Sunny," Anne said in English. "Can you say 'Polly wanna cracker'?"

On my shoulder, Sunny cocked his head and squawked. "Polly wanna finger!"

Chapter 7
(Zephyr)

I hadn't heard a foul word spoken about the Earthlings until their animals got out. It was with shock that I stopped outside my office to listen to the gossiping coworkers who hadn't noticed me yet. My lower arms were full of important paperwork, and my top arms held rapidly-cooling drinks for two superiors, but I stopped like someone had just announced that we'd be reprogramming the entire building in trinary code.

"The humans are dangerously incompetent," said the tall gentleman with his back to me. His voice dripped with disdain. "If they can lose track of this many of their own animals at once, then we want no part in further trade. I'm embarrassed to work in an office even remotely associated with them."

"Have they put out a statement yet?" asked a woman who I couldn't see over the man's broad shell. "Any attempt at explaining it?"

"Not that I've heard. And I wouldn't expect a very good excuse. These were their creatures, their responsibility. There's been no natural disaster to break the cages or blackout to release the locks, nothing of the sort. I can't think of a single thing that would leave them blameless."

"Could anyone else have gotten ahold of that many Earth animals?"

"Hardly. No one could—"

I broke in. "Smugglers." When they turned to look at me, my dawning horror kept me talking. "It wasn't enough for the criminals to sell addictive food that *kills people*—" I clacked my beak skyward in respect for the dead. "But now they're bringing us animals from offworld and *losing them*!"

The two coworkers didn't have much to say to that, but this kind of evil had clearly not touched their own lives.

They wouldn't understand.

"Can you please bring these to the front office?" I asked, thrusting the drinks forward. "Where did you hear about the animals? Is it on the news? I'll put these away myself." I babbled, juggling mugs and paperwork. My coworkers seemed taken aback enough to accept my urgency at face value. The man took the drinks, and the woman directed me to the live news update that would have more information.

I thanked them both. Then I ducked back into my office, threw the papers in the general direction of the desk, and slammed the door behind me as I ran for the media room. Some people got out of my way, while others had to be dodged around. I fancied myself agile and quick, able to move at close to human speeds when pressed. The fact that that comparison might not be a favorable one for long just added to my haste.

Every human I've met has been nothing but honorable, I thought as I ran. *They do not deserve to get burnt by someone else's fire. Especially those abominable lowlifes!*

Heads turned when I skidded into the media room, but when I ran to a terminal instead of announcing some new development, everyone went back to work. I tapped the controls with impatience. While the live feed loaded, my thoughts skipped to the "touch screen" that one human acquaintance had shown me, which hadn't been adapted for Rockback hands yet. I wondered now if it ever would.

The feed popped up, looking much like the coworker had described it: a flying eye's view over a public garden with an inset recording of the action from earlier in the day. The place was calm right now, but it had been exploding with fast animals not long ago. I'd never seen creatures like that before. Definitely from Earth.

I stood there, listening to the account of the events and completely ignoring the chair at my side until a clock chimed with the end-of-shift tone.

Startled, I looked up to confirm the time, thinking wildly about the many things that I had planned to finish today. The documents on my desk — or near it — would have to wait.

This couldn't stand.

I had sought out every bit of information that was publicly available, and I needed more. Also, a plan of action. But I was sure to come up with that soon enough. First, I had to talk to someone who knew more than I did.

Already planning madly, I shut off the terminal and raced back to gather my things.

I might just be conveniently sick tomorrow, I thought as I ducked under the widespread arms of someone gesturing while they talked. *Better practice my cough. Or not. At this point, I don't care if they believe me.*

Leaving a trail of confused coworkers, I rushed out of the building and down the road to Silverwright's. I had eaten there numerous times, both before and after they became the much-lauded first restaurant to serve human food. I'd even tried some of the new cuisine, though I honestly didn't think much of it. Not that I would ever say so anywhere the owner could hear.

Because that was who I was there to see. She had no reason to talk to me, lowly nobody that I was, but I hoped that curiosity on her part would do. And insistence on mine. I was on a *mission.*

Once inside the high-ceilinged building with black and gold decor, I found an eager crowd waiting to eat. Somehow I hadn't expected that. I chafed waiting in line for a two-seat table. Normally I would spend the time admiring the weekly rotation of art on the walls, painted by Tertia Luminescence Silverwright herself, but today I was far too preoccupied. I looked at nothing and over-groomed my cuticles with my beak.

When the waitress finally showed me to a table, I asked to see Lumi in my most polite tones. I made sure to use her common name and didn't elaborate. I stressed that it was important. The waitress said she'd check whether Lumi was available. I curled my toeclaws under the table and hoped.

Nothing to do but wait. Sip the complimentary water, nibble the seasoned beetle wings, taste the air. Look at the other guests, some of whom were trying alien food for the first time. No humans were here at the moment. That was hardly a surprise, though. Only a few of them lived nearby, and they had other places to eat now.

I looked up when someone approached the table. It wasn't the waitress. This middle-aged woman with the gold-and-teal shell paint of an artist and the confidence of a god could only be Lumi. I sat up straight and spread all four arms in subservience. I had seen her before, but never up close, with the focus of her attention solely on me.

She nodded and settled into the second chair, folding two hands on the table. "What is your important matter?" she asked.

"Smugglers," I said, immediately bungling the encounter. I hadn't even introduced myself. Nothing to do but press on now. "Everyone's blaming the humans for losing those Earth animals, but I know it was smugglers, not them."

Lumi looked amused. "You know that, do you?"

I restrained myself from gesturing wildly. "Who else could it be? Law-abiding citizens have no way to acquire animals from Earth! And the humans claim they didn't come through official channels; these aren't even the right type of animal to bring here."

"Have you asked a human directly?"

"Well, no," I had to admit, "I haven't had a chance. But all my experience with them says they are *honorable*, not the sorts to bring animals here in secret!"

"'All your experience,' you say."

"I work in accounting at the Embassy," I explained hastily. "Part of my department oversees paychecks and such. Sometimes I get to talk to them in person. They're always very nice!"

"I would expect no less," Lumi said. She folded her other hands around the first. "So, what do you want of me?"

I waved my hands broadly. "Fix this! I know you have connections!"

"Ah," Lumi said, leaning back in the chair. "Do you now?"

"Don't give me that look; everyone knows that." I took a deep breath. "I apologize. This is important to me."

"Why?"

I took in her focused expression before speaking. "My cousin died from an illegal substance," I said. "The smuggling trade is to blame. His loss wrecked my family, like many others. And now the smugglers are branching out to animals that don't belong on this planet, which are already causing untold damage, and might disrupt the alliance with the first alien civilization we have ever encountered." I bit the air fiercely. "I would peel the shells of those responsible if I could."

"I see," Lumi said, picking out a beetle wing. "And is there something specific you expect me to do, or are you just here to yell at the only person you can think of?"

I deflated at that. "I — do you know how to find the people who lost the animals? There's probably a bounty…"

She waved a hand while she crunched down on the wing. "Don't strain yourself. Tell you what. You do me a favor first, and I'll see if I can point you toward someone whose shell deserves peeling."

My heart leapt. "The ones who lost the animals?"

"I'm not promising anything," Lumi said. "But I'll see what I can do."

"Thank you!" I gushed. "What favor do you want?"

She leaned in conspiratorially, as if we hadn't already been discussing topics that might conceivably get me in trouble. I probably should have been quieter.

When I leaned in too, she said, "I'm looking for someone with knowledge of offworld tech. Can you think of anyone like that?"

"Well, the humans," I blurted.

"Can you bring one here for a nice meal and a chat?" she asked, smiling widely. "No charge."

"Sure, I can do that!" I exclaimed. "Is tomorrow okay? Everyone's probably gone home now, but I can try to find one during work hours. I don't know where they live."

Lumi sat back, still smiling. "Tomorrow is perfect. I'll be here all day. Now, why don't you take your pick of the menu? My treat. I'll see you again tomorrow."

Before I could thank her properly, she was up and striding away, her shell glinting in the light. I said my thanks from a distance. She didn't turn.

Jittering with nerves, I picked up the menu without seeing a word on it. Tomorrow. Tomorrow I would find a human and then learn some valuable information.

I even knew the perfect one to ask. She was always friendly.

Chapter 8
(Robin)

After the adventures of the last couple days, I was glad to handle something normal at work. Even more glad that it was my turn at the zoo across town and that no animals were missing there. I triple-checked, but each Earth creature was accounted for. That meant I could throw myself into the usual tasks and pretend there wasn't a crisis unfolding.

Thankfully no big projects were waiting for me today. The permanent human staff usually handled most of that, with occasional assistance from those of us who rotated in from the vet center. None of the Earth animals on exhibit needed medical attention today, so it was all a matter of routine care (hoof trimmings and such), followed by a wardrobe change and some interaction with the public.

I was a bit worried about that part. The crowd was distinctly smaller than normal. But the youngsters were just as excited as always.

"Hey there, kids! Want to meet some animals from my planet? This one will let you touch her if you're nice."

The turtledillo children oohed and ahhed and reached out timid hands to brush the fur of the most exotic of Earth creatures — a very tame pony. Her name was Dusty, and she didn't bat an eye at even the most shrill-voiced alien child. Of which there were several today.

"It's so *weird!*" shrieked the closest one, waving all four arms in excitement.

"Yup," I said. "She came all the way from Earth. Want to pet her? She likes it if you stroke her like this." I ran my fingers across the short fur. (Petting was good; scratching was bad. Someone had realized early on that Rockback claws were often extremely sharp, given the fashion preferences of the individual in question, so we had strict no-scratching rules.)

Two other kids took me up on it while their parents watched from a few steps behind, near the edge of the wood-fenced enclosure. The loud one just danced around the sunny area, commenting on how the pony was the most bizarre creature ever. Luckily there was no pony poop on the ground to dodge around, just a bin of aromatic hay and a water trough.

When I'd first learned which animals humanity would be contributing to this zoo, I had an unprofessional giggle fit. I'd expected tigers and elephants, the type of impressive beasts that were staples of zoos at home. But everything Earthly was impressive to these folks, so logic had dictated that we send only the safest choices.

That meant pets and livestock. We had cats and dogs, pigs and ponies, two horses, and a small flock of chickens. I'd heard that sheep were next on the approved list, but there was no sign of them yet. Ponies remained one of the most popular, thanks to their temperaments and petting-zoo experience. We could have set up a pony ride, and they wouldn't have minded, but early discussions had found that the average turtledillo would be more frightened than excited by the experience.

"Why are its feet like that?"

"Those are called hooves," I explained. "Imagine if you just had one toe on each foot, and the claw was big and flat."

"Weeeeird."

"A lot of animals with hooves are a big help on my planet," I said, flicking a glance at the parents. Still not scowling, good. "They're good at pulling and carrying things. Some of the bigger ones even carry people!"

"Woah," said one child.

"How?" said another. "Do you lie across its back?"

"No, we ride it!" I struck a wide-legged stance. "This

little pony is much too small for me, but there are two *horses* around the corner that way. They're taller than I am."

"What!"

"That's so big!"

"Yup. If you're still here this afternoon, you can watch me ride one. There's a sign that says what time it happens."

The kids looked like I'd promised to ride a shark: impressed and alarmed in equal measures. I knew from experience that it was the idea of being on top of any large animal that scared them. They weren't natural climbers, these guys. Wobbling around at twice their own height would have been terrifying.

"Mom, can we watch?"

"We'll check the sign."

"I wanna see too!"

I smiled at all the approval. You wouldn't think humanity's reputation had taken a nosedive at all. I'd been braced for an empty zoo, with no audience for when I put Flora through her paces. My riding skills were not expert-level by any means, but I could stay in the saddle well enough, and on normal days the turtledillos loved watching a qualified human ride a horse about.

Positive signs, I told myself, *Positive signs.* I finished up the petting zoo session and moved on to the next thing. The day was still young. While logic said that the only turtledillos to be visiting the Earth animals were those with a favorable opinion of Earth, I wasn't about to assume anything. For all I knew, protesters would show up to insist that all of the animals get shipped back.

There were a few dirty looks at the first show-and-tell, from zoo visitors who sneered at the golden retrievers and kept walking. Oh well. They didn't get to see how well a dog can catch a tennis ball, or how happy these two were to run a simple obstacle course and earn crunchy treats.

I only had two people stay for the second half, which was definitely their loss. The elderly couple were delighted to learn how a chicken worked. And when I presented them with one large wing feather each (shed, collected, and cleaned beforehand), they couldn't contain their joy.

"This is an honor!" said the shorter female. "We will get a display case made immediately!"

I was humbly waving off the gratitude when the taller female continued.

"These will be incredibly valuable in a few years when there are no more." She looked at me kindly. "I hope you get some similar souvenirs to take back to your homeworld."

"I... Thanks. I'll see what I can do." I didn't argue with their assumption, simply waving them on their way and gathering up Flapper the Bold in silence. No one else walked by while I returned the chicken to her pen.

The rest of the morning followed in that vein. No drama, but subtle moments that made me wince internally. The only time someone had even asked about the escaped animals, it was a quiet question while I walked from one exhibit to another. I answered honestly that we still didn't know what had happened, but the situation was being handled. The solemn young man nodded and left it at that.

By lunchtime, I was on edge. I half expected to hear a mob in the parking lot: either more reporters or the portion of the general populace with negative opinions of Earthlings at the moment.

I peeked past the ticket-takers to see. No crowds. Whew. I skedaddled off toward the employee area with thoughts of sandwiches and apples.

Halfway there, I was brought up short by someone familiar running toward me. It was Zephyr the accountant, he of lavender-gray shell paint, good problem-solving skills, and a love of chattering away like the wind he was named for.

"Please come to a free lunch," he said, panting to a stop. "Do you have time right now? It's important."

Taken aback, I said, "I've got a bit of time. Why is a free lunch important?"

Instead of answering, Zephyr waved me closer, which meant bending nearly double. I sat down on the low rock wall outside the gift shop and listened.

"I talked to Lumi," he said, as if that was significant. "She has connections. One of her siblings upholds the law, and the other two break it. She *knows* things about the smuggling underground!"

I looked at him sharply. He hadn't been part of the conversation yesterday. "Is that where the animals came from?"

"There's no one else it could be!" Zephyr said. "Lumi is going to use her connections to do something about it, but she wants to talk to you first."

"Why me?" I asked. "Because I found the first one?"

Zephyr waved three hands. "No, no, she simply needs an expert on offworld technology. She said the meal is free, so let's hurry!"

"Wait, what kind of offworld technology?" I asked. That could mean anything. "Why can't she use her influence to hire an expert?"

"She is!" Zephyr insisted. "That's you! This is how she operates: on favors and word of mouth. And she'll help us take down the *smugglers!*"

He said it like he had a personal vendetta against them. "You're sure it was them?" I pressed.

"Yes!" He clawed at the air, stopping the motion with another hand — the equivalent of pounding a fist into a palm. "The cracked-in-the-egg mushbeaks," he hissed. "They're responsible for any number of illegal trades that have shot up to dangerous levels in the past few years. If I could get my claws on the person who sold them that stealth tech, I'd rend them to ribbons!"

I took in the way he was glaring off into the distance. "You don't say."

The tirade that he let loose involved the death of a family member from eating too much of a banned food — this sounded something like the issues with mercury poisoning back home. Apparently, when the super-tasty and super-illegal delicacy had become easy to buy on the street, that relative had learned the hard way why it was banned.

And Zephyr had never forgiven the smugglers for it.

"…Tie rocks to their feet and drown them in the sea!" he concluded, waving all four hands dramatically. I nodded. He slumped against the wall, catching his breath and looking dejected.

"All right," I said, standing. "Let's go see Lumi."

He brightened immediately and scrambled upright. "Yes! They have a new lunch special today and everything! You'll have to tell me how it compares to the original Earth dish; it's supposed to be very authentic." He was off and talking as eagerly as usual, though with an undertone of determination that hadn't been there the last time I'd seen him.

I was more than a little determined myself. Someone who could help take down the smugglers who were apparently responsible for the disaster? Yes, please.

Now, if only this wasn't a massive trap by the criminal underground.

Chapter 9
(Robin)

If it was a trap, it was a tasty one. I sat at a table with Zephyr and sampled the new dish: a surprisingly decent sushi platter, much better than their attempt at pasta the month before. It was all alien ingredients and cooked seafood with nary a sign of raw Earth fish. As far as I was concerned, that made it better. No amount of assurances of its safety would make me feel comfortable risking parasites from a meal they'd only been making for a week.

It even tasted a bit like crab, which was impressive given the fact that no Rockback fit for polite society would harm their world's version of crabs. The capital city of Sea Soul Haven was named after the bay, which housed many of the things. Apparently, some turtledillo in prehistory had looked at the little beasties with armor like their own and decided they were "sea souls."

I didn't know if they were aware that humans ate similar creatures on our own world, but I wasn't going to be the one to tell them.

"That's good!" I said to the waiter. "It reminds me of a restaurant back home that substituted ingredients. Tell the cooks well done!"

He left with a smile and a lift of his beak that translated to a polite bow. I'd found it funny when I learned that turtledillos bow in the opposite direction from humans, but it made sense when I thought about it. For us, bowing puts our heads low and our posture at a disadvantage in battle. For them, raising their chins bared their less-armored underbellies. Science.

Zephyr wasn't interested in science and barely in the

food. He watched the fancy room anxiously for Lumi, though we'd hardly been there a few minutes. The cooks had made my food first, as they always did. I felt guilty for jumping the line, but none of the other diners begrudged an alien visitor a short wait time. One of the perks of being human here — an arrangement that would hopefully not unravel completely before we could do something about these smugglers.

A noise from Zephyr made me look up. I followed his gaze to see the proprietor of the restaurant approaching, serene as ever. She had her pet with her: a bright yellow ribbon of fur draped around her neck that looked like an animated feather boa with aspirations of becoming a ferret. I'd met him before on my other visits, and he was always a joy.

"Honored guests!" Lumi said, pulling out a chair to sit with us.

"Hello, Lumi," I said. "Hello, Brainless." The featherwhip replied with a squeak that was just this side of too high-pitched to hear, and scratched with one tiny foot at a stubborn blue patch in his yellow leg fur. "Did somebody help with the painting?"

Lumi chuckled. "That's one word for it. I was going to have a new seascape for the back wall, but it'll take some touching up now." She craned her long neck to look fondly down at Brainless, who was still scratching away at the paint in his fur. "He's due for a trim anyway. And how did you like the new dish?"

I said polite things about it while Zephyr made a masterful effort at not exploding with impatience. While I was anxious too, maintaining a calm front was part of the required skill set for representing Earth. I did my best to be as relaxed as Brainless, who gave up on the paint and flopped across Lumi's shoulders. Not a speck of color was out of place on Lumi herself, not even in the near-invisible seams of her shell ridge alterations. She'd apparently hatched a Tertius instead of a Tertia, though that was no more than an interesting factoid now.

"So," Lumi said with a dramatic pause. "I'd like you to fix something for me."

"What kind of thing?" I asked. Zephyr straightened up eagerly.

"The kind of thing that is exotic and broken," Lumi said evasively, "Which you are likely to know something about."

I frowned a little. "I can't say yes if you don't tell me what it is."

She smiled. "I'm sure the why is more important."

"Okay, why?"

Lumi cast her eyes sideways. "Your friend here is seven flavors of furious at smugglers in general. Are they also an enemy of yours?"

I spoke slowly. "If they caused the current animal crisis, then yes, absolutely."

"I understand they did," Lumi said. "And fixing this broken thing of mine will be the start of their end."

"Why me?" I asked. "Why not go to someone official?"

Lumi looked at me directly. "This may be hard to hear, but I don't trust the officials. I know too much."

I sighed, then took a deep breath. "I get the distinct feeling that agreeing to look at this mystery thing could get me in the kind of trouble that would have me shipped back home in disgrace. Illegal, yes?"

Lumi spread all four palms, lined up along the table's edge. "I promise you it is not. You'll understand once you see it."

Zephyr caught my eye. "It can't hurt to look, right?"

I looked back at Lumi. "Can you really promise me that I won't get in trouble for being part of whatever you refuse to tell me?"

"There's no risk here," Lumi insisted. "Just a small thing that is broken, which can help expose the villains if fixed. And I don't trust the official repair people."

"But you trust me, who just eats at your restaurant."

There was that smile again. "And who works on a

61

foreign world, passing every test your people have devised."

"Okay, fair point."

Zephyr made good puppy-dog eyes for a guy who looks like a turtle. "Please, just see if you can fix it?"

Against my better judgement, I said, "All right, fine, I'll take a look at it. Just promise me that this is legal."

"It is."

"But you still won't tell me what it is."

"I distrust the listening ability of the people who can make their vehicles invisible."

"Okay, that's fair too."

Lumi pulled a card from the belt pouch that blended in with her scales. "This is the location of where to meet my friend," she said, "He will escort you to the item." She showed both of us the address written there. "Can you remember it?"

I nodded.

"Yes," Zephyr said with a vicious clack of his beak.

"Then be there tonight when the glow-flowers bloom," Lumi said. A poetic way of saying the equivalent of 9:00 PM back home. Those glow-flowers were all over the city. I spent a moment wondering if the rabbits would get sick from eating them, then put the thought away so I could say goodbye to Lumi.

"Enjoy the rest of your meal," she said.

"Thank you. We will."

"And we will *be there*," Zephyr declared.

Lumi just smiled and glided toward the door, with Brainless settling in to sleep. I wondered if she'd meant to invite Zephyr along with me. Well, this was shady enough that I wouldn't object to having backup. Such as it was.

"I'll bring my knives," he whispered across the table. "I have a collection. Nobody will get away with double-crossing us tonight."

"I'll be glad to have you with me," I told him honestly.

Chapter 10
(Robin)

"Do you want a knife?" Zephyr asked as soon as I stepped inside his apartment. My impression was of low ceilings and more brightly-colored, angular decorations than I'd expected from the guy's businesswear. It smelled like fruity soap.

"I want to say we won't need them," I said as I bent to avoid the ceiling. "But it's good to be prepared. Do you have any that I can hide in a pocket?" I demonstrated how much storage space there was in my brown high-collared coat, which I wore with my braid tucked down the back. As far as I could tell, that long hair was my most identifying feature to the average turtledillo. There would be no disguising my species, but I could at least make an attempt at disguising *which* human I was.

On Zephyr's insistence, I accepted a slender pocket knife that reminded me of an ice pick. It seemed designed to pierce a turtledillo's natural armor. I didn't ask where he had gotten it.

I also didn't ask, moments later, how he expected me to fit comfortably in his tiny car. Luckily for us, I fold up well. The back seat was barely wide enough for me to sit sideways, knees to chin, hoping that he would drive safely. The seat had a weird texture that wasn't quite worth complaining about, and the floormat stank of fuel. I dearly hoped there wasn't a leak.

As we took off, Zephyr talked about things he'd uncovered — the celebrities who had died of overdoses similar to his cousin, the children who had been sold dangerous things, the bystanders who had wound up in the wrong place at the wrong time. The way he talked, it sounded like there was a far-reaching network among the Rockback criminal element, possibly with all the clout of a few organized crime rings I could name. The fact that the local criminals appeared to be working with offworld smugglers made it more alarming.

This could be huge, I thought from the back seat. *If an underground empire like the Borznats or the Wheelers is getting a foothold here, then it'll be worth risking my career to stop them.* We rode in silence for a while. *I just hate not knowing what we're walking into.*

The ride seemed to take forever, but when signs appeared that we were getting close, it was somehow far too soon.

For me, anyway. Zephyr was as hyper as a squirrel. I had to remind him to calm down a little, so people wouldn't wonder what his problem was. He nodded and took a few deep breaths, driving with exaggerated care and looking for street addresses. There were none, of course; this was that kind of neighborhood. Directions given here were more along the lines of "turn left at the collapsed red building, turn right at the broken statue, and go under the bridge made of abandoned construction materials."

It was not classy, is what I'm trying to say.

It was also super dark because *of course* the glowflowers here were wilted and faint. The signs of various skeezy businesses lit the streets. Pedestrians hurried by with quick steps, looking over their shoulders.

I started to wonder if Zephyr's car would be a target for break-ins. I had a hard time telling how its style matched up to those I saw parked nearby. It was in good shape, which made it look valuable, but I hoped that it wasn't a model that would start losing bits the moment we walked around a corner.

Zephyr parked in the brightest spot we could find. Everybody knew that criminals were more likely to steal things in the dark, where no one could see them. I assumed it worked that way with turtledillo psychology, at any rate.

Speaking of turtledillo psychology, I learned something interesting that night. Or rather, I had it confirmed. See, there's this human idea of scary aliens with mandible mouths, and I'd heard that the beak-faced turtledillos had a similar uneasiness about our flappy human lips. Silly, I know, but I'd wondered about that and never had a good chance to ask a friend if they found my face unsettling.

But I got the perfect opportunity.

It was when we'd left the car in the distance. Zephyr spotted a landmark and hurried ahead, right around the corner and into a trio of armed muggers.

He made an undignified squeak, trying to jump back but finding himself faced with several knives more dangerous than the one in his pocket. The leader was already demanding money.

They didn't see me. It was perfect.

I stepped out of the shadows, arms wide as I loomed over them, bellowing with all my might. "Rarrgh, booga booga! Hablablabla, grr! Thbbbt!"

The muggers stared up at me for a heartbeat, with the widest eyes I'd ever seen, then bolted for their lives. I yelled after them, blowing raspberries and adding in some dog barks for good measure.

When they had disappeared from sight, I collapsed into laughter, leaning against the side of the building.

"Did you see their faces?" I asked Zephyr, who was regaining his own breath. "Hoo! I thought they were going to pee themselves! That was excellent!" I stayed there chuckling while Zephyr pulled himself together.

"Yes," he managed. "That was well done. Thank you."

I waved it off. "Oh, my pleasure, absolutely. I've always wanted to foil a mugging. Tell me, what was scarier: the rarr or the thbbt?"

The turtledillo gave me his honest opinion (the thbbt), and soon we were on our way again, though this time much more carefully. I peeked around corners first (higher than the average mugger would be expecting). We had no more trouble. I was almost disappointed. But, as the rules of such things go, a second encounter surely would have gone much worse for us, so it was probably for the best that we didn't meet anyone else.

When we reached the building that Lumi had directed us to, I found it to be decidedly Earthlike — the sort of construction that I'd have thought they'd learned from us, if I wasn't pretty sure the alliance was too new for that. At any rate, that side of things wasn't my expertise. This nightclub was big and sturdy, made of poured concrete with blacked-out windows, a glowing red sign, and a bouncer out front with locals milling around under a corrugated awning.

Zephyr's pace slowed. But he squared his armored shoulders and strutted forward with me towering behind him. He probably thought he looked important, with his businesslike stride and tall alien as backup. I let him think it. I was pretty sure that he wasn't impressing anyone.

Certainly not the bouncer. That beefy individual looked like she could have taken on the entire street and come out on top. Her shell was painted a fire-red that was much like the sign. I found myself noticing how the larger-than-average arm muscles caused her natural armor to separate a little, which was surely a weakness. I wondered how that factored into knife fights, but set the thought aside for another day. The bouncer regarded us with the same unruffled gaze that everyone was graced with.

Zephyr stopped right in front of her. "Lumi sent us," he said, still trying to be cool.

The bouncer replied with a quick look up and down for both of us, then a step aside to open the door. "You'll find Rumble at the back," she said. "He's expecting you."

Zephyr nodded a crisp thanks as if he had expected no less and strode past. I thanked the bouncer, wanting to whirl around and booga-booga the onlookers, but I nobly resisted. I did hear the conversations start up as the door was closing, though.

Indoors, we found a dark, loud hallway with red-orange lights, a ceiling that was only slightly too low, and ventilated air thick with Rockback body odor. (It honestly smelled better than human BO; how unfair is that?) The floor was painted matte black. The walls were covered in abstract fiery patterns that were surprisingly artistic, tapering upwards into smoky clouds on a gray ceiling. I almost tripped while I looked up at it. Zephyr saw nothing, striding along in front of me. I recovered just before we turned a corner to see a dance floor full of turtledillos. They were more graceful than I'd honestly expected. And the music wasn't bad — not much more than drums, but a good beat. Most importantly, the ceiling was higher here. Same decoration scheme, though, with spots of light moving over everything in specks of red, orange, and yellow.

Zephyr clearly didn't care. He looked to make sure I was following, then began weaving his way through the crowd at the edge of the dance floor. We passed red-curtained booths and doorways to private rooms that I didn't want to speculate about.

I didn't have to. Zephyr caught my attention to jerk a disdainful thumb toward them. "This is one of those clubs that sells illegal entertainment on the side," he told me over the music, yellow lights passing over his face. "It's only illegal because rich people commissioned the films to be available to only them, but they got sold anyway." He sniffed haughtily. "These are barely criminals."

With that, he strode off toward the back of the dance floor. I readjusted my impression of the place and followed. A sitting area filled with black couches lined the wall, which was likely where this "Rumble" character waited.

The crowd parted with impressive speed. I couldn't say whether it was awe, fear, or the prudent desire not to be stepped on by someone so much taller than they were. Either way, it suited me just fine. Zephyr plowed ahead, and I followed, stepping carefully. Wouldn't do to trip now.

We made it to the couches without incident. Zephyr narrowed in on the likely choice of Rumble: the large fellow seated in the middle of the biggest couch, flanked by guards and sycophants of one type or another. As we approached, he waved for us to join him.

I wondered again just what I was expected to fix, especially in this sort of place. Did the dance floor use offworld lights? How did any of it fit in with stopping the smugglers?

"Welcome," said Rumble in a subterranean bass that made his name choice immediately obvious. He spoke with authority and an easy confidence that made me respect him on an instinctive level. Some things are universal, I guess. He surely would have had a harder time of it if he'd been graced with a squeaky-balloon voice. "Lumi never disappoints. Would you like a bite before we get down to business?" He waved a single hand toward the bowls scattered across the mirrored table in front of him. I could only guess what sort of insect-based delicacy they contained.

Zephyr answered for me. "No, thank you," he said firmly. "We'd rather get right to it. This is important to everyone."

The larger turtledillo regarded him with amusement. "And you are?"

Zephyr stared right back, radiating as much confidence as his tiny accountant's frame could muster. "Secundus Zephyr Mudlark, problem solver. Lumi tells us that this broken thing of yours can bring down the smugglers from offworld, and I cannot *wait* to see it."

Rumble laughed. "Aren't you just precious?" he asked. "You've got fire in you; I'll give you that. Sure you wouldn't rather knock shells in the back room?"

Zephyr stood stiffly, trying to formulate a response to the sudden and — to me, at least — completely unexpected proposition. It's hard to tell when a turtledillo's blushing at the best of times, what with the scales covering much of their faces, and the uneven lighting in here made things even more complicated. But I was relatively sure that Zephyr was blushing.

"I thank you for the offer, kind sir," he finally said, much to Rumble's amusement. "If the circumstances were different, perhaps. But our mission tonight is of the utmost importance. The smugglers deserve a violent end."

The large fellow laughed again, patting his smaller neighbor on the shoulder — who I just now realized was a slender male. I really needed to start paying more attention to shell ridges.

"Well said, lovely," Rumble said. "And what about you, Tree-top?" he continued, turning to me. "Are you driven by a deep hatred for smugglers as well?"

"If they're the reason all of my coworkers and I might get shipped home in shame, then yes," I said. "Will you kindly tell us what you need fixed and how that will stop them?"

He levered himself to his feet. "Come see for yourselves." With bodyguards and hangers-on in tow, he led the way down a hallway that got quieter with each step away from the dance floor. The ceiling was just high enough for me to stand up, though I had to duck through several doors as we walked.

Rumble spoke without looking back. "It's a rare day when someone threatens my territory and doesn't treat a warning shot with the respect it deserves. I guess times have changed. Used to be you could run a fine illicit business, bothering nobody but the law-grubbers, and only have to snap at a few upstarts now and then. There hasn't been a full-on street fight in a fingerless number of years."

I mentally ran that through my idiom translator, remembering how many fingers the turtledillos had to count with while Rumble went on.

"But now!" he said, "Now these invisible mud-eggs are bringing offworld merchandise in, causing problems for everyone. They step on more turfs all the time. With how long their list of enemies is now, our original plan was to unite the gangs and beat them into the dirt once and for all — send the message that they're not welcome, despite the traitors who keep signing up to do their distribution. But!"

He pointed upward with both right hands. "Most of those bosses are cloaca-kissers who can't be reasoned with."

One of the bodyguards snorted but held his silence. I privately wondered about the translation for the insult. It could just as easily have been "butt nuzzlers." Though, I supposed, it amounted to the same thing.

Rumble was still talking. "The new plan is to let the police do the hard work for us. They just need to be able to find the offworld eggholes." He looked sharply at me. "That's the part we'll need your expertise for. In here."

He told most of the crowd to wait for him outside another low doorway, bringing only a couple of the bodyguard types with him. I held my questions and followed into what proved to be a high-ceilinged garage/ workshop sort of place. The door locked behind Zephyr. The other door, a large one for vehicles, was already shut. No windows. A number of single-seater aircars lined up along the wall, painted in the same fiery color scheme as the building's decor.

In the center of the room waited the fabled offworld tech. Before Rumble said a thing, I recognized it as (A) a hovercycle, (B) beat to hell, and (C) not made by either of our species. Judging by the shape of the seat, it was designed to fit somebody with a long thorax and multiple legs. Either arms or tentacles, too. Probably one of the insect-like species.

Of course the criminals are from a creepy race, I thought. *Why do you have to be a stereotype like that, you smugglers? You're letting down the rest.*

"We managed to score this when we clashed with the mud-eggs," Rumble said. "It was already a little broken; otherwise, we never would have seen it. The creature that was driving it got away with the goods it was trying to sell in *our* territory, but we kept this scooter." He picked up a wrench and stepped forward. "Let me show you what the problem is."

With deep misgivings about how much he expected me to do, I followed.

"When we got it," Rumble said, "This part here showed a chart of some kind that marked where the softshells and their ships were. A stealth-breaker of the highest order." He looked at me significantly. "If we'd had this kind of tech when they first showed up, they would never have gotten a foothold."

I was curious about what kind of turf Rumble was protecting — did the offworlders have better holovids than the restricted films he sold? Or was it purely a physical territory? But this didn't seem the time to ask.

"We're hoping," Rumble said, "That we can use this thing to track them down. Either we shred their ship enough that the invisibility shuts down, and the police take 'em out for us, or we carve off enough pieces to show those thick-headed officials that they'll have to believe the report of where the ship is. But the problem is," he said while pointing with the wrench, "It stopped working. Somewhere between grabbing this thing and getting it back here, the chart disappeared. I told the crew not to touch it, 'cause they might break it worse. I'm hoping you can fix it proper. We need that chart."

"Well," I said, "Let me take a look." This was *not* my area of expertise in the slightest. But, since I was there, I might as well see. With Zephyr urging me on, I looked for buttons or other obvious controls.

Buttons, yes. Squishy ones. Makes sense if these folks have pointy exoskeleton claws. No idea about the language, though. Is that a language? Has to be. And, of course, everything's black, not color-coded. That would be too easy. Well, this one's big and looks important. Is it too much to hope it's a power button?

I pushed it. Nothing happened other than the blank screen moving in a way it probably wasn't meant to. Wondering about loose wires, I lifted the screen into a more likely-looking position.

It lit up! I made a happy noise at the same time Rumble did, then we were both overshadowed by an explosion outside the building.

Rumble swore and raced for the hallway. He directed

one of his guards to stay with us (and with the valuable hoverbike), then he was gone in a slam of the door.

Before I could do more than exchange worried looks with Zephyr, something made a distinct zapping sound.

My muscles locked up, and I toppled over sideways. More zaps put Zephyr and the guard on the floor with me. All I could see was a patch of oily floor and the back of Zephyr's head. I listened with everything I had, picking up a mighty ruckus of some sort out front, which almost covered the sound of the door locking from the inside.

The big rolling door opened, and that wasn't quiet at all. Someone shouted in the hallway. Ran toward us. Found the door locked.

Then I was being dragged by my feet toward the open door. When I got close, my frozen eyes caught a glimpse of an empty nighttime street. I was dragged out onto it, then up a ramp of some sort, and an invisible spaceship bloomed into view around me.

Whoever was pulling me dropped me in the cargo bay before going back for Zephyr. I heard multiple feet. Insect-ish. Zephyr slid to rest beside me. Back in the building, the broken hovercycle creaked, but the small door creaked louder, and the invisible person gave up on the bike before Rumble broke the door down. All those footsteps pattered back into the ship along with words in a chittery, chattery language that I wasn't even close to fluent in.

The door to the hallway crashed open. The door to the ship closed in silence.

We were well and truly captured.

So much for my worst-case scenario, I thought, trying not to panic. *This wasn't even on the list.*

Chapter 11
(Robin)

The invisible smugglers worked fast. I would have been impressed with their coordination if I wasn't busy fearing for my life. How long had they been watching us? If they wanted the bike back, why grab us first? And where were we going?

I slid several inches as the ship rocketed forward. The jerkwads hadn't strapped us down at all, and the floor was speckled with dirt. *If this is the kind of care they put into everything,* I thought with scorn, *Then I'm not surprised they lost all their animals.*

After a lengthy silence in which we angled upward slightly, the smugglers exchanged words in their foreign tongue. A chair creaked as one got up and tap-tapped back to us. A dim light clicked on nearby.

I found myself turned over onto my back, still in an awkward pose, with Zephyr similarly positioned next to me, angled for a good view of the bug-eyed face that hovered over us.

I hope we're not about to be eaten, I thought unfairly.

We were not. I realized that this was a species I'd seen before, though I couldn't remember the name. This individual was blue-black with lighter blue tips and roughly human-size, so probably male. A female would have been bigger. I knew that much but little else.

The alien began talking in passable Rockback with an accent and a hissing lisp. He wasted no time on niceties.

"You will catch animals for us," he told me with a wrist talon pointed at my head. "If you do not, then we will gut this one and sell his plates offworld." The talon gestured to Zephyr. I didn't doubt that the smuggler would do it. And there probably was a market somewhere for turtledillo shell segments, which didn't bear thinking about.

The smuggler was moving toward me with a strange device. I couldn't tell what it was until it touched my shoulder and restored my ability to speak. I coughed instead, licking dry lips and thinking madly.

The smuggler told me, "You are no good to us if you don't cooperate." The driver shouted an interjection, and the speaker added, "Never mind, you are probably good for leather. But that's not worth much. Answer now: will you capture the animals for us, or do we kill the both of you now and start skinning?"

Put that way, it wasn't much of a choice. I would have liked to say something rebellious, like every action hero I knew of, but that wouldn't do me any good. Dying now was out of the question. I wrapped myself in false confidence and answered in the affirmative.

"I will catch the animals," I said.

The smuggler leaned back, out of my field of vision. I still couldn't move my eyes. "Good," he said. "Do not disobey. Your friend here will suffer for anything we don't like." I heard more footsteps and miscellaneous scrapes. Something cold fastened about my neck with a click. "This is a shock collar. Do you know what they do?"

Crap. "Shock me, I assume."

"Yes. Any time you need mild disciplining. Would you like to know what it feels like?"

"No, I believe y—" My jaw clenched as untold volts tore through me. It was incredibly painful. Everything was on fire, and I couldn't breathe.

After a long few seconds, the electricity cut off. I lay there panting and sweating, unable to tell if I had soiled myself. That hurt a *lot*. Mild disciplining, my ass.

"Obey," the smuggler instructed me.

"Yyess," was all I managed through jaw muscles that were still more than a little stiff. I wanted to voice a few select insults, but it wasn't worth getting shocked again.

I was sure thinking them, though.

The smuggler didn't bother to do the same routine on Zephyr, simply leaving him frozen there as insurance on my good behavior. He still didn't secure us against sharp turns either, which was more than a little irritating when the shuttle took a steep dive. We slid again. The jerk just went back to the seat up front and let us.

I swore quietly, glad I was able to talk. Not that there was much I could do with that right now other than reassure Zephyr. I wasted no time in telling him I would look for the first safe chance to escape and get him out with me. These bastards wouldn't be getting away with it.

Zephyr couldn't answer. I hoped he believed me. Neither despair nor blind rage would do him any favors when his paralysis wore off.

I hoped it would wear off. There was no way this was healthy.

Shadows flashed past, making me try to blink. I realized that they were trees lit by moonlight. We were in the forest.

The shuttle slowed in midair, coming to rest on the ground so smoothly that I didn't realize we'd landed until the smugglers both got up to walk around and open the doors. With the lights turned up, I saw that the driver was female: a good head taller than the male, colored in purples and reds, with sharper blade-arms.

Both aliens were just as beat up as the hovercycle. Did Rumble's people manage that?

My jaws were working normally again, though nothing else was. "What happened to you?" I asked.

"A crash," said the male sourly.

"We couldn't get fuel at our usual stop," the female elaborated. "Surviving the landing at all is something you should respect."

The male was staring directly at her like he wanted her to stop talking but didn't want to say so out loud.

"Why couldn't you get fuel?" I asked, because no one had told me to shut up yet.

"Blockade at the station. Also not my fault."

"Anyway," the male cut in, "That is beside the point."

I connected a couple dots. "The people fighting the cops at the space station meant no one is allowed in? Or just extra security, so they'd realize what you were carrying?"

The male triggered the shock collar at that, and I had a few seconds of electricity-filled regrets. When I could breathe again, he waved the controls at me.

"Pay attention."

I did. The two smugglers presented me with a variety of tools and some very simple instructions: catch the animals. Bring them back to the shuttle. Don't try to escape.

"Why can't you catch them?" I asked, hoping they didn't zap me for asking more questions. "Why me?"

"You will be faster," the male said.

"You're expendable," added the female, getting another glare from the male.

They turned back to business, explaining each of the tools that they had for me. There weren't many, but they looked useful: a net-launcher that was supposed to be silent, a remote-activated paralysis disc the size of a manhole cover, several noisemakers on different frequencies that would attract certain animals, a pair of night-vision goggles that had a fighting chance of fitting my head, and a collection of muzzles and collars. It would do.

The two aliens would not be joining me. They carried me out of the ship before undoing the paralysis, apparently taking no chances that I'd try something desperate. They set me down face-up, then checked my pockets thoroughly. I'd really hoped that they'd skip that step — my phone would have summoned the cops in no time. But they found it and the dagger Zephyr had given me, along with the nearly-empty wallet I'd brought along and a variety of pocket detritus. They took it all, retreating with another reminder that they wouldn't hesitate to use the shock collar.

I agreed to behave. They released the paralysis. I collapsed when they did, smacking one hand on a rock.

The ground was spongy with fallen leaves. I sat up with a groan and a few more quiet curses, rubbing my hand as I looked around.

Yep, this was a forest at night. It smelled like mud and was super dark. Those goggles were going to be crucial. I looked back at the shuttle — invisible again — and my captors, who stood in front of it with the collar controls held threateningly.

"Get up."

I got up. It was a little painful, but I felt things loosening up by the second. At least I wouldn't have to hobble around the forest, chasing cats and rabbits and who knew what else. Zebras.

I turned to ask them what kind of animals I should expect. They were gone, apparently having stepped back into the ship. I sighed. Fishing the goggles out of the pile of supplies, I tried to formulate a plan.

Didn't come up with much.

The goggles made the forest green and brightly-lit, as opposed to black and full of darkness. Good. Now, where were these animals that the smugglers expected me to find?

A look around was of no use, so I gathered up the gear into a bag (which the smugglers had provided, but not bothered to use themselves; rude), and I started walking. It occurred to me several steps in that there could easily be other things in this forest than escaped pets. I had a cursory familiarity with the most common of the native animals — mostly to better deal with Earth critters who'd run afoul of them — but I had very little idea of what to do when faced with some nocturnal beastie with more teeth than sense.

Here's hoping I find none of those, I thought resolutely. *Now, should I start calling out for kitty-kitty and see what happens, or just be stealthy? Well, on the chance that those beasties are about, I think I'll be staying silent for now. The smugglers can't expect me to catch what I can't find.*

So I kept walking, sweeping the area with my eyes and listening to every sound. I wondered what the odds were of convincing the smugglers to let me come back in the daylight. Probably not good.

Then, to my surprise, I found an Earth animal. Half of one.

The rabbit haunches lay in a dark puddle that was as green as everything else to my goggled eyes. I spent a long few moments frozen cautiously in place, listening, before I approached. Nothing snarled or jumped out to scare me away from its prey.

I carefully set the bag down, then pulled out the net-launcher and eased my way forward. It was the closest thing I had to a weapon.

A detailed look at the gory sight told me that the rabbit had been killed by something predatory with sharp teeth, and that this had been several hours ago. The body was cool. (Hand sanitizer was near the top of the list of things I would have loved to have right now, right after phone and stun gun.)

Well, there's not much I can do for this one, I thought. *The smugglers probably only want the live ones. Probably. How am I supposed to tell them when I've caught something, anyway?* I looked around for the invisible ship, with a predictable lack of results. The forest here was sparse enough that the shuttle could float between trees without moving a branch. I had only a rough idea of how big it was.

All right, executive decision. Moving on. And NOT bringing this guy as bait. I stood and moved away, returning to the bag of gear. Still no signs of life.

Then something whined. I froze.

There it was again. *That sounds suspiciously like a dog.* I left the gear where it was, tracking down the noises with my trusty net-gun at the ready.

Something moved under a bush. I crouched down and did my best to see into the dense foliage. A dark lump of some sort huddled in the center. It could have been a dog.

"Hey there," I said gently. "You wanna come out? I won't bite if you won't."

That was a very canine whimper. The lump shifted, then crawled toward me. I stepped back just in case it was a doglike alien beastie.

It was a beagle. Young adult, favoring one front paw, with a dark patch on its muzzle that might have come from the rabbit.

Well, beagles are hunting dogs, I reminded myself. "Hey, buddy," I said, holding out a hand. "You okay?"

The dog limped over to my hand and nuzzled it, whimpering and licking. I set down my net gun and stroked the poor thing before taking a look at its injured foot. Just a bruise, by the looks of things, but I'd want to be sure in better lighting. There were no visible cuts, and the bones didn't feel broken, though it was hard to say in this green darkness.

I retrieved the bag to fish out a collar and a leash, which the dog appeared familiar with. When I had these fastened in place, just as I was starting to wonder what to do next, a blinding glare appeared behind me.

I screwed my eyes shut, keeping one hand clenched on the leash while I pulled off the goggles. The dog whimpered again and crawled to hide behind my legs.

Yep, there were the smugglers, right on time. With floodlights that made *their* lives easier, never mind my burned retinas. They ordered me to get the dog into a storage crate. I did, wanting to give it a full checkup and a bath instead. That was definitely blood on its face, but there didn't appear to be any cuts. I checked out the paw quickly to be sure — good enough. Then the male smuggler shut the door of the crate and ordered me back into the woods.

I went, though not before giving them explicit instructions about what sort of care the animal would need. They ignored me. Not really a surprise.

Back into the green-tinged night. I was honestly impressed that the dog had been close enough to stumble upon; I didn't expect to find anything else.

I was wrong again.

This time, it was porcupines.

A herd of them. Do porcupines travel in herds? The group name is probably something dumb like *passel* or *gruntling*. But yeah, it was a herd. My vet training didn't cover porcupines. I wasn't pleased about any of this.

I heard the snuffling and the rustle of leaves first, then approached slowly enough that they didn't see me right away. I actually had enough time to crouch, set down the gear, and stand up again with the net launcher before one of them noticed.

A dozen pairs of eyes suddenly stared at me while the air filled with angry grunting. I edged forward as if I knew what I was doing. They did a threat display that involved a lot of quill-covered tails waving at me.

I fired the net gun, which was as quiet as promised but not super accurate. It *sort of* snared one of them while the rest waddled away at top speed. I rushed forward to do … something.

Ever wrestle a porcupine? It was a first for me too. And it was every bit as unpleasant as you might expect. My only saving grace was the fact that the net had caught the porcupine's head, which meant it couldn't see where I was in order to spike me. So, I somehow managed, through luck and undignified scrambling, to grab hold of the net and pull it to where it actually held the squealing creature against the ground.

I held it there, panting. *Now what?*

There probably wouldn't be any help coming from the smugglers. Even with their paralysis tasers, they seemed to be extremely unwilling to put themselves into the action. Maybe because of their injuries. Maybe they were just jackasses.

Either way, it was up to me. And the leashes that were *almost* close enough to reach.

After a lot of struggling, squealing, and thrashing, I edged across the dirt to where I could hook a foot around the bag's strap and pull it closer. Then contort myself to free a hand without letting off pressure on the net, and yank a leash out.

Or, more accurately, grab one leash and spend more time trying to untangle the others that came with it, one-handed. While not letting the porcupine escape, or get me with its quills.

Finally, I freed a leash. I threaded it through the edge of the net, hoping the porcupine would cooperate enough to let me tie it up. Predictably, it didn't like this. Threading one side of the net wasn't so bad, with my feet straining to hold the other side down like the most awkward game of Twister, though the other side was a near miss of quills to the arm.

"Hey, I got it!" I yelled at the sky. "Come and get the dang thing! It's not going anywhere!"

For a moment, nothing moved, then those floodlights appeared to my right. I managed to close my eyes and turn away before my vision was completely washed out.

The smugglers appeared with another crate and very little sympathy for my difficulties. Before going out again, I demanded gloves but was refused on the grounds that they didn't have any. Reasonable, I suppose, but still annoying.

"I really need Zephyr's help," I said. "And it's not like we'll be able to escape, what with the shock collars and you guys following us all invisible."

They weren't buying it. Back to work for me; further complaining would be met with a zap from the shock collar. I gave up and went, faking a limp for sympathy that I didn't get.

The rest of the porcupines were predictably long gone. I did my best to track their footprints in the leaves, but other than the original scattering, there wasn't much to see. I kept walking for lack of anything better to do.

The forest seemed a bit brighter up ahead, smelling more like wood chips than mud. I trudged onward, pressing through a spiky mass of bushes to find an odd clearing with fallen trees that looked like they had been politely pressed aside.

I stopped, taking in the sight. It had to be the crash site – the ship was probably still there, broken and invisible. And I couldn't let the smugglers know that I realized that. I pretended to hear a sound off to the right, then moved away at a stealthy pace like I was actively stalking something. Who knew; there might actually be porcupines there.

There weren't, but after a long bit of walking, I reached muddy ground that held footprints better than the leaves, and that was helpful.

Gotcha! That herd of prints probably belonged to the porcupines. Probably. I followed it. And this time, when I found them, I had my net gun ready.

I'd been considering doing a deliberately bad job on this capture, just so the smugglers would see how much I needed assistance. But as it turned out, I didn't need to try. As soon as the net left the gun, they all saw it and scattered. I had to run after them, belatedly wondering just how many nets were stored in that launcher.

Three, as it turned out. That third net snared the biggest porcupine in the herd, and when I went to launch another to seal the deal, nothing came out.

So, back to swearing and struggling. At least now, I'd done it before, not that that really helped. The local plantlife turned out to be more useful; I wrestled the critter into a shrub, and managed to pin it there while I tried to slip a hand under it without getting spiked. I'd remembered that there were no quills on the underside of the tail. When the porcupine tried to hit me and missed (woo!), I laid a hand on the ground. The thick tail smacked onto my palm. No pain. I closed my fingers, moving along the grain of the quills, and soon had a solid grip. That was a thick, meaty tail.

I hauled the 30-pound animal from the bush with one hand on its tail and the other wrapped in the net that tangled the rest of it. I knelt just inches from a mud puddle and yelled for the aliens to show up and take it from me.

The porcupine joined in with angry noises that would have been cute under other circumstances. I hadn't really heard a porcupine's voice before today. It sounded like a person doing an impression of a teddy bear that could *almost* talk. A furious one.

The floodlights blinded both of us, and I complained along with the porcupine.

When the unwieldy armload of spikes was safe in a cage with water, I insisted again that I needed Zephyr. This time the smugglers actually listened. Or maybe they'd been arguing with each other about it while I struggled about in the bushes. Either way, I approved of their decision.

"What's the plan?" Zephyr muttered, scowling fiercely while he tugged at his own shock collar.

An abrupt lightning strike of pain said they'd tased us both. It hurt just as much the second time.

"Don't touch it," hissed one of the smugglers while we twitched. "Now, get out there and don't try anything."

They don't know I found the ship. I kept my teeth clenched while I regained muscle control and limped away from the shuttle. *At least, I don't think they know. Now what?*

Zephyr wheezed a bit as he followed me. As soon as he cleared the door, a gust of displaced air said it was shut with invisible silence. I considered telling him about my discovery, but I was pretty sure that the shuttle's sensors were good enough to overhear us. Instead, I reassured him that I wasn't hurt and that this would be easier with six arms instead of two. Thankfully, the smugglers had had a second pair of goggles, so he could walk without tripping over everything.

We set out after the new tracks in the mud, discussing plans. We would find the herd silently, then plant the remote-activated paralysis disc, and hopefully move around to the other side and scare them toward it. Or one of us would, while the other laid in wait with the controls.

It was a pretty good plan. It might have actually worked. But luckily for us, that was when Rumble's crew showed up. Dark shapes of airships flitted through the trees from multiple angles, waiting until they surrounded the invisible shuttle to flare fiery lights.

"Exit the ship, you mudborn—" the rest of the loudspeaker tirade wasn't fit for polite company.

"It's Rumble!" Zephyr cheered beside me. "He got the

stealthbreaker working to rescue us!"

That didn't seem 100% accurate, but I didn't correct him. I scoped out trees to hide behind instead. Pretty sure the local crime lord was more interested in taking out a rival than in saving people he'd just met.

Yup, the threats did nothing. Rockets followed. Zephyr and I dove for cover as small explosions lit the woods even brighter, impacting the shuttle several yards off the ground. They did no damage that I could see.

I hope Rumble has a Plan B, I thought, peering through leaves from where I crouched with Zephyr. *Maybe he's going to herd them toward the police — Oh, there they go!* One way or another, the shuttle had taken off at top speed. I could only tell by the trail of explosions and the way Rumble's group of airships flashed off after it.

Suddenly, the forest was dark again. And very quiet.

Zephyr spoke first. "Any idea how to get these collars off?"

Chapter 12
(Robin)

The shock collars weren't as high-tech as I'd assumed, but they were stubborn buggers. As far as I could tell in the dark, they were leatherlike straps with electronic elements and a covered locking mechanism. They'd probably stand up to an animal scratching at them, and they might or might not shock us if we tried to take them off.

Sure hope not, I thought, inspecting Zephyr's collar while he looked at mine. "Do you have a knife?" I asked, not expecting much.

Zephyr shook his head. "No, they took everything. And I keep my claws manicured to a proper smooth point, so that's no good. You?"

"Same. Either way, let's get moving in case they come back. I have an idea about where we might find something sharp."

"Did you find garbage in the woods?" Zephyr asked, adjusting the night-vision goggles that were much too big for his head.

"Better than that," I said as I gathered up the gear. "Pretty sure I found where the smuggler ship crashed."

"What?!" That yelp would have woken half the forest if the animals weren't already scared off by the heavy artillery. He clamored for details.

I told him what I'd seen, both in person and on the news, and we set out at our best pace toward that mysterious clearing. Zephyr would have led the way if he could. Poor guy could barely see out of the goggles, but he was *ready*. For what, that remained to be seen. Maybe to tear the ship apart by hand for therapy's sake. It'd probably make him feel better. Heck, I wouldn't say no to a little therapeutic damage myself. But that wasn't at the top of the list.

"Assuming it's still there, the ship might have things we can use," I said, stepping over a log in the silent forest. "Tools to get the collars off, maybe even a communication system that can get us a rescue."

"Maybe weapons in case those smugglers show their faces again," Zephyr muttered. Then we reached a break in the tree canopy, and he brightened. "Is that it? That has to be it. Come on!" He hurried forward.

"Wait!" I said urgently enough that he actually stopped. "The ship is invisible," I reminded him. "And probably damaged. If we go running in, we could run straight into a jagged piece of something."

"Good point." Zephyr cast about and came up with a fallen branch. "Now, let's go." He waved it in front of himself like a kid at a piñata party, stepping along at a more reasonable pace.

I couldn't find a stick of my own, but I did still have the empty net launcher. I dug that out of the bag and followed.

We edged forward this way, testing the air, listening for any signs of airships or animals. There were none, just green-tinted silence. Eventually, we reached the fallen trees and could get a better look at the imprint that the ship had left on the forest.

"It must be right there," Zephyr said, waving his stick. "Right in the middle." I agreed. If it was anywhere, it would be there. We moved in more carefully, aware that there could easily be a broken wing in front of our faces. Zephyr started tossing things underhand: twigs, small rocks, messy handfuls of mud.

I was looking for rocks so I could show him up by throwing overhand with my long human arms when he yelped in surprise.

"I threw a stick right *there*," he said, pointing with both left arms. "It just stopped at the peak of its arc and fell instantly! No sound whatsoever!" He scrambled to throw another.

I saw it this time. It was exactly like he'd said: the stick stopped dead, its momentum cancelled by contact with the ship. Without so much as a tap, it dropped to disappear among the tree trunks.

"O*kay* then." Wanting to keep the net launcher, I scooped up some mud and flung it in the same direction. The mud hit and slid, not splattering like I'd expected. It did leave a brown smear hovering in midair, though.

Zephyr laughed and grabbed up some mud of his own. Soon we had dark streaks outlining the side of an invisible spaceship, nestled among the fallen trees at something of an angle.

Then I threw one mudball that disappeared. "Hey, I think I found a door!"

"Where?" Zephyr demanded. I pointed, threw more mud, then followed the eager little turtledillo as he scrambled across the tree trunks with stick in hand. I held the net launcher out in front of me.

Zephyr grabbed a leafy branch and pressed it to the invisible surface next to a mud streak. The leaves rustled as they compressed. I caught up and tapped the net launcher against the ship.

Tried to, anyway. It stopped suddenly in the *strangest* way.

Zephyr turned his branch around and gave the area a mighty whack. The stick halted in midair, with no sound and no bounce-back. The expression on Zephyr's face was a funny one.

I reached out with apprehensive fingers to find a wall that felt smooth and slightly cold, but oddly undefined otherwise. I rapped my knuckles on it. Silence, and my hand didn't bounce. So weird. My whole arm was just suddenly still.

Zephyr had finished marveling at the technology. He edged forward with one hand on the ship and the other pressing his branch against it, searching for the door. I followed with careful steps. This was not the time for a broken ankle from falling off a log.

"Ha!" Zephyr exclaimed when his stick disappeared from view. He felt around some more, then stuck his head into the empty air. "This is it!" he said, his voice suddenly echoing. "Come on; there's even some light in here."

"Careful," I whispered, the thought only now occurring to me. "It might not be empty!"

Zephyr made a distracted noise as he climbed over the edge of the doorframe, vanishing from sight. I caught up and stuck my head after him.

"Wow," I said as the interior of the ship popped into view. "This is it, all right." I climbed through the doorway onto the crooked floor, which smelled more like fuel than Zephyr's car did. "What a mess." Now that I could see it, the place was full of cracks, and the door had been ripped halfway off the hinges. I was glad that we hadn't approached from the other direction. We would have had to navigate around it.

"There's a light from over here," Zephyr said, pressing on down the hallway. I looked back the other way, my goggles showing only green darkness. This was an odd sort of entrance to a ship, I reflected as I walked with bent knees on the crooked floor. There must have been a bigger cargo bay elsewhere. This was purely for people.

And the hallway was a wreck. Those oh-so-amazing inertial dampeners only went so far, apparently. They could handle mudballs and even trees, but a full-force impact with a planet was too much. Though they did blunt the damage at least; a normal ship wouldn't have left more than a crater and shrapnel.

Still amazing, I thought. *The question is, what happened to everybody else on board? Were there more smugglers? Did ALL the animals escape?* It seemed likely since the ship was quiet. Though with the paralysis guns, that didn't mean much.

And that doesn't mean none of them came back here for shelter, I reminded myself. I opened my mouth to tell Zephyr the same thing, but he'd reached the next room, and his attention was elsewhere.

"Look at all the tools they left behind!" he enthused. I stepped forward and had to agree. That was a lot of stuff hung on the walls, strewn across tables, and fallen from open cabinets. I had no idea what any of it was.

"Let's see if there's something to use on the collars," I suggested. "Before they come back."

Zephyr scoffed. "They're not coming back," he asserted. "Not with Rumble after them. They can't hide anymore, and it's only a matter of time before they're blasted out of the air." He threw his stick aside and began digging through the tools.

I looked at him with a raised eyebrow. "Those rockets didn't seem to be doing much," I pointed out.

Zephyr waved a hand dismissively. "Those were probably just to scare them away from us, so Rumble could use his *real* ammo."

"Uh-huh."

"He knows what he's doing," Zephyr insisted. "I'm sure he'll have the rotten smugglers taken out in no time."

"And what about the animals on board?" I reminded him.

That brought him up short. "Oh. Right. Um, well, Rumble probably disabled the ship without destroying it, so they could be taken alive. He's clever enough for that."

I opened a cupboard. "You seem quite the fan," I observed.

Zephyr made an indignant gesture. "He was nice!" he exclaimed. "A man of integrity, despite operating on the shady side of things. I'm sure he's valuable to have as a friend. And that voice, hmm…"

I laughed. "Zephyr, do you have a crush on the man with the illegal business?"

"No!" he protested in a high voice. "I'm reasonably impressed; that's all. As I said, he was very nice."

"And very much hitting on you."

"He was a gentleman and complimentary!" Zephyr sputtered. "And hardly a criminal, as I said. Just someone with a niche and dubious business, which he is interested in protecting from incursions by villainous smugglers who surely have a vast network of resources to draw upon. Rumble is to be commended for standing up to the likes of them."

I chuckled and left it at that. I hadn't realized earlier that Zephyr was actually tempted by Rumble's offer. Somehow I got the feeling that the deep-voiced turtledillo would be amused by the little accountant's infatuation.

"A-hah!" Zephyr exclaimed, pulling free a pair of shears. "These look promising!"

They did. They also looked like they were built more for humanoid hands than mantis pinchers, or even the little wrist talons. I made a note to be prepared for other species among the smugglers.

"Let me try them first?" I suggested.

"Are you sure?" Zephyr asked, clinging to his prize. "I'm good with scissors too, you know."

"Ah, but have you freed panicky animals from things that they've tangled themselves up in? Repeatedly, while being a panicky animal yourself?"

He had to admit that he didn't have that exact type of experience, and he handed over the shears. Then he let me use them on his collar, since we didn't have a mirror around for me to use them on myself. I rotated the collar, looking for the least dangerous-looking place to cut, and finally settled on an area near the latch. Being extra special careful after the little speech I'd just given, I slid the shears into place, held the material away from his neck as best I could, and sliced through it in one clean go.

"Huh. That was easy."

I let Zephyr cut mine off. It was just as easy that time. Zephyr ceremoniously flung the collars against the far wall, then set about searching for anything he might want to keep. I did the same. Some of this stuff looked useful, and we didn't know how long we'd be out on our own. Assuming no rescuers appeared, the walk back to town promised to take hours at best.

"Did you hear that?" I asked after a muffled thud.

"No?" Zephyr said, arms full of things.

"Mmmaybe we should search the ship," I suggested, not wholeheartedly liking the idea myself. "It could have been just a broken bit falling off. Or not."

Zephyr put down his armload and selected two things: they looked like a taser and a flashlight, though these were shaped weird for pinchers to hold. Lucky for us, fingers could hold them too.

I traded the bag of useless gear for a taser and light of my own, then led the way. We still wore our night-vision goggles and didn't need the flashlights yet, but if we met any hostile animals whose eyes were adjusted to the dark, it might give us a moment's advantage.

There were three doors to this room, including the one we'd entered from. Cautious peeks through both of the others showed similarly dark areas. Zephyr spun in place and randomly pointed left, so left we went.

We found a kind of conference room, an alien bathroom, and a ransacked kitchen. Here we stopped, less concerned with animals as we were with the fact that it was nearly dawn, and we were hungry.

Most of the food was either spilled, spoiled, or so alien that I couldn't make heads or tails of it. But some was recognizable to one or the other of us, and we managed to cobble together a meal. It was, in my professional opinion, super gross. Almond butter on fish jerky kind of gross. But it was food.

Then, finally realizing how tired we were, we made the executive decision to hole up here for what remained of the night. It was a long walk to the woodland's border. Goggles or not, it would be easier to find our way back to civilization in the morning. And the forest was dangerous now that we didn't have an invisible spaceship following us around. Zephyr was particularly worried about large predators that I'd never seen in person. We hadn't heard any other suspicious noises, though that didn't mean much. After checking the room for hidden critters, we barricaded the doors with tables and set about gathering hand towels to use as pillows and an attempt at blankets.

I took off my goggles, loosened my braid, and was asleep before Zephyr finished settling into place.

Chapter 13
(Robin)

I woke to the horrendous scraping sound of the door being forced open by something very strong. Scrambling to my feet in the dim light, I retreated to the far corner of the room alongside Zephyr, where we both realized we'd trapped ourselves. We snatched up the most dangerous things we could get our hands on — for him, a wrench, and for me, a flashlight. I aimed it at the door without turning it on yet, hoping that I'd be able to stun the whatever-it-was long enough for Zephyr to throw the wrench at it. Or something.

Just as I remembered that turtledillos weren't built for throwing, the door opened the rest of the way. Something large hulked in the darkness. I switched on the flashlight and yelled wildly.

Zephyr yelled too, and the unlikely creature in the doorway flinched, then thundered into the hallway with heavy steps. Listening was difficult over the blood pounding in my ears, but I thought it had stopped right around the corner.

Still screaming, Zephyr huddled next to me. "Ahh! Ahh! What was that?!"

I answered with wide eyes. "That was a gorilla," I told him. "The smugglers took a *gorilla*."

"Is that bad?" the turtledillo asked, waving his wrench. "Do they eat people?"

"No," I said, looking down at him. "They *are* people. Just a different kind. And there's going to be eighty flavors of hell raised when people find out that these guys kidnapped one to *sell* offworld."

"So it's not going to eat us?" Zephyr lowered his wrench, looking back at the doorway.

"No," I said, taking a hesitant step forward. "But we might have scared him enough that we could get hurt if we're not careful." I raised my voice, trying for gentle and apologetic in my native tongue. "Hello?" I called. "I'm sorry we scared you. We were scared too. Can you hear me?"

There was a pause long enough that I started to doubt my training. All gorillas were supposed to recognize English; the people who had started the reservation-resorts for these particular Citizen Animals had been English speakers, and it had stuck. But this one wasn't responding.

A dark head peered around the corner. I made sure to point the flashlight at the floor. This lit things up well enough that we could all see each other, and no one was blinded.

"Hello," I said again. "Sorry about that. Are you okay?"

The gorilla grunted, bobbed his head, and made a hand sign that I recognized from long-ago classes: "Yes." The next one was less obvious but clear enough: "Scared."

I nodded in exaggerated fashion. "We were scared too," I repeated, hoping I knew enough Gorilla Sign Language to get through this conversation. It was slightly different from the standard signs that everyone learned in school. I'd never expected to meet a gorilla, much less talk to one solo on an alien world. "My name is Robin," I said, pointing to myself. "This is Zephyr. He's a friend." I used the Rockback word for his name, but signed it out in GSL at the same time, hoping that made sense. Translating between three languages was hard.

The gorilla edged forward, still looking ready to run. And, conversely, ready to rip the wall open if startled. Silver fur showed over his shoulders, making him a male of at least twelve years old. *The most dangerous twelve-year-old I've ever met,* I thought.

The gorilla signed something that I recognized as a

bird symbol, then pointed at me in a questioning way. It took me a moment, but then I nodded and agreed, "Yes, Robin like the bird. And he is Zephyr like a breeze or wind." I also repeated Zephyr's name in both languages.

Zephyr whispered urgently. "What's it doing?" he asked, and I remembered that he wouldn't have understood any of that.

"Talking in sign language," I told him. "Give me a minute, and I'll translate."

The gorilla was already volunteering his own name. The sign he used stumped me — an embarrassing thing so early in the conversation — and I had to ask him to clarify. The additional signs took me a minute to put together.

"Fire ... animal ... flying ... Dragon? Your name is Dragon?"

He nodded vigorously. I kept my surprise to myself. Of *course* the spacefaring gorilla would have a name that cool.

I told Zephyr what his name was, having to explain the mythological Earth creature, then having to interrupt that explanation when Dragon wanted to know where the "giant stinging bugs" had gone.

Guess he's met the smugglers in person, I thought. Doing my best to be clear and brief, I explained that as far as we knew, the only two "stinging bugs" had been scared away by some people who looked like Zephyr. We didn't know if they would be back.

It was at this point that we heard distant voices outside. I couldn't make out words or guess the species. The three of us looked around in unison; this kitchen had no windows. I certainly wasn't eager to stick my head past the invisibility field if I didn't have to. What other options did we have?

"Maybe it's Rumble!" Zephyr exclaimed. He dashed into the hall, only pausing briefly before sidling past the large gorilla who regarded him with suspicion. I translated and followed as Zephyr ran down the tilted hallway in search of a window. Dragon stuck close, his heavy footsteps echoing my own.

None of the rooms had windows. Only sturdy metal walls with a few blank screens that might have been digital windows, but of course, they were all dead. Zephyr hurried on. The ship's living area wasn't all that big, and we soon found ourselves in the cockpit.

This didn't have actual windows either, but it did have computers that were still partly functional. One monitor flipped through readouts of the ship's systems, one was stuck on a layout of the ship that might have been useful if I'd had time to study it, one was broken, and one showed the sunlit forest directly in front of the ship.

Distant turtledillos with guns picked their way through the trees. Not Rumble's crew, by the looks of it. These guys were painted in hunter's camouflage, wielding firearms that looked far too eye-catching for any underground crime ring to use.

"Is one of those the owner of the forest?" I asked.

"Well, it's not Rumble," Zephyr said in clear disappointment. "What does this mean? It's flashing." He pointed to the monitor that had held changing images a moment ago. Now it held two green triangles growing closer together with a flashing red border.

"If this was human tech, I'd say it's an alarm of an approaching ship," I said, glancing instinctively at the ceiling.

Dragon grunted for a translation again. As I obliged him, Zephyr came to his own conclusion.

"If that's another ship, then those people will *see it*," he said, pointing at the screen. "And so will any watching cameras at the edge of the forest! Unless it's invisible too."

"Right," I agreed. "We can't tell from in here. Let's find the door." I turned to Dragon and said in English, "More bad bugs are coming. We need to see if the good people — like Zephyr — will see them too. Come on!" Then I ran for the side of the ship that was torn open. Dragon and Zephyr followed.

Nothing stood out at first. The hole was big enough to

show blue sky, but the spaceship that must have been approaching was nowhere to be seen.

"Invisible," Zephyr spat.

Then a square opened in the sky, and something mechanical reached toward us.

"There!" I said.

Dragon grunted loudly.

"They don't see it!" said Zephyr. "They're not yelling! How do we get them to look this way?"

"We yell first," I said. "Dragon! We need to be loud!" Without waiting, I launched into every full-voiced animal impression I could think of. If those turtledillos prowling the woods were searching for Earth animals, there was no way they would miss this.

Especially when Dragon roared next to me. It was more than a little terrifying; the sound shook my lungs and put my eagle screeches to shame.

Zephyr flinched, then started screaming. It wasn't an Earth animal, but it added to the racket.

I listened for a moment. Startled shouts reached my ears. My satisfaction was short-lived, though. The mechanical arm retracted into the ship above, to be replaced by what was clearly a weapon.

"Oh no — Get inside, get inside!" I exclaimed, pushing the others back under cover. "I think we started a fight!"

The muffled pop of turtledillo guns joined the shouting. I raced back to the cockpit and its viewscreen. By the time I arrived, with Dragon thundering behind me and Zephyr scuttling after, the screen was full of gunfire. None of the turtledillos looked hurt yet, but I wouldn't be making any bets.

The ship vibrated. I gripped the console as the floor tilted ever so slightly. Then a strange light filled the screen, barely-audible screeching sounded, and the vibrating increased.

"What's happening?" Zephyr asked, nearly falling over.

"I don't know!" I said.

Dragon whined, then growled and punched the floor as if to make it behave.

The turtledillos were still shooting, barely visible through the glare, but they were also edging backwards.

And getting smaller.

"Oh dear gods, we're lifting off!" I exclaimed.

"What?" Zephyr demanded. "No!" He yelled at the screen, "Shoot harder, you idiots!"

I looked wildly around the room for ideas. Dragon signed, <Stinging bugs make building fly again!>

"Yeah," I said. "I guess we should have run for the trees instead. Though we might have gotten shot."

The light on the screen shone brighter before shutting off completely, then the floor dropped six inches and slammed sideways.

All three of us fell over. Everything was shouting and thudding and stuff falling on us. I ended up curled into a ball, protecting my head while alien coffee cups and pencils and crap rained down. Things fell off the wall that I couldn't even begin to identify. It occurred to me that this cockpit had never been designed to handle inertia of any kind.

Wonder why.

When everything was still, Zephyr sat up first, undaunted in his natural armor. "Everybody okay?" he asked.

"I'll live," I told him, uncurling and looking to Dragon, who was signing madly. *Huh,* I thought. *Never seen a gorilla swear before. It's a red-letter day. But at least he looks all right.*

I asked him in English to be sure, and he assured me that he was unhurt but *very* mad at the bug people.

"Yeah, me too," I agreed. "Maybe we'll get to hit them and tell them so."

Another thump shook us. Again I heard voices outside the ship, but these didn't sound like turtledillos. Uh oh.

<Bug people!> Dragon signed, getting up with a growl.

"Wait, wait, wait," I exclaimed, "It sounds like there's a lot of them. Let's be quiet for a minute first, okay?"

Dragon grudgingly agreed. Zephyr edged away from the gorilla, looking nervous. We all stood and listened to the chatter.

I had no plan at this point. I just knew that charging out there in a towering rage was an easy way to get shot in the face. And I very much liked my face. There had to be a way to do this safely.

Zephyr whispered, "Why did they take us? Are they only after the ship, and they didn't check if anyone was on it?"

I shook my head. "I don't know. I hope it's just the ship, and they'll be open to putting us back where they found us. Or outside the forest. Near the police. But hey, I'm not picky."

The room tipped again without warning, and we scrambled to hold on. The floor moved slowly upward, and then down, then the room shuddered.

I heard bug voices again. All clicks and hisses, unsettling sounds. I didn't want to be prejudiced, of course, but it was unnerving to my human hindbrain. The fact that I knew they could kill us on sight didn't help.

A new vibration and sideways motion. I clawed my way up to where the viewscreens were still partly operational.

The view out the front showed what looked like a distant warehouse ceiling, slowly moving past. Windows let in sunshine — at least we hadn't rocketed up to space. I blinked as a doorway whooshed by close to the camera, leaving us in a new room and making me wonder exactly how much of the ship had actually come with us.

The motion stopped. Again we were lifted and set down carefully. Voices resumed. Bangs, clangs, and the creaks of metal panels filled the air. Sounded like the ship was being dismantled. A draft gusted through the room; the hull was breached nearby. A pair of big-eyed faces appeared in front of the camera. I flinched, but they couldn't see me.

"Guess they are after the ship," I said, glancing at my companions. "You guys still okay?"

Dragon joined me before Zephyr could. The big guy had a musky smell and was surprisingly warm, like a furry heater appearing two inches away. Apparently personal space was less of an issue in gorilla culture. Good to know.

When Dragon reached over my shoulder with a grunt, he made three gestures toward the screen: he pointed at the buglike aliens, made a fist, then flipped them off. I told him that I agreed wholeheartedly.

"We should arm ourselves," Zephyr said from the other side of the room, rooting through the fallen trash. "They'll reach us soon, even if we don't make a move."

He had a point. I looked around to see if anything looked useful. But as soon as I turned away from the viewscreen, a louder voice shouted in clicks and screeches and the dismantling stopped. Footsteps clattered away.

"Think it's safe to leave?" I asked.

"We'll have to try," Zephyr declared. He had already pulled something weaponlike from the floor and Dragon was heading for the doorway, having gotten the idea despite not knowing the language. I shrugged and picked up an alien wrench, following the others out into the hall. Maybe we could stop by the kitchen and get that net launcher.

Nope. The kitchen was gone. The hallway turned one corner and cut off abruptly, leaving us staring out at the interior of a cluttered alien warehouse.

Quiet swear words and mutterings of surprise were the order of the hour. We ventured forward like puppies encountering snow for the first time, stepping off the edge of the hallway and down onto the floor like we expected it to go away at any moment. Nothing happened other than sounds of industry from the next room.

I stepped away from the ship enough to see how much had actually come with us. As I watched, the invisibility field flickered before retracting toward the point of the ship. This chunk was *small*. "Wow. We got lucky."

Zephyr turned to look, and jumped visibly. "That almost cut us in half!" he yelped. "They definitely didn't know we were there!"

"Yeah," I agreed. "Let's get wherever we're going before they come back. And hey, at least the rest of the ship is probably visible now too!"

"Even if it's not, I'm sure those people can find it," Zephyr agreed. "It's still covered in our mudballs. Now, all we have to do is survive to find a way home."

"Yeah, speaking of which," I said with a deliberate look around, "This doesn't look like the inside of a spaceship." The angles and joints of the ceiling looked distinctly like quick-construction meant for early colonization efforts. Or temporary housing after natural disasters. Or, apparently, criminals.

Zephyr followed my gaze and hissed in sudden fury. He scrambled between crates and boxes to glare at a logo up close. I didn't recognize it: a red symbol on a pinkish wooden crate, some alien glyph that I couldn't read.

"What is—"

"My cousin," Zephyr said slowly, "Bought the poison that killed him in tins with this symbol."

"Oh, man." I didn't know what to say. "I'm s—"

He hefted his maybe-weapon and stumped off. "Let's wreck the place."

"That might be a bit hasty," I said, hurrying after.

Dragon signed a question at me.

"The bad bugs killed his cousin," I told him. "And they keep things here. Zephyr wants to break something, but I think we should escape before they kill us too."

Dragon raised a fist in reply, ready to slam it into the nearest box.

"Wait, wait, wait," I begged. "We need to at least see where we are. See how many are going to come shoot us, and which way we'll need to run. So we can destroy as much as possible before they catch us."

Dragon listened, and when I repeated the entreaty in his own language, Zephyr did too. I breathed a little easier.

"There, that's a window. Let's look."

I found another wooden crate underneath it, glad to see that it looked strong enough to hold our weight. The window was so high that it might have been deemed "not worth it" if we had to do any acrobatics to see out of it.

The view outside showed a grassy blue plain with cliffs on the far side. As far as I could see either way, actually. Dragon said nothing, but Zephyr muttered something about blasphemy.

"What?"

"They put their smuggler's base in the Footprint of the Moon!" he exclaimed. "How *dare* they!"

I wracked my brain for knowledge of important landmarks. "That's a canyon, right? A crater-looking place with a river in the wet season?"

"Yes!" Zephyr said. "How dare they!"

I had other thoughts. "They must have some of that invisibility tech shielding the place from satellite view. The Footprint is pretty big, right? Because it looks like this base is in the middle. That leaves us with some terrible odds for running to safety before we're spotted."

"If we wanted to," Zephyr retorted, setting his beak stubbornly.

Dragon opened a crate with a loud creak, making me flinch. Then an engine sound from the next room gave me an idea.

"Compromise!" I said in desperation. "Let's peek into that hangar. Gimme a second." I darted toward the door, weaving between crates on my long human legs, hoping that neither of them caused a ruckus. I crouched to peer around the doorframe, trying to breathe quietly.

All right, that's the hangar portion of this place, I thought, scanning the vast area that held half a dozen small shuttles. *Ceiling hatch is still open. Side door is closed. Looks like other storage rooms there. Oh hey, everybody's doing a group huddle by the huge boxes. Hmmm.*

Zephyr joined me, with Dragon ambling behind him. "What's your plan?" Zephyr whispered.

I pointed. "Let's hijack a ship. We can shoot up the place with it, then escape afterwards. Hopefully."

While I was half hoping he'd say no, what a ridiculous idea, he just nodded. "Good enough. We'll need proper weapons, though."

"What's yours do?" I asked, pointing at the thing he held.

Zephyr rotated it. "I think it's a paralysis gun." He seemed mostly certain. The handholds were definitely made for mantis-like wrist joints to slot into. I realized that the little fingers those bug aliens had on their wrists were a similar size to Zephyr's. Perfect fit. "We could test it, but they might hear."

I looked at my wrench, then around at the room full of boxes and tools. "There's probably other useful stuff here, but I don't know if we have the time or the knowledge to find it."

Dragon started haphazardly opening crates. These lids were quieter than the first, so I just winced slightly. With a worried look at the doorway, I moved to peer into boxes and look over the tools laid out near our ship segment.

Those were the most promising. Alien tech or no, some things had clear purposes and obvious On switches. Also, the aliens had duct tape. Or at least something that looked like it.

One quick invention montage later, peppered with glances toward the door, I had a plasma cutter taped in the On position, tied to a cable. With Zephyr and Dragon standing back, I made sure no one was watching, then started spinning it.

I took aim and launched the thing out into the hangar, where it soared in a heroic arc to land on the far side of the room in a cart full of breakable things.

The bug aliens flinched at the shattering crash. We raced out the door as quietly as possible. I was certain that one of the bugs would see us — those eyes surely had a better range of vision than mine did — but the broken stuff seemed important. They were much too busy yelling at each other to notice.

We ducked behind a cart near our chosen ship: a sleek pearlescent thing. The cart was empty and the loading hatch of the ship was open, with boxes visible inside that held another label Zephyr recognized. He hissed to himself, nearly incandescent with rage. But he followed my lead when I was sure our way was clear.

All I carried was another cutting torch. We got lucky. No one saw us creep into the ship's hold. There we found deep shadows and crates to hide behind, with enough space for all three of us. The shouting was still loud as we settled into place, with Zephyr's shell bumping against the wall and Dragon almost knocking over a box. I tried to catch my breath in silence. Infernally lucky.

I don't know how long we waited there. I'm sure it was a shorter time than it felt like. But the bottom line was, no one found us while the alien smugglers cleaned up the mess and assigned blame and probably looked into the other room. No one checked the ship, or at least no one did more than peer through the doorway. The hatch closed.

I breathed a little easier. But only a little.

Zephyr shuffled in place. "I think they've started the engines."

I nodded. "Yeah. I can't tell if we've lifted off or not. This ship probably moves fast, so we'll be gone as soon as it does."

"We should catch them by surprise," Zephyr said.

"Right," I said, still full of doubts about this plan.

Zephyr was already out of his hiding place, hefting the paralysis gun. "This way," he said, striding toward the interior door.

I slid out and urged Dragon to join us. The gorilla was happy to.

<Fight bad bugs?> he asked, hands flying in the dim light.

"Yes," I said. "Hopefully, we can figure out how to steer the ship. Or convince one of the bugs to fly it for us. Honestly, our odds are not good."

Dragon just grunted and followed the trail that Zephyr blazed between crates.

I glanced ahead at the little turtledillo. He was walking with purpose, every inch the badass action hero in the body of an adorable little accountant fellow. I kept my opinions to myself. He had a cousin to avenge, and I had a planetary alliance to salvage. I followed closely, listening for anything that sounded dangerous. All I heard were Dragon's footsteps. (Which were, admittedly, dangerous, but not the kind I was concerned with.)

The door to the rest of the ship was a big one. Zephyr guessed about the button before I stepped forward, and luckily for all of us, he guessed right. The door rattled as it slid aside.

I hid with my cutting torch held at the ready, but Zephyr and Dragon didn't. When no sounds of battle greeted my ears, I stepped back out to join them in entering the corridor that looked like the ones in the half-a-ship that we'd just left. Definitely the same technology base at work here.

Why did the smugglers want to get that bit of the ship back? I wondered. *To keep it out of enemy hands? Then why not take the whole thing? I guess it wouldn't fit in the cargo bay, but still. Why that part?*

It occurred to me that the thrice-be-damned inertial dampeners were probably housed in the cockpit area of the ship. When they cut it free, they shut it off, and that explained all the stuff falling on us earlier. Not to mention the invisibility field.

That kind of stuff has to be valuable. All right, it's starting to make sense. But I can't say how they'll react to finding us now. Prooooobably going to shoot us and pretend they never saw us.

We made our quiet-footed way down the hall. Distant bangs, footsteps, and voices soon filled the void, getting closer with every moment.

There was nowhere to hide. A corner waited up ahead. I hoped it led to a safe room and not a gang of murderous smuggler bugs.

As it turned out, it was a bit of both.

A yellow-orange bug person walked toward us around the corner, only to pull up short when Dragon roared at him, I brandished my torch, and Zephyr shot him with what was indeed a paralysis gun. It was very effective.

The guy locked up, teetered, then slowly fell onto one side with an awkward thump. Zephyr laughed in delight. Dragon bared long teeth at the frozen enemy, sniffing him from up close, then making a dismissive noise and a rude gesture before moving past.

"Sorry about that," I said in Rockback as I walked by. "But you really shouldn't have kidnapped us accidentally. And stolen a bunch of animals from Earth. And lost them in an alien forest. Not to mention smuggling the other stuff." I stopped, turned back to give him a good kick, then moved on. "Asshat."

No one else walked into the path of Zephyr's paralysis gun, more's the pity. The hallway was empty when we turned the corner. Several doorways lined the sides — dark, threatening portals that could spill enemies as soon as we turned our backs on them. Zephyr walked first, proudly holding his gun at the ready, until Dragon decided the turtledillo was going too slowly and thudded on ahead. Zephyr protested but let him be. I didn't argue the decision.

Near the end, a doorway was open, with bright walls instead of darkness. Dragon ambled up to it and stuck his head around the corner. Whatever he saw must have looked safe since he promptly swung inside. Zephyr and I hurried after him.

The room felt like someone's private cabin — that was probably a bed, that was a weird chair, and those were cases for belongings. But the most eye-catching thing was the porthole on the wall, which showed a view of space. A familiar planet was rapidly dwindling in size.

"Oh," Zephyr said in a small voice, lowering his gun. "How do we get back?"

"I... guess we ask nicely."

"Right." He raised it again and headed for the door.

"Let's go."

I scanned the room for a better weapon than the cutting torch but found none. Just a distressed gorilla.

<Not Earth?> he asked with a whine, pointing at the window.

"No," I told him. "Our best plan is to convince the bad bugs to take us back. We might have to scare them a bit."

He was out the door before I was, almost stepping on Zephyr.

The ship wasn't all that big, though it had a lot of ominous dark rooms. Conserving power, I guess. Zephyr led the way toward the end of the corridor with his gun-thing at the ready and Dragon looming over him. I kept an eye out for surprises with my torch raised.

We reached the door without incident. The hall branched off into another empty corridor, as quiet as the first; though who knew how good the insulation was on these walls? I sure didn't. Anything could be happening in the next room.

If Zephyr had any doubts, he kept them to himself. With just a moment's hesitation, he pressed the probably-a-button to open the door. Correct again. It slid open.

Startled insect faces turned to look at us from every direction. Too many for such a small room.

Zephyr took aim, and they swarmed us.

I yelled, waving my torch like I was warding off bats, but Dragon roared and charged into the cockpit.

The bugs immediately lost interest in me. Dragon swatted them aside in fury, which might have been heartening to see if not for the delicate electronics on every surface.

I can't say for certain who did the damage — it could have been a bug alien sprawling back, a monstrously strong fist, or even a shot from Zephyr's paralysis gun. It probably wasn't me. Probably.

It definitely changed our trajectory, if the windshield opposite the door was any indication. The stars all slid sideways. A silver shape wove into view that I recognized with a start: it was the only space station in this neck of the woods. Were we that far already?

The next things to come into view came faster: pieces of broken spaceships, followed by space rocks and miscellaneous garbage. Just as I remembered the floating junk heap that spacers complained about, our ship slammed into something. Apparently.

I say apparently because the inertial dampeners made sure we didn't feel a thing, though the view jolted something fierce. I did sense a whoosh of air, which cut off abruptly. The piercing red lights and the whooping alarm seemed to be bad news.

The way every bug alien scrambled from the room was worse. I pressed myself against a wall.

"What happened?" Zephyr asked as Dragon stumbled to a halt.

Creaks echoed through the floor. "Damage!" I said. "Run!" Then I booked it after the smugglers, hoping I wasn't about to die. Neither death by bug alien nor by explosive decompression sounded like a great choice. My guess was that the ship had lost a piece and sealed the leak, but badly. The walls were creaking around me.

Dragon caught up, and I turned guiltily to make sure Zephyr was coming. He was, though panting hard already. Tiny legs.

But we were there, wherever there was; I heard shouted bug language around the corner. I slowed to look carefully.

Dragon didn't. He just charged again with another bellow, leaving me to scramble after.

Round escape pods lined the walls. Panicking bug aliens of every color scrambled into them, doing their best to evade the terrifying thing roaring in their direction. Dragon landed one solid punch on an exoskeletoned shoulder, sending the gray mantis person sprawling into a pod. The door shut instantly, leaving Dragon to beat on it in rage.

I looked around wildly as those creaks got louder and Zephyr stumbled up to join me. Several pods left. No telling how much time.

"Hurry and get in!" I said to Zephyr. He nodded as I darted toward the closest one. As soon as I left him, I heard a thump and yelp. I whirled to see one last bug alien wrench the gun from Zephyr's hands, holding it in spiky brown arms while kicking the little turtledillo with one leg of many.

I yelled and ran. Dragon beat me there.

The alien smuggler took aim at Dragon, but couldn't focus on all of us. I threw my torch. Zephyr headbutted him, knocking him off balance, so the shot at Dragon went wide. My torch also missed, but it gave him something else to think about while Dragon closed the distance.

The bug guy made a clear decision. He ducked and ran for the pods, dodging the gorilla's grasp and giving Zephyr another kick on the way past. The turtledillo was knocked off his feet, but I was confident that his shell was strong enough to take the hit.

I was also lucky to be out of the bug's way since I was ignored in favor of escape. Two heartbeats later, the escape pod was gone, and the ship creaked ominously around us. A door slammed into place on the hallway we'd come from. Horrendous wrenching sounds echoed through the ship, and air gusted sideways.

"Let's go!" I shouted. Dragon scooped up Zephyr and carried him like a football toward the nearest pod. I followed.

They stepped inside, and the door shut in my face.

Dragon turned to stare in panic through the window while I tried not to panic myself.

"Push the button!" I shouted, pointing at the red thing on the far wall. "I'll get the next one!"

Dragon nodded solemnly, not pausing to set down the struggling Zephyr before pressing it.

The pod blasted away into the night.

The ship creaked louder, and I heard the sound of

crumpling metal.

I threw myself into the next pod, slammed my hand on the button, and fell over as the pod jetted away. I know there's no sound in space, but I could have sworn I heard a kaboom behind me.

I hoped the pod had good navigation abilities.

Chapter 14
(Zephyr)

When Robin was shut out of the tiny room, I confess I didn't notice immediately, caught up as I was in struggling free from the arms of the monstrously large creature-person. This led to an undignified descent to the floor. Then something beeped, and the room moved, making me tumble against the wall and lay there blinking in confusion.

Though it shouldn't have been a surprise, the face that appeared close before me was something of a shock. Large, dark, utterly alien, and too close for comfort. For the split second while my eyes focused, the creature made quiet grunting noises, then I'm afraid I ruined the moment by shrieking in startlement.

The creature jerked back. I scrambled away over a curved bench and hit the wall of the very tiny room, spinning to behold the offworlder that regarded me with equal alarm.

After a moment of heavy breathing from both of us, I said, "Sorry. You scared me. What happened?"

Those massive hands moved in several quick gestures that I didn't understand in the slightest. I realized that we wouldn't be able to say a thing to each other without a translator.

The room was otherwise empty. "Where's Robin?" I asked, hoping he recognized the sound of the human's name. He seemed to, getting more animated in his gestures and finally pointing at the window in the room's only door.

I got to my feet, still a bit lightheaded, and climbed up on the bench where I strained to see out the high window. A field of random detritus greeted my eyes, with a mostly-intact ship in the center. Part of the front end was sheared off. Numerous tiny shapes were moving away from it in all directions.

All of this was shrinking in size, and I realized that we were in one of those tiny shapes; the rest must be full of smuggler aliens — blast their shell-less hides — and hopefully, one human. I didn't know why Robin wasn't in with us, and I couldn't ask my current companion. What had she called him? A dragon, named Gorilla? No, the other way around.

"Dragon?" I said, to which he looked at me sharply. Good. "Zephyr," I stated, pressing all four hands to my chestplate.

He nodded somewhat impatiently, making a gesture with his two hands that looked like reeds moving in the wind. Then he grunted and held up one hand like a beak that opened and closed, pointing out the window.

"Robin? Yes, I hope she made it out safely," I said, aware that my other words likely wouldn't mean much to him. "Where are we going now?"

When I stopped making sounds that he knew, the gorilla turned away from the door to look at something on the far wall. I followed his gaze to a viewscreen and some form of control panel. While I lost no time in scrambling toward it, my larger companion easily beat me there and started poking at things. Assuming he couldn't know how to work it, I started to protest, only to click my beak shut and let him work. What did I know about this alien's technological familiarity?

Whether through skill or luck, Dragon caused the screen to change from indecipherable charts to another view of the outside. A dotted line appeared, which seemed to predict the path we were to take through the rocks and garbage that still lay ahead of us.

Dragon sat back with a grunt of satisfaction. We both watched things slide by. I kept glancing back at the ship in the distance. Suddenly we were in the clear, and ahead of us floated the distant glittering object that could only be the fabled city in space.

I forgot our predicament and pressed forward for a better look. This was something that all of my friends hoped to see someday. Contact with the humans was still such an exotic thing, with all parties careful not to offend anyone. Only the highest-ranking officials and diplomats had been allowed offworld. Surely that would change. We all knew there were many species coming and going through the space city; it was only a matter of time before the average Rockback would be able to take a trip into the sky and join them.

But I got to be ahead of the crowd. This was beyond exciting, despite the circumstances.

As I was taking it in and watching the improbably large structure grow closer, the screen changed on its own. A human face appeared, wearing a stern expression and speaking to us sharply. He (I think it was male? Face hair?) broke off mid-word, peering at us in surprise. I realized this was a two-way viewscreen. Another human appeared behind the first, adding more words in a language I didn't know. These sounded like questions.

Dragon was gesturing beside me, no doubt explaining things. I chimed in for good measure, but the expressions on those two faces didn't become less puzzled. The first one said something else to us, which meant nothing. The screen abruptly changed back to a view of the approaching space city. I looked up at Dragon. He made a gesture that looked impatient and possibly rude, then sat down on the floor to wait.

I turned back to the screen, trying to recapture the magic of my first glimpse of the space city. It was much closer now, and I could make out the shapes of many tiny ships stationed around it. Several were peeling away from their formation to head in our direction. This made me a tad nervous, but the ships didn't shoot. Instead, they gathered around us in a protective huddle and did something that made our tiny vessel shake.

Suddenly we were taking a different route to the

station, around the side to where a door slid open for us. We were being escorted in.

Whether as prisoners or honored guests, we had yet to discover. I had no idea what life was like on that space station.

Chapter 15
(Jacinta)

I stifled a sigh of annoyance as I confirmed that no, there were no stray bits of glass stuck in the golden elbow joint in front of me. This was a repeat customer who had just happened to catch me on a street corner with a few minutes to spare and a very flimsy excuse to talk.

"You're sure? Oh, I could have sworn there was something grinding in there after I hit the table. Shattered like anything, I can tell you," the cyborg said, laughing and waving his other hand. He'd come in to office hours before with a variety of exotic mods that needed attention, but today he looked mostly human, aside from the metal skin with intentional seams. His eyes were clearly able to see more than the usual human range. He reminded me of a frog.

A very talkative frog named Loyll who had trouble getting to the point.

"It wasn't some street gang that caused the ruckus that time, either; it was ranking members of the Hive!" He bent the elbow and kept talking. "They're just terrible, don't you think? These ones wanted seats at a restaurant, and didn't mind having their bodyguards literally throw people outside to get them! I was lucky to hit the cafe table and not a car!"

I put my tools away, balancing my pack on a handy trash can. "Yep, they're a menace, all right."

"So glad you agree! You know, they stole something from me, and the police have been no help in retrieving it."

"That's a pity." I was sympathetic but not surprised. "I understand a fair few cops are on their payroll." Con had always had grievances about that from his work as one of the honest ones, and it sounded like a losing battle. Probably made the recent feuding awkward too.

"Yes, yes," Loyll said, waving a hand like warding off a fly. "I've tried finding trustworthy individuals to help me get it back, but the police are either corrupt or too afraid of their coworkers to dare cross the Hive openly. That's why the station is closed until the Seers arrive to weed them out. Someone actually got a call through, or made a report, or whatever it is they do — and most likely that person has already been killed for it — and that's lovely for the station's integrity, but a problem for *me.*"

I closed up my pack and politely waited for him to reach whatever he was leading up to. Cars honked behind me, and the trash smelled like stale pizza.

"I need my stolen item back *now*. I can't wait for every thinking being on this station to have their thoughts sifted."

"I understand the Seers are very fast," I said. While I'd never been on the receiving end of their invasive telepathy, and I knew how unpleasant their tentacular mind-meld was rumored to be, personally, I couldn't wait for the Seers to arrive. Getting that crime ring uprooted was going to do wonders for my stress levels.

"Not fast enough!" Loyll insisted. "Honestly, I would pay impressive money for someone to help me get it back before they arrive. Very impressive. All it would take is some skill with electronics." He gave me a significant look. "Like a toolset and skillset that could cut through a security system?"

I shook my head, not hiding the sigh this time. "No thanks."

"But you would be so good at it!" he wheedled. "Surely, it wouldn't take you much time. I can show you the back door to their enclave and everything. I'll pay you enough to set up your own independent business, working with anyone you please."

I refused again, looking out across the light traffic in hopes of spotting my ride. Of course I wasn't going to *break into the Hive's central property*, not for any amount of money.

This shouldn't have been a surprising answer. But he kept at it, stressing what a good deed I would be doing, how pleased the Seers would be with me after the fact, and how much money he had. I doubted all of that, especially since he wouldn't even tell me what the item was.

"It's important," he said. "Precious to me. Something that should never have fallen into the possession of any kind of criminal network, especially one as powerful as this one. And unethical! Did you know the Hive is on record for threatening to hit a volcano with orbital bombardment? In order to bully a colony into giving them natural resources?"

"Yeah, they're pretty bad," I admitted. "But I'm afraid you'll have to wait for the Seers to sort things out." Ah, there was my ride. I shouldered my pack. "Sorry I couldn't help. Good luck!"

Vittr's taxi pulled up right on time, glittering in the lights, and I got into the front passenger seat with all haste.

Loyll waved after me in an attempt at being upbeat. "All right, but if you change your mind, you can find me at the spaceport. Berth number 354. Hope to see you!"

I waved back and said nothing. Vittr likewise held his silence until he'd sped us off into traffic. Then he had questions.

"Did shinyface want you to doing illegal mods?" he asked. "Lockpick attachment for hiding in closet from the Seers finding secrety secrets?"

I arranged my pack in the footwell, grateful as always that it was a multi-species model car. "No, he just wanted me to break into the Hive's home base for him."

Vittr burst out laughing. "What? Shinyface is soft in the head!"

"Very possibly," I said. "I never did find out how much of him is metal and how much is meat." With a sigh, I leaned back against the cushy headrest. Vittr's seat was entirely different from mine, adjusted to fit his buglike shape, though with a similar headrest. That was important in case someone else on the road crashed into him.

Vittr would never cause a crash himself, oh no. And he

117

would be the first to tell you so.

"Softminds ask Vittr stupid things as well," he said. "Find places to hide selves, hide shady dealings. Not enough brains to think it through. If Vittr shows them hiding spot, then Vittr will know! Defeats entire purpose!" He shook his head. "Numbskulls."

"The stress is making everyone lose it," I said, thinking over the chaos of the last few days. Citizens panicking over minor crimes, big-time criminals trying to break into places either to escape or to hide, and just … idiots making life hard for the rest of us.

Vittr detoured to pick up a fare: a non-cybernetic human waving him down from the side of the road. I didn't mind the delay. Vittr was giving me a ride to a job on the other side of town, which I hadn't expected to be called in for today; otherwise, I would have gone out in a company car instead of on foot. It wasn't much of a rush. The business owner with the busted shopfront would have disagreed, of course, but no lives hung in the balance. It could wait a few minutes for this guy to get settled.

"Yes, be getting in car," Vittr was saying. "Is short drive to shopping centers. How is your living in trying times?"

The man collapsed into the seat, tossing his bag on the floor with a gust of fresh shampoo scent. "I'd rather not talk in the taxi, thanks."

"Is okay," Vittr said as he pulled away from the curb. "I talk for both of us."

"No, no conversation."

"Is only conversation with both peoples talking. Is lecture now. You have paid for Vittr's wisdom."

I kept my eyes forward, but I could hear the guy sigh in frustration.

"What's the price for Vittr's silence?" he asked.

Vittr didn't miss a beat. "Triple fare."

"I'll take the wisdom."

"Already you are becoming more wise!"

I had to stifle a laugh. The passenger kept his mouth

shut while Vittr launched into a cheerful tirade against the current state of things, ranging from the cost of fuel to the detours he had to make thanks to the riots. He didn't need to go into much detail about those. But he did stress how irritated he was personally with the leaders of the biggest crime ring, who had the bad taste of being troublemakers of the same species as Vittr himself.

"Are bringing bad name to all!" he exclaimed, tapping the controls with what amounted to a wrist on his mantis-like forearms. "How dare! Was bad enough doing crime quietly, but now is bringing down high muckety-mucks to bother whole space station, and we hardworking types have to suffer for it!" He paused to make eye contact in the rearview mirror, making sure the man was paying attention. "You have likely never given ride to self-important tourists prevented from returning home on time. Or business peoples cranky about missing appointments. Station lockdown is hard on all, but taxi drivers deal with every rudeness! Is unfair."

The man murmured noncommittally. Vittr was undaunted, continuing on to offer his opinion about many things. When we reached the fellow's destination, he paid Vittr, gave him a terse thanks, then hurried on his way.

"Happy time to you!" Vittr called after him, getting no response.

I sat in quiet amusement while Vittr flicked his antennae in the equivalent of a shrug before pulling out into traffic again. My own destination wasn't much farther. I'd been tasked with repairing some of the damage I'd seen inflicted during the food court kerfuffle the other day. I would have thought that the shop owner would have gotten someone to work on it immediately, but I had the impression that there was some kind of holdup with the insurance.

"Here is familiar friendly food place," Vittr announced. "With familiar mess, made by inconsiderate larvae. Good luck with the fixing." He pulled up at the curb.

"Thanks," I said, picking up my pack. "We should really plan another get-together, one without inconsiderate larvae."

"Yes," Vittr declared, giving the controls a decisive whack. "Lightball game, or dinner chat at very least."

I got out. "Maybe we can go to that place with the holographic things built into the dinner tables."

"No one will beating Vittr at the table games!"

"I'll check with the others. Thanks for the ride!" I closed the door and waved him on his way, back into traffic at a speed that he would insist was entirely reasonable. I turned to take stock of the damage.

It was extensive.

I definitely don't have enough supplies for this, I thought. *Even with the van, I would have had to make multiple trips. That part's not standard, and that looks custom... Ah well, let's see if I can at least get their lights back on.*

Someone shouted behind me in the food court, and I flinched. But it wasn't a gun-wielding menace, just an everyday jackass.

I took a deep breath. The Seers really couldn't come soon enough.

Chapter 16
(Robin)

When the escape pod shot away from the ship without exploding, my first thought was *Hooray, I'm not dead.* My second thought, which occurred to me as I sat up, was *Where the hell is this pod going?*

A look out the back window showed the Crud Cloud far in the distance; I couldn't tell what had become of the damaged ship or the other pods. Well actually, if I looked far enough to the side, I was pretty sure I could make out a couple headed the same way as me, just not terribly close. I hoped that Zephyr and Dragon were in one of them. They had to be, right? We'd taken pods right next to each other.

On the wall opposite the door, I found a viewscreen that looked like it might be useful. Further inspection showed it to be frustratingly alien, with controls that made no sense and charts that were next to useless. I couldn't tell if any of it was a way to steer the pod. For all I could tell, it was instructions to an in-flight meal cooker.

Doing my best to guess at the alien system of intuitiveness, I pressed buttons that I thought I understood. I was wrong and only got more charts. I tried again and finally got a view of the sky.

Or more accurately, of the planet that I was about to crash-land on. It filled most of the screen.

Panicking, I tried again to find a way to steer the dang thing, or contact the planetary defense, but no luck. I blasted forward at an alarming speed, and soon I could see flames of reentry lighting up the outside.

This was a veeery anxious few seconds. I had to watch the outer layers appear to burn up, trying to decide whether it would be better to lay flat on the floor or wedge myself between the bug-alien bench seats and the wall. It was only when I realized that the pod was slowing did I calm down a little.

I hid behind the bench anyway, but my odds of surviving didn't feel quite as dismal.

It was a good thing I did that since the landing was no cakewalk. The pod *rolled* on impact, which it definitely wasn't supposed to do, and might have been due to my button-pushing. I managed to stay in place for a few revolutions, but eventually was flung out into the room to bounce around painfully while the pod rolled to a stop. Good thing that floor was soft. The walls weren't.

I swore my sweariest swears, and took stock of my injuries. Many bruises, but nothing seemed broken.

Hallelujah.

I got to my feet with a wince, careful of sore neck muscles and something wrenched in my back, not to mention the new angle of the floor. I had to step on the control panel to reach the exit.

Granted, this is better than getting stuck with the door against the ground, I thought as I clambered upwards. *And it doesn't look like I'm underwater. So far, so good.*

The viewport on the door showed only gray-clouded sky. Hoping that the locks unlatched automatically, I prodded the weird-looking thing that passed for a handle. It took a couple of tries to figure out which way to turn it, but I finally managed to pop the door open.

It swung back silently, which was almost anticlimactic. I would have preferred a dramatic hiss.

At least a creak of hinges, I thought. *Oh well. Time for my grand entrance! Here's hoping I didn't land on anything important.*

I peered over the edge, ready to duck back down. But there was no angry crowd of locals, hungry pack of beasties, or other obvious threat on the ground outside, so I climbed up for a better view.

Rolling hills of farmland greeted me, smelling of churned-up dirt and lit dimly by that gray morning sky. (It was morning, right? I hoped I was still on the same side of the planet.) Rows of mysterious wicker structures loomed nearby, with a few trees and whatnot scattered in the background. This was a scenic place with no close-packed houses to be destroyed by the impact, but with civilization near enough that I wouldn't starve trying to walk there. The auto-navigation had chosen well.

Now, as long as I haven't destroyed some really valuable crops, I thought as I turned to look behind me. A long furrow of flattened plantlife lay where the pod had bounced and rolled. I winced but reflected that at least it hadn't hit one of those wicker things. Turning back, I threw a leg over the side and began the climb down.

A dust plume in the distance caught my eye. *Here's hoping that isn't super-angry farmers,* I thought. It appeared to be a vehicle speeding in my direction, though it was still a ways out. I slid down the side of the pod and fell in a heap when my abused joints protested the landing.

Grateful for the time before the car arrived, I got to my feet and tried to make myself presentable. It occurred to me that I didn't know what had happened to the other escape pods — I looked around but didn't see anything past the hills.

No signs of explosions and fires, so that's probably a good sign, I decided. *Guess I'll ask the locals if they saw where the others landed. Assuming they speak the language. I don't know what continent I'm on. This might be super awkward.*

I hope Zephyr and Dragon are doing okay. At least one of them should be somewhere they recognize.

Chapter 17
(Dragon)

Dragon wait for door to open. Little shell-man make talking sounds, but no real words, so Dragon ignore. Door open, show humans wearing uniforms and nervous body language. They speak in mouth words, but not respond to signs. Dragon sigh and walk past in search of someone smarter. Room is big and empty, with only flying-room sitting in middle of floor.

Shell-man follow Dragon, still making not-words. Humans give him no answer either.

Instead, one hurry toward new door, looking over shoulder to make sure important guests follow. Dragon nod and do so. Shell-man still talking.

Other humans walk behind — would probably make good helpers if could understand signs like civilized people.

More humans wait on other side of door, holding still like scared children. Dragon stop to sniff one, curious about stillness. Human nod politely, say nothing. In uniform like others, with buttons and hat.

Dragon like hat. Take hat. Fit well enough. Human open mouth to say something, but close mouth instead. Dragon keep walking.

Look important in hat. Now just need pockets. Pockets are civilization.

Lead human open door and gesture for guests to go inside. Dragon go first, with shell-man (finally quiet) tapping after. His feet have claws that sound like tiny antelope. Dragon huff in private laughter at idea; shell-man is timid like antelope. But seem to think self brave like lion. Is funny.

Inside room are two humans and one moving pile of snot that somehow make talking sounds. Impressively human-sounding sounds too; Dragon spend long few moments investigating weird snot-person. Smell like river water. Move constantly. Would probably taste bad. Talking, but not saying anything important.

Oldest human ask about spaceships, and Dragon reply with flurry of signs. Wealth of information. All he could ever want. But human is stupid like others, and not understand signs. Dragon huff in impatience and walk over to look at potted plants.

Humans try to talk to shell-man, but not understand each other. Plants tastes bad. Room boring. Still no one able to talk properly.

Dragon take matters into own hands. Approach each human in turn, sign clearly <*Do you understand me?*>

None do. Dragon head for door. Humans object; Dragon ignore. Sign to humans in hallway, looking for communicator. Other humans follow out of room. Dragon look back and see shell-man coming too. Maybe communicator will talk to him too.

Lucky shell-man. Get communicator first. New human hurry in from other hall, talk in shell-person words. Shell-man happy, talking much. Dragon unimpressed. Consider trading hats, but no others look better. And no vests or pouch-belts to be had. Space station humans badly prepared. When Dragon finally talk to smart person, will complain.

Dragon about to leave again when shell-man trot forward and wave for Dragon to follow. Humans walking somewhere. Dragon take rightful place in front, only behind human who knows way. Other humans and snot-person make space.

Walk is short, down hall to big metal room like other, with no flying-room but with table of food instead. Dragon walk to table and start eating. Familiar fruits first, human snacks next, then try weird things. Purr happily.

Plenty for everyone, but shell-man not join at table.

Dragon turn to look, and find door shut. Room empty.

Footsteps walking away. Shell-man making upset noises on other side of door.

Dragon in cage again.

Throw down food and roar.

Chapter 18
(Zephyr)

I thought at first that the humans had simply made a mistake, locking Dragon away — perhaps they hadn't meant to lock the door — but when my protests were ignored, I began to worry.

"He won't take well to being trapped there," I insisted. "He was stolen from Earth in a cage, and I don't think he likes them!" A sound of thunderous rage from behind the door punctuated my speech. "See? He's going to break your door!"

The human behind me said something terse, which the translator behind her repeated as "Be quiet." I turned to look, offended, and found myself shoved forward by the business end of a blast gun. "Keep walking."

Shocked, I did as I was told. What was *happening*? Loud banging shook the corridor, but the humans ignored it. I couldn't tell if they had left any of their number to guard the makeshift prison. When I tried to look back at where we had left Dragon, the gun pressed between my shell plates, so I subsided.

We walked in silence for a few more paces, then they ordered me to stop while several objects of unknown function were pulled from a small closet.

Ah, to make space for me. When the human prodded me forward again, I lunged to bite her on the knee. I would escape and free Dragon, then we would find someone reasonable — but she wore armor. My beak slid off with a clack.

The rudest of kicks sent me sprawling on the floor of the closet while the door latched shut. This left me in mildewy near-darkness. The lead human said something in a commanding voice, which the translator repeated as an order to stay quiet. The group of them exchanged a swarm of words in their own language. I listened for any familiar sounds but heard none. Dragon hammered away down the hall.

The huddle broke up, and most of the humans left. One of them stayed, no doubt to guard the door from accidental rescue, and that guard wouldn't answer me no matter how I pleaded.

This wasn't looking good. I searched the dim closet for anything that might help my predicament, but they had cleared it thoroughly. Empty shelves were all I found.

This can't be normal, I thought in agitation. *Unexpected guests from planetside should be cared for, and their family contacted, not shoved in a closet like a dirty secret.*

It occurred to me to wonder if in fact I was a secret, and why that might be. It took no great stretch of the mind to make the connection between the smugglers and the only place nearby that they could stop for fuel.

I tucked my chin against my shell at the sudden chills I felt when I remembered the threat to gut me and sell my plates offworld. This was offworld. Was this who they meant?

Oh, this is bad. The smugglers obviously have allies among the officials here — I assume these are official uniforms, and those were guard ships outside — but at least I know that they don't have complete control of the station; otherwise, they wouldn't have to hide me. The question is, who am I hidden from, and how can I find them?

I got part of my answer a moment later in the form of loud noises: a wrenched-off door tumbling down the hallway. Dragon's roar of defiance echoed after it. The guard outside shouted something, shot twice, then turned and ran for her life.

"Dragon!" I yelled over the din of footsteps and smashing. "Dragon, I'm in here!" Familiar heavy footsteps thudded toward me while weapons blasted in the distance. "Dragon!" I pounded on the door.

The handle twitched, shuddered, then tore free as the door was flung open by the outraged Earth monster that I was very glad to see.

Dragon grabbed me and ran, barreling down the hall on three limbs with me clutched to his side like an infant. Gunshots behind us made me curl up instinctively and grasp his coarse fur. I hoped the gorilla had some idea where he was going, but I knew with a sense of despair that he was probably as lost as I was.

Lost or not, he blazed quite a trail. We plowed through several unlocked doors and upended a variety of furniture, leaving bedlam and exclamations in our wake. At least the voices sounded more startled than angry, and the gunshots had stopped. So much for keeping us a secret.

Dragon shoved another door open and galloped through, this time into what sounded like a crowd of people. I uncurled in alarm at the screams. Dragon hardly slowed, just dodging around the various humans and others who didn't get out of the way quickly enough.

I caught tantalizing glimpses of beings I'd never seen before, aliens from the far reaches of space, but I had no time to stare. We raced across a wide open area with many entrances and a balcony at the far end. I thought I recognized the shouting of the humans with guns pursuing us, loud and authoritative among the hubbub.

Instead of running down a hallway, Dragon rushed toward the balcony.

I expected him to slow. To look for escape routes, or maybe to turn through a hidden doorway.

When he vaulted over the railing into thin air, I screamed loud enough to make him grunt in irritation. But we didn't plummet to our deaths; the hand he'd placed on the railing still held it, and we swung down and away from the abyss, to the level below. He let go at the right time to kick past the lower railing and land with a running start on the floor.

I couldn't tell you if there were startled people here too. I was busy trying not to pass out in terror.

Eventually, I could hear again over the blood pounding in my ears, and I raised my beak from where it had been buried in musky fur. The thought surfaced in the back of my mind that I hoped I hadn't poked Dragon in the ribs too badly. If I had, he showed no sign.

No sign of stopping either, though he panted as he ran. Surely we would reach somewhere to get out of sight. He probably thought the same thing since when a large tuft of plantlife appeared, he made straight for it.

This proved to be the top of a tree near another balcony. I thanked all my lucky scales when Dragon stopped this time, looking over the railing before jumping. I looked too; we were one level away from the floor, at a central open area with a ceiling that projected an illusion of blue alien skies. More important than the levels above were the plants below since they had the makings of a lovely tended courtyard garden, with shady groves and off-color green hedges everywhere.

It looked great. I almost managed to hold back my shriek when Dragon jumped over without warning.

This time he clung to the railing while grabbing a branch with his feet — I hadn't realized he could *do* that — then he climbed down quickly without needing to use the arm that still held me close.

We hit the ground and trotted off at a more sedate speed, shielded by trees. I stretched to look up the way we had come and couldn't tell if we were still being pursued. Probably. But with any luck, they wouldn't be able to find us.

I had no idea what we would do next. Dragon hadn't put me down; maybe he had some sort of plan. I would have loved to know it.

On reflection, his plan may have been nothing more complex than "find somewhere safe to hide," but whatever it was, everything went out the window when he saw a human doing the same gestures he used.

He made a sound of delight, then started running again. It took me a moment to figure out where we were going. But when I saw the fingers flashing up ahead, I was almost as relieved as I would have been if I'd heard my own language. Someone we could communicate with! Who might not be in league with the smugglers!

Of course, I had no guarantee of that, but I'd take the chance. I *really* didn't want to die today.

The human in question was conversing silently with another — this one covered in a startling amount of metal, some of which actually looked attached somehow — and the one making the gestures wore a reddish uniform very different from those of the shady officials. An open bag on the ground between the two held umpteen things I couldn't identify. The pair hadn't seen us yet, though we were hardly subtle in galloping across the terrain. As far as I could tell, the one with the metal seemed to be getting help in fixing part of his headgear.

As I watched, the one in the uniform removed a new tool from the bag, did something with it to the other human's head-metal, and that seemed to fix the problem. The metal-clad human smiled and nodded, speaking with his mouth for the first time since I'd glimpsed them. They were still too far away for me to hear the words exchanged, but the odds were good that I wouldn't have understood them anyway.

But Dragon seemed to. He ran faster, covering the ground at a rapid pace. Even at that speed, the human with the metal had said goodbye and moved off before either of them noticed us. Only the fact that the one in the uniform had to repack her bag of tools kept us from having to chase her down.

I was pretty sure this was a her. She had those chest-things that I forget the name of, which Robin had assured me were the closest analogue to proper shell ridges that her species had. At any rate, it didn't really matter right now. We had to talk to her without scaring her off.

Dragon hooted, doing his best to gesture as he ran, one-handed still. The human finally spotted him, and to my eternal relief, she didn't run for the bushes at the sight.

Maybe the gestures helped.

She remained standing there by the bag of tools, looking a little wide-eyed, when Dragon skidded to a stop, dropped me in a hedge, and set his hands truly flying. I sank deep enough for it to be undignified.

After a moment, the human responded in kind. This gladdened my heart, though most of my attention remained occupied with trying to crawl free of the plant that wasn't strong enough to support my weight. Finally, I managed to thrash free of the bruised leaves — an unpleasant smell — and set my feet on solid ground. This was a welcome feeling indeed.

The human spared me a glance but kept her attention on the fast conversation. I stood there, content to catch my breath while they talked. This area was quiet and peaceful. Somehow we'd managed to outrun the gun-toting villains who'd pursued us. I hoped they kept their distance.

I also hoped that we had found an ally and not someone who would turn us in. I studied the uniformed human. She appeared to be on the job in some capacity, maybe having to do with the fixing of things. That other human had seemed happy with her assistance.

She's level-headed enough to treat this bizarre encounter with grace, I assessed. *Very professional. She's ... I don't know, shorter than Robin? Thicker build, darker flesh, is that significant? Oh, I hope she can help! I wish I knew what they were saying.* I began to fret with impatience while the conversation dragged silently on. The longer we stayed here, the more likely our pursuers were to catch up with us.

Then suddenly, the pair stopped talking and turned to look at me. I looked up, at a loss. The human said something in what sounded like Robin's language. All I knew how to say were a handful of names and various exclamations. Oh, and...

"Take me to your leader."

I had no idea why the human laughed when I said that. Robin had assured me it was a standard interspecies greeting.

Chapter 19
(Robin)

I mentally went over several possible greetings as the hovercar came to rest in front of me. It was a rattletrap affair, not able to keep its tail above ground for long, dragging a dust cloud behind it. I did my best not to cough as the dust washed over me. Two smallish turtledillos got out and approached.

"Greetings," I said, squinting at the dust. That's as far as I got.

"You're a human, yeah?" blurted the taller one. "Like from t'other end of the sky?" He spoke with a different accent from the city folk I was used to, and his companion did the same. Both wore yellow-brown shell paint that was flaking around the edges.

"What do you out here?" he asked, peering at the mess behind me. "Did you crash your sky-car?"

"Something like that," I said. "How far—"

"Is it true you can squeeze through a hole t'size of y'head? And survive being cut in half? Springleaf says both halves turn into new humans, but I know that's trash."

"No, though if there's a good medical crew—"

The other one chimed in. "Does your spit really corrode metal? And poison a folk if y'bite one?"

"Well, there's bacteria—"

"How fast do it work?"

I put my hands on my hips and bared my teeth. "Would you like to find out?" They were silent for a heartbeat. "How far to Sea Soul Haven from here?"

They both pointed in slightly different directions, contradicting each other as they explained how to get there.

Apparently, this was a lengthy journey. When they were getting to the part about the fields of long grass where dangerous wild animals were known to spring out at people, a peal of thunder interrupted them.

I looked up with some concern. The sky was a darker gray now and the wind spun by quickly. Buildings huddled far in the distance, but only those woven dome things were close. My dented escape pod had to be more rain-proof than them. But I didn't like the odds of weathering a lightning strike inside it.

The locals had a different concern. They chattered about wind-borne shrapnel, urging me toward the nearest wicker-looking thing. I limped after the pair. The wind didn't seem dangerously strong yet, but they knew more than I did about the local hazards. If this dome of loose sticks was the safest place to be, I wouldn't argue. (I did wonder, since many of the gaps were big enough to stick an arm through, and a large opening yawned at the top, but I held my silence.)

"Hurry in!" the tall one said, pulling open the door and waving me forward. "Careful of hitting y'head, and don't step on the sparklings."

I obligingly ducked through the doorway, watching the ground for "sparklings," whatever they were. Rows of narrow-leafed plants greeted my eyes. They were a deep green with weird-looking fruits just starting to sprout — these had spines, ridges, and the tiniest sparks of electricity dancing along them.

I kept well to the sides of the room.

The turtledillos didn't follow me in. Instead, they shut the door and leaned against it, whispering urgently to each other. I listened, indignant, as one found a stick or something to wedge the latch shut, and they talked about ransom money.

I considered simply reaching through the wall to try and punch one of them. I was pretty sure I could do it, but I knew how hard their shells were. It would likely just hurt my knuckles.

Besides, I thought as I looked up, *No need.* The round skylight at the top of the room was more than big enough for me to fit through, and the walls offered plenty of handholds.

As I was picking out the best route, another hovercar roared up outside. My captors greeted the newcomers with forced casualness. My view between the sticks was limited, but the other person apparently hadn't noticed me yet. The first two agreed that the fallen "sky-car" was exciting, and claimed to have seen some alien beastie running off thataway.

Before I could decide whether to yell something or not, other cars joined the growing crowd. None of these people seemed overly concerned about the thunder or the wind. All they wanted to talk about was the Amazing Alien Thing that had fallen on their neighbor's land. What had come in it? Was it dangerous? Where did it go? Where was that neighbor anyway?

The crowd relocated to cluster around the escape pod. Peering through the branches, I saw the first two turtledillos waving animatedly and pointing in the direction they claimed the alien had gone. Compared to the others, they looked scrawny and ill-groomed. And no one was paying the slightest bit of attention to them.

Wonder why, I thought drily. *They're such honest upstanding citizens.* I stepped back and made my way over to the far side of the room where the handholds looked best, and started climbing. It was a little painful, what with my various aches and the arched shape of the wall, but I managed. It was trickiest near the top. The higher I got, the more I worried that my hands would slip and drop me onto the spiky, sparking alien crops below. I hooked my arms around the branches and moved up slowly.

Finally, I reached the hole. Getting out of it was harder than I'd thought. I had to get both arms over the edge, grab hold of the metal railing that was *of course* only on the outside, then swing my legs over the abyss until I could wriggle upward to freedom.

A whole platform with railings and a staircase greeted my eyes. What the heck.

I guess they want to water the plants without getting in spark range, I thought as I lay on the platform, my heart beating wildly. *Wonder how big the things get?* After a few moments of catching my breath, I sat up to take in the scene.

The crowd of turtledillos was still growing, though they were all looking away from me. I crept down the ladder and circled the building to approach from the side opposite the road.

The two little liars spotted me first and did their best to blend into the crowd. Moments later, someone else noticed the tall figure walking toward them (with only the slightest limp), and the group's focus shifted instantly. Before they could figure out how to react, I adopted my best Emissary From Earth voice.

"I am DISPLEASED," I thundered, striding forward with purpose. "Is it common to hold offworld dignitaries for ransom here?"

The crowd scrambled to apologize, shooting each other wild looks and wasting no time in realizing who I was staring at. The two lowlifes were halfway to their car before multiple hands grabbed them and hauled them in front of me.

Now, I'm not fond of acting like a vengeful god or anything along those lines. I didn't want to get these guys curb-stomped by their neighbors. But I also didn't want the community to think their actions were okay. I settled for giving them a good scolding, and leaving their verdict in the hands of the locals, who would "share the consequences of further *disapproval.*"

What could they possibly do to make it up to me, they asked?

They could give me a ride to the nearest shelter from the weather. It was getting worse. They fell all over themselves to offer vehicles, hurrying to tie up the two delinquents in the back of their own truck. Someone else would drive that.

Moments later, I was crouched in the back of another truck, since I wouldn't fit in the passenger seat, and I was holding on grimly as the driver sped toward a farmhouse. Many others had piled into the back with me. Despite the wind, they had many questions. Especially once they stopped worrying that I was going to smite them or something.

The locals assumed I was there on official business, here to find the dangerous beastie that had fallen from the sky, and it took some explaining before they understood that I *was* the beastie. They immediately clamored for details. It wasn't hard to tell they'd never met anyone from offworld before.

"Can y'really jump over a house?" one asked.

"No, but I could probably climb it," I said honestly.

"What about over this truck?"

"No, but I could vault over the hood if I got a head start."

"Is it true you can imitate t'sounds of any animal?"

"Well, not *any*..." I began, but the truck stopped before I could do any of my favorite impressions. When I turned away from the conversation, I was surprised to find the convoy halted in front of a single truck blocking the road.

Someone muttered that it was the owner of this farmland, who hadn't given any of them permission to be here. I started to worry.

A middle-aged turtledillo woman got out of the truck, wasting no time in striding toward us. "What in t'name of t'first egg is going on here?" Her shell paint was the green of fresh leaves.

The neighbors all answered her at once, yelling from their own trucks, which made for an impenetrable wall of sound. She waved her hand, and they subsided like guilty schoolkids. I stood up in the truck bed. To her credit, she didn't blink at what must have been an unexpected sight.

"One at a time. That's no way t'behave in front of an honored visitor." She frowned at the others, then addressed me directly. "I 'pologize for this rabble. What brings your honored self to my farm?"

"Thank you," I said, hiding how relieved I was that no one had been shot for trespassing. "It's a long story, but my sky-car crashed, and I need to get to the capital soon, or at least tell them where I am. It's urgent." I realized as I spoke that the clouds would have obscured the scene from most watching skyships, though they might be able to pinpoint my location with electricity readouts — wait, no, the plants probably interfered. At any rate, the authorities could do with some assistance in finding me.

The farmer was ready to help. "Well, you're welcome to send them a message from m'home," she told me. "At any rate, let's get y'out of this weather. Tall as you are, the sky sparks might take a liking to you." The soft corner of her beak quirked in a smile which disappeared as she turned to address the crowd.

"All right, you lot, y'know better than to trample all over m'land. Get. I'll bring our honored guest indoors."

Somebody piped up about the two troublemakers, which got them a fierce glare from the landowner.

"*You* two," she said, stepping to the side to get a better view of where they were trussed up. "I told you last time that if I caught y'here again I'd shove sparklings 'tween your plates and drag y'home behind m'car. I'm sure this lot will want to cart you off to the sheriff as soon as the weather allows, but I say next time it's the sparklings for you."

At her dismissive wave, the truck carrying those two took off down the dirt road, followed by others. I waited until the way was clear to climb down. Once I was safely on the ground, I bid polite goodbyes to the locals who'd ridden beside me. Everyone waved in excitement as they left.

Soon enough, it was just me and the farmer, whose name I didn't know. She fixed this as soon as we could hear each other over the motors.

"M'name is Prima Beetle Soilmaster," she said as she waved us both toward her own truck, which was the same green as her shell paint. It was also big enough that it might just have leg room for me. "By what name should I be calling yourself?"

"Robin Bennett," I said, following. "It's a pleasure to meet you."

"And t'meet you!" Beetle said. "First alien we've had in these parts. No surprise t'see everyfolk in driving distance coming for a gander. Say, d'you need to close the top of y'sky-car? The rain'll get in."

I looked over my shoulder at the distant escape pod, which was visibly open, and shook my head. "Let it," I told her. "To be honest, it belongs to someone who wronged me greatly. They deserve a little rain damage."

The turtledillo barked a laugh (a funny sound, really) and opened the driver's side door. "I'd love to hear the storying behind that," she said.

"I'll tell you what I can," I said, reaching the other door. "Some details I probably shouldn't say right now for security reasons." I folded myself into the passenger seat with as much grace as I could muster, trying not to hit any bruises. Success.

"Of course," Beetle said magnanimously. "I'm not wanting t'pry." She started the engine and sped away from the crash site, in the direction of what was probably her home. Thunder sounded again.

I hoped the escape pod filled with water.

Chapter 20
(Dragon)

Dragon glad to find smart, civilized human. Human fixer-of-machinery, no less; was helping cyborg when Dragon approach. Good. Fixers and helpers always good to find.

And this one listen well when Dragon explain problems: taken from Earth by bad bug people, crash on other planet, meet Robin human and Zephyr shell-man, taken again into space, end up here. Chased by bad humans. Fixer help?

Fixer help. Name self "Jacinta," say will get to safer hiding place, then find good people to talk to, instead of bad people.

Dragon make sure fixer know of shell-man, who say silly movie greeting to make fixer laugh. Laughter good. Fixer not know shell language, but like Zephyr anyway. Take phone from bag, explain calling friends, start talking to it.

Dragon wait, watching bushes for bad people. Shouts in distance, but none up close. Shell-man look nervous. Have heart of mouse with owls overhead. Dragon try to comfort; pat on back, but startle him more. Dragon sigh, give up. Watch for trouble.

Fixer put away phone and say friend with car on way. Good. Dragon spend time answering fixer's questions about bad men — what clothes and hair humans wear. Dragon not pay attention to boring details. But show nice new hat to fixer; maybe that useful information.

Fixer say yes, helpful. Bad people wearing clothes of *good* people; this big problem.

Dragon again unimpressed with people in charge of

space station. No knowledge of sign language, bad people in with good; obviously many people failing at jobs.

At least fixer seem competent. She explain all things to Dragon's curiosity, even bag of tools. This give Dragon something to do while waiting. Soon car with friend beep from other side of bushes.

Fixer tell Dragon to stay quiet while she talk to friend. Dragon agree, ready to grab shell-man and run again if need to. Shell-man stay close. More nervous than before. Dragon would explain, but no language between them.

Fixer come back, tell them to hurry. Dragon pick up shell-man (only slightly noisy), and follow fixer around bushes to car. Is small car of shiny rainbows, very bright. Maybe enough room for Dragon to fit. Fixer throw bag into trunk, open door for Dragon, looking around for bad people. Dragon stick head inside car.

Driver is bug man. Dragon snarl and jerk back, turning to fixer accusingly.

<Bug man! Like stinging bugs that took Dragon from Earth!>

Fixer hurry to calm Dragon. <Different bug man,> she sign. <Good bug. Not with bad bugs.>

It take some convincing, but Dragon finally get in car when fixer spot bad people in distance. Dragon push shell-man in and shut door, find seatbelts like humans love on Earth. Fixer get in front of car with bug, say to drive fast.

Bug drive very fast. Bad people not follow.

Dragon watch space station go by.

Not impressed, but maybe get better.

Chapter 21
(Jacinta)

I'd had my share of problems sprung on me since the lockdown started, but this was the winner so far. An alien from a newly-contacted world in the company of a *gorilla*, of all things, running from security in a public park. Never have I been so glad for standard spacer sign language training. It always comes in useful: talking with the hard of hearing, talking in loud environments, talking with clients like the one I'd just finished with, whose augmented hearing was on the fritz. But I'd never talked with a gorilla before. Luckily his signs were close enough to standard that I could figure them out. I kept my cool, though it was a stretch.

The fact that this guy and his little friend (What were they called? Armadillo-turtles?) were hiding from security was honestly not a surprise, given the current state of things. But it sure made life tricky. My first thought was to get them somewhere they could hunker down until the Seers could sort the corrupt officials from the trustworthy. My second thought was the safehouses that Con liked to brag about. My third thought was transportation: these two wouldn't be hitching a ride on my emergency mechanic jetpack, and they needed to get out of sight fast.

Now, who did I know who drove fast?

Vittr arrived in three minutes flat.

It took almost as long to convince the pair that no, really, he was one of the good ones. Vittr showed admirable restraint in only muttering darkly to himself about all the ways the crime family was soiling his species' good name.

Finally, we were all belted in and rocketing off down the road. I craned my neck, watching for pursuit. There had been a couple people in security uniforms jogging around the far end of the park, but none seemed to watch us leave.

I sat back in my seat and made more calls. I could communicate with the gorilla, but the little alien's language was just a wash of noise to me. Those guys weren't expected to make an appearance off-planet for some time yet, and I was willing to wager that precious few people on this station would have put in the time to learn their language.

People like a diplomat from another species, trusted with paving the way between her own people and a great many others. Lucky me, to have such a person as a friend.

Lucky me, to be a mechanic who ranged far and wide on the station, meeting people and making friends from all walks of life. Maybe tomorrow would bring a disaster that only my book club could solve. Or the nice folks from the class on cooking with offworld ingredients. They'd probably be up for some adventure.

Roka answered her phone and immediately rescheduled the rest of her day. The most pressing thing she had planned was sitting in on a meeting among her own people about terraforming a moon, and there would be just oodles more meetings about that before the approval went through. Missing this one was fine. She agreed to join us ASAP at the same secluded place I'd already asked Con to head for. Vittr would undoubtedly get there first.

I was not disappointed. We zipped from an area of warm sunlit ceiling panels into one of cool blue twilight, and dodged a few slower cars on the way into the tunnels of the decorative labyrinth.

This place had been designed as the equivalent of that sunny park for a species that preferred more dim lighting, but it was honestly used more by human teenagers looking for privacy. At any rate, it didn't hold much in the way of spying opportunities. Line of sight was short.

Vittr slowed when he drove through the bead curtains, grumbling threats that the decorations had better not damage his car. Driving a cautious speed now, he eased us through the mazelike collection of luminescent fountains, plants, and all-weather cushions. Finally, he stopped at the big room with the fountain that sprayed overhead, which dripped too much for anyone to seek it out on purpose.

At least the drips were only on one side of the room. As suspicious as our two guests looked when they exited the car, I doubted they would take well to surprise dampness.

"Why don't you two make yourselves comfortable while we wait?" I suggested to the gorilla.

He huffed in agreement and claimed several firm cushions, spreading out regally.

The little guy followed him to settle down on another. He rocked a moment, looking like he might topple backwards, but he recovered with the kind of too-smooth calm that said he hoped desperately that no one had seen it. I did him a favor and looked away.

Vittr filled the air with opinions and casual complaints. "Room is smelling of pond water. Mildew maintenance is woefully behind in their work, but is to be expected with this kind of fungus-friendly space."

I was glad that he had something new to grumble about.

Con arrived in an on-duty car and a cheerful flurry of tentacles — the first he parked beside Vittr, and the second he startled the guests with. I hadn't told him over the phone exactly what to expect, for fear of someone overhearing or even recording his calls. So he was a little surprised now to look past us and see two species that had absolutely zero business being on this space station.

"Who-the-what-the-how?" he recited, flailing theatrically before calming down when he saw the little guy flinch again. The gorilla just stared like Con was a mystery that needed unbroken eye contact to solve. To be fair, Con certainly looked bizarre to any Earthling eyes who'd never seen a Strongarm before. He was wearing his uniform vest today, with all the subtle tech armor that that entailed, and his hat too. But that just made him look like a particularly civilized octopus.

I told Con the short version of the explanation. He agreed that I'd done the right thing. And yes, he knew of a safehouse that he could swear to be free of crime connections. His friend had set it up personally.

He made the call, and Roka arrived while he was on the phone. I hurried to fill her in.

Her face lit up around the breathing mask when I made it clear that we needed her to translate for a species that her people hadn't officially contacted yet. She'd been studying the language in hopes that this newest species would venture out among the stars sooner rather than later.

"I am *honored*," she told me, sketching a bow before hopping over to where Zephyr sat. I'd told her his name, and I hoped that it hadn't gotten mistranslated somewhere, between him to human to gorilla to me, and now to Roka.

We were in luck. If I'd thought Roka looked delighted moments ago, it was nothing compared to this poor guy's visible joy at meeting someone who spoke his language instead of English. They were off and talking, and if his name had gotten accidentally turned into Fart or Tornado, he hid it well.

Chapter 22
(Robin)

I learned several things about the weather systems in turtledillo farmland that day. First, thunderclouds were a common sight; second, rain and lightning followed predictably enough that no one ran for shelter unless they weren't paying attention; and third, the interesting things that happened when water flooded the croplands made sure that *everyone* paid attention. Oh, and fourth: the gathering storm knocked out any means of getting a phone call through to the many people who would be looking for me. Beetle assured me this was temporary.

Her speedy driving got us to the farmstead before the rain hit there. Barely. When I unfurled painfully from the truck, I turned to see those gray clouds dumping on the area we had just left, with petrichor on the breeze.

Puddles were already gathering in the low spots. I fancied I could see sparks of electricity starting to jump. It occurred to me that I was fortunate the locals had found me so quickly. I didn't like the idea of waiting out a lightning storm when the ground was electrified.

Beetle ushered me into the house, and I was happy to join her. I hadn't seen any more of those sparklings growing over here, but that didn't mean the puddles would be safe. Besides, I wanted to see what a turtledillo farmhouse looked like.

From the outside, it was a low structure made of bricks or rocks or something else that came in grayish square chunks. The door was predictably short, making me wince as I ducked and put a strain on my sore neck muscles, but the sight of the interior was enough to distract me.

The city buildings I was used to were all stark and tidy, very professional. Maybe the city decorators wanted to make it clear that no one on the premises worked in the mud. Maybe it was something complicated. At any rate, this place was far more colorful and interesting than most of downtown.

Plants were everywhere — growing in pots and vases and things that were obviously not meant to hold them (pretty sure I saw a sturdy hat on the windowsill) — and a few clusters of fragrant herbs hanging from the ceiling that told me I wouldn't be spending much time on that side of the room. I had a hard enough time standing up straight as it was. I didn't need to be bumping my head on crispy leaves too.

The floor was tiled in several shades of dark rock, with woven rugs thrown over most of it. I belatedly realized that there had been a doormat to wipe my feet on. I stepped back and did so, glancing at Beetle to see that the turtledillo was too busy tidying up her home to notice.

"If I'd known a guest from t'sky was coming, I would've made t'place look a bit nicer," she said, scooping random things off low tables and stashing them out of sight down the hall. "Make y'self comfortable! Would y'like any food or drink?"

I would have liked to politely refuse, but I realized that it was nearing lunchtime, and I hadn't eaten since last night. I was never one for skipping meals. As soon as I thought of it, I was distinctly hungry.

I admitted as much to my host, and Beetle wasted no time in opening every cabinet in search of something a human could eat. We finally settled on the alien equivalent of a peanut butter and jelly sandwich. I got the feeling that Beetle would have liked to offer me something grander, but I was just glad to find something edible. Plenty of Earthlings before me had come to the conclusion that while the bulk of turtledillo cuisine was technically possible to digest, there was a strong chance of diarrhea from the meat dishes. I blame the alien insects that they're so fond of.

Chocolate-covered crickets, these are not.

While Beetle threw together a simple bug-free meal for me, I took off my coat and settled onto the biggest of the beanbag chairs that passed for furniture. It was a little soft for my taste, without much back support, but I piled another smaller one behind it and was comfortable enough. Food appeared on the table in front of me with flair, and I happily dug in.

I was taking my second bite, mumbling my appreciation, when footsteps and voices outside heralded the arrival of other family members.

"Ah, I wondered where they got to!" Beetle said, hurrying out to meet them. "Looks like groceries!" She intercepted the group, murmuring what was surely a warning to be on their best behavior, then led them back in to meet me. I swallowed my bite of food and waved as they entered.

A whole family of turtledillos crowded in the door, with adults of multiple ages directing two sets of children. Most of them carried woven straw bags, and the adults quickly deposited these on the nearest countertop to greet me properly while the children ran right over to stare.

"Wow, a real human!"

"How d'you live with only two arms?"

"But look how many fingers!"

"What are you wearing? Is that because y'don't have a shell? Doesn't that hurt?"

There was no answering every question, so I did my best. They listened when I talked, then burst into new questions as soon as I finished a sentence.

"What's that in your mouth? Is it like a beak on the inside?"

"How do you eat without a beak?"

I was busy explaining teeth to the children when the adults joined us. The littlest kids quieted down reluctantly, obviously still afire with curiosity. The teenagers pretended (badly) to be jaded about the whole thing. They all hushed up and let their elders ask the questions now.

After introductions that I was never going to remember, the adults talked with a little more politeness, all wanting to know why I was here.

I told them the short version, stressing the urgency and describing my two friends who had also escaped the smugglers by getting shot into space.

"Have you seen anything else fall from the sky?" I asked.

"T'were two more," volunteered an adult, looking to the others for support. "Two, right?"

"I saw two."

"Over t'hills, somewhere thataway."

All four of the younger kids leapt to their feet. "Let's go look for 'em!"

"Ah ah," scolded a granny. They froze in place. "'Tis *raining*, childs."

It really was. I hadn't noticed just how loud it was getting while everyone talked at me, but now that there was a beat of silence, it was pretty intense.

The kids reluctantly sat back down. "We'll go out after," one said. "Yes?"

"We should," added a teenager. Those four joined the younger set in convincing the adults to do something that I'm pretty sure they were going to do anyway.

"Yes, of course, we'll go," said Beetle. She was met with a chorus of hoorays.

I lifted a hand for attention. "How long do you expect the rain to last?"

"Oh, a while still," Beetle told me. She interpreted my grimace correctly. "I do 'pologize on behalf of our weather systems for the holdup."

I assured her that I didn't take it personally. "I'm just concerned that the smugglers might have a way to follow me. The escape pod could have a homing beacon on it." I kicked myself for not thinking of it sooner, but what could I have done? It's not like I knew how to disable the thing.

The granny waved both left hands in dismissal. "This weather damps out every bit of talk-tech there is," she assured me. "They won't be tracking you now."

"I hope not," I said, my head full of invisible gunships seeking the house. I tried to convince myself that the crackling rainclouds would give them grief too.

"Oh, believe it!" the granny said. "Let me tell you of t'time some big city folk convinced the sheriff t'try out new tech that would definitely work!"

I smiled and listened. The storm grew stormier by the minute. I kept looking from face to face for signs of alarm and found none, but that barrage on the roof sure did make me uneasy. I was impressed there were no leaks. The rain sounded loud enough to drive its way through concrete.

But the locals had built to account for wild weather. Nothing leaked, no one worried, and they all spoke a bit louder to be heard over the racket. Thunder followed lightning at almost the instant it struck. The hits were close; I found myself wondering if this building held a lightning rod that I hadn't seen. And what about those rickety-looking structures out on the plains; were those lightning-proof? They must be.

I asked, and the family was happy to explain it all to me. Beetle and her husband Sunrise — the primary homeowners, as far as I could tell — brought out lunch for the rest of the crowd while this went on. A different grandmotherly sort offered to help, but was gently denied; the rest of the family got to talk to the visiting alien.

And they did talk. I ate while listening, and I learned that all buildings in the lightning zone had conductive structures of one sort or another: the metal staircases on the wicker things did the job in the lowlands, and there were numerous threads of metal worked into the farmhouse itself. Outbuildings had similar pipes and bars concealed from view.

"T'only time sommat gets built without lightning veins is when a body wants it t'burn down!" laughed a teenager. "Not that anybody would do such on purpose, mind. No, no."

This led to a spirited discussion of epic feuds in years

past, the sort of dirt that would have been uttered in hushed whispers by the diplomatic types I interacted with in the city. This sort of honesty was fun. I wondered what they would tell the neighbors about me when I left.

Probably that I talk funny and don't know much about lightning, I guessed.

The storm was still raging when everyone finished lunch. I expected the various family members to occupy themselves with indoor tasks while they waited it out, and I wasn't wrong. They bustled about in every direction. I sat uselessly on the beanbags, looking from face to face.

Beetle approached with a polite suggestion. "If you be looking for ways to pass t'time, there are a few simple tasks that could use assistance," she said, spreading all four palms in a gesture that probably meant something. "Simply as a suggestion, of course."

"Sure, happy to help!" I said. With a slight wince at the bruises, I got to my feet. "What can I do?"

I could join the teenagers in de-spining the sparklings, that's what. Beetle showed me to the room where they sat at laughably low tables, armed with gloves and going to town on several large tubs of the things. As Beetle announced to the four of them that they should show the friendly alien what to do, I searched for signs of sparks. The plants looked dried out and safe-ish. No sparks.

But yes, spines! Oh my, were they vicious. I eagerly accepted the gloves that Beetle found for me.

"See this part?" asked a teenager. He held up a bundle of thick leaves and ran a gloved claw over the serrated edges. "If it gets into flesh, it works its way deeper. Even without the sparks, they're hateful little things."

"I am *very* glad I didn't trip and fall on them earlier," I said, struggling with the gloves. "That sounds like untold ages of pain. Say, don't suppose you have any bigger gloves?"

They didn't. Of course, it was too much to expect them to have anything that fit my long human fingers, of which I had far too many. But it was awkward. Like wearing two-pronged snow mittens made for children.

"Will you be all right with those?" Beetle asked, hovering by the door. "I can find sommat else for you t'do."

I waved her off. "I'll make do. Thanks. Now, where should I sit?"

The kids made space for me, Beetle went off to do other things, and I learned the fine art of sparkling processing. It was hard. There were pliers to help grab the spines, though of course the kids only used them on the toughest ones, and these were super awkward with the gloves. I could reach farther than anyone at the table here, but that didn't do me much good. My two arms were no match for the experienced teenagers' speed.

"Slow down," I joked. "You're making me look bad."

The four of them laughed and agreed that I was doing that without their help.

"Well, okay, I'll give you that," I said. "But I think I'm doing pretty good for my first day at it. And with your silly little short-fingered gloves!"

They replied that it was my own fingers that were silly, and so the conversation went. The kids plucked three sparklings to each of mine, and I kept them laughing with commentary about the whole thing. They listed some of the uses for dried sparklings: food, fiber arts, and an acquired-taste spice from ground up spines. Ground *very* fine.

We even had a fun discussion of our two cultures' number systems, each based on the number of fingers we had in total — ten for me and twelve for them. All the while, rain drummed on the roof, elderly turtledillos worked some other task down the hall, and other adults came and went. I tried not to think about Zephyr and Dragon out in the lightning storm, and the smugglers getting away with their various shenanigans. I couldn't do anything about it for the moment.

To my surprise, the moment was a brief one. Rain was still bucketing down when an adult appeared at the door wanting a word.

Apparently, they'd thought up a plan to run by me.

Chapter 23
(Robin)

"Now that t'storm core has passed," Beetle told me, "Local talk-tech is back online. Not any long-distance stuff," she hurried to add when my face lit up, "Just house-to-house and the like. But that might be enough t'get you somewhere that *can* reach the capital."

"Great!" I said, beginning the process of unfolding my legs from under the stepstool-height table. "What's the plan?"

The plan, Beetle explained, took into account the fact that offworld ships were very likely watching the area for any sign of me. A single truck driving through the rain could be easily tracked.

But not when dozens were involved.

"Our best bet is mass confusion," Beetle said. "If I can call in enough neighbors for a hectic convoy, is that sommat you'd want to be trying?"

"Yes," I said. "Absolutely. How long will it take to arrange?" Standing up still hurt a little, but I was more than willing to put that aside and focus on this exciting development.

"Not long. We've got a list of folks t'call just ready and waiting. I'll tell the elders to get started." With that, Beetle hurried out of the room.

Everything turned into eager chaos, with the teenagers shoving sparklings into tubs and casting their gloves aside.

"T'nearest folks drive fast," one told me. "They ought t'be here in no time!"

"Is it safe to drive now?" I asked. "That storm is still going."

"Oh yeh, t'part of storming that can kill a body is short," she said. "T'part that hexes the tech is longer, but now it's safe t'get you out to the nearest boosted comm center."

Was this a dedicated radio hub, I wondered, or maybe that sheriff's station they'd mentioned?

Nope. A restaurant. But a very important one.

"They've got t'best food—"

"—And t'best gossip—"

"And t'most powerful comm hub for a half-day's drive!"

A grandpa appeared at the door. "Enough beaking; our honored guest has t'get ready."

The teenagers objected that they had been sharing important information, not talking my ear shut. (Turtledillos don't have human-style ear flaps, just reptilian ear holes. This flavors their idioms.) At any rate, the grandpa wasn't impressed.

"Come gather up your fabric," he told me, ignoring the youngsters completely. "Did you bring anythin' else with you?"

"Fabric? Right, my coat. Thank you. No, that's all." I could have explained that I don't normally fall out of the sky so ill-prepared, but decided against it. Instead, I asked about the bathroom facilities, bracing myself for an awkward experience.

I'd seen Rockback toilets before. This one wasn't too different from the city kind, just *dinky*. Ever see one of those training potties for little kids? Perfect height for a two-year-old? I got distinct training potty vibes from this bathroom.

But honestly, I've had to make do with worse. I had plenty of memories of space travel on multi-species ships to keep me company while I used the facilities. Washing my hands was silly too since the sink barely reached knee height. At least the ceiling was tall enough for me to stand. Barely. (The doorway, not so much. But the bathroom itself I could stand up in.)

I rejoined the hustle and bustle of the living room,

stepping over more than one child on my way to grab my coat. Settling it back into place, I felt just a smidge more reassured. Hard to underestimate the hugging powers of a familiar coat. It had dried mud about the elbows, but it still smelled like my favorite laundry soap.

After scant minutes, I heard motors outside. The teenagers weren't kidding about the speed of the neighbors.

I said my goodbyes in a rush, thanking the teenagers for the lesson as I was ushered out the back door. An uncountable number of hands waved me on. I'd always found it funny that turtledillos make the same farewell gesture as my own home culture, but this wasn't the time to think about it. A roiling, darkly dramatic rainstorm blew raindrops and the smell of wet dirt outside.

I pulled the collar of my coat up around my neck, grateful for the awning the size of a two-car garage spreading overhead. It was great on two counts: I only got a smattering of raindrops about my ankles, and it hid me from view of the sky.

Here's hoping the smugglers don't have x-ray tech, I thought as Beetle pointed me toward a hovertruck painted a screaming purple. Apparently, this was the fastest vehicle around. Or maybe the fastest driver.

The passenger door swung open from the inside. "Greets!" said the turtledillo woman in the driver's seat, who wore purple-blue shell paint and a wide grin. "Quatra Moondark Waterwheel. Best t'meet you."

I returned the greeting and folded myself into the fruit-scented passenger seat while the wind whipped past. Beetle closed the door for me and shouted instructions to Moondark. Other hovercars and trucks rumbled by under the awning, starting up a procession much larger than I'd expected. I didn't see which car Beetle got into. Moondark gunned the engine and slid into the crowd like a fish in a fast-moving stream.

I told myself not to worry about how close she got to the car in front of us. These vehicles probably had excellent shock absorption. Probably.

At any rate, they were just as fast and chaotic as promised. Cars and trucks edged forward and back, passing and re-passing each other, swapping positions as we barreled down a muddy road in the downpour. Every time we passed a road, at least one or two peeled off. Sometimes new ones joined us. We appeared to be covering the entire web of roads with vehicles, all weaving and circling, hopefully disguising which one held the human.

Moondark stayed solidly in the middle of the pack at first, then nudged her way up near the front. She talked as she drove, giving me a running commentary of all the landmarks I couldn't see past the sheeting rain. I made noises of approval and held onto the seat with what I hoped was a casual death grip.

We had just passed a major road where the trio of large trucks in front of Moondark's had taken a hard right, when the rain noise stopped suddenly. Then it returned.

I held my breath for a heartbeat. "What was that?"

Moondark craned her long neck to see past the edge of the windshield. "Look!" she said. "Hollow spot in t'rain!"

"What?" I looked. She was right: there was a moving patch of air where no raindrops fell. Instead, they hit something large and invisible, up in the sky, and sluiced off the sides. I felt immediately colder. "Oh, jeez. It's following them."

"Is that one of t'invisible ships?" Moondark asked with far too much enthusiasm. She gunned the motor and sped forward through the mud. "We'd best put some distance 'tween us!"

"Yes please," I said, twisting in my seat to watch the trucks' taillights shrink into the distance. It occurred to me that the smugglers might blame me for the loss of their ship. Our hectic plan was working so far. I just hoped I hadn't gotten some innocent farmers killed.

But no explosions glowed to life, and there were no more signs of pursuit. Vehicles kept coming and going. After a while, the rain calmed from an unholy torrent to a friendly patter — either the regularly scheduled storm was slated to end, or we were outrunning it. Just a few more white-knuckled minutes, and a town of sorts came into view. (A little one. That's the sort.)

"There 'tis," said Moondark, pointing at a faded red building. "The Edible Flower, best eatery in three days' ride. Let's get you inside. We'll have to treat y'to some eyeflower hash after you've contacted your people. Nothing like it."

I said something polite and noncommittal as I shook life back into my fingers. We pulled under a fancy awning along with several other trucks. The rest just blasted past. Moondark said they were waiting for the all-clear on the radio, which would also come from this exceptional foodplace.

"Sounds great," I said, undoing the seatbelt that didn't really fit. "As long as the villains in the sky aren't listening for radio waves, we should be set. Is that Beetle?"

It was. She appeared from what I recognized as her own truck (with Sunrise driving) to lead a cluster of locals in escorting me from the truck to the restaurant. Moondark left her truck and followed. Nothing shot us.

"Nimble!" Beetle declared as she shoved the doors open. "Today is the most important use of your phone!"

My impression of the restaurant interior was: red theme, flowers everywhere, the distinct smell of pancakes with berry sauce, many low tables, and a handful of surprised turtledillos staring at us.

The one behind the counter fixed me with a speculative look and nodded. "Right this way," he said. "You lot have a seat, and tell me t'story in a moment."

Several polite hands at my back urged me forward. I didn't argue. With my head still full of invisible spaceships, I hurried after the proprietor's speedwalk that managed to look dignified somehow. Must have been the posture. He had clearly seen weirder things, which made me wonder what.

Through two sets of doors and a privacy screen, I

beheld the much-touted comm station. It was more than a little baffling at a glance; all I understood about the room were the beanbag chairs and the blank video screen on one wall. Everything else was a mess of buttons and thingamabobs and doohickeys, with something that looked like a digital papyrus scroll. Maybe it was a phone book.

Thankfully Nimble was ready to do the dialing for me. He didn't even ask questions other than the phone code. I told him the code for my workplace, and that was enough to get things going. The tech made a rainbow of quiet sounds while it spun into action.

"Turn this all the way when y'finish," Nimble muttered while it connected.

I nodded, and he withdrew. Whether to wait outside the door or go demand gossip, I couldn't say.

A human face appeared on the screen: Jasmeet the receptionist. "Hey!" he said as he recognized me. "Where have you been?"

"Kidnapped!" I replied. "By the same offworld smugglers who brought in all the animals. I have some crucial testimony to give. Who can you connect me to?"

Thus began a chaotic few minutes of Jasmeet calling on other lines and yelling at people in the next room to 'get in here now, dang it, this is important.' Between all the wrangling, he got the rough idea of what had happened. I told him about Zephyr and Dragon still out there in another escape pod, and about the baddies who could pop up at any moment to rain lasers or paralysis rays on us all.

Jasmeet told me in turn that the ship in the forest was indeed visible now, though debate raged over whether the official offworlders (us) were working with the illegal ones. Massively irritating, that.

But not as bad as the next bit of intel, courtesy of somebody official on Jasmeet's phone.

"Wait, hang on," Jasmeet said, switching channels. The screen swirled in a "please wait" pattern until he returned. "Okay, yeah, the big meeting is tomorrow. They could decide to end the alliance over this."

It didn't bear thinking about. We would be sent home in disgrace that would follow us for the rest of our lives and beyond. Assuming, in my case, that I didn't get zapped first.

"What will it take to convince them it wasn't us?" I asked in desperation. "I can show them where the smuggler's base is — it's hidden in the Footprint of the Moon! Tell the police to ransack the place!"

Jasmeet winced. "That's one of the private-property landmarks, isn't it?"

I swore. "They've got to get over these property laws! Surely there's an override for emergencies. How much time do we have?"

"Not much," he said. "It's first thing in the morning. And direct proof is the only thing that will sway them."

"Like what, a hog-tied alien ready to confess?"

"Yeah, that might do it."

"By tomorrow morning."

"Yep."

"Fine, I'll see what I can do."

"Wait—"

The knob made a click when I turned it, and the screen went black. I took a deep breath before pushing out into the main room where I hoped the locals were still interested in helping me.

Chapter 24
(Zephyr)

It was wonderful to speak with someone who knew my language, however imperfectly. This bizarre creature crouching on a single leg was clearly new to it, but I wasn't about to complain. I tried to minimize my staring at her. This was easier than I would have thought, since there were more than enough other strange sights everywhere I looked. The gorilla lounging beside me was odd enough, but nothing compared to the creature made of many tails and a hat. Insectile aliens I had seen before, and humans were commonplace. But the others were bizarre. And so was the architecture, honestly: all dim light and glowing fountains. I tried not to be too distracted from the conversation.

I told this "Roka" my story over the pattering of the fountains, doing my best to speak slowly and use simple words. The one-armed alien was a good listener. In return, she told me that the tentacle person would be supplying a safe place to hide. Some authority figures were on the way with the ability to see a person's thoughts, and they would sort out everything.

That sounded wonderful. These people were so kind. The human even came up with a ration bar that wouldn't make me ill, when I mentioned how long it had been since I'd eaten. The bar was chewy and vile. I didn't complain.

When I was ushered toward the car I'd come in, I went eagerly. Especially since Roka the translator was coming with me while Dragon rode in the tentacle-man's car. The human went to translate for Dragon, and we were off. I spent the drive talking with Roka. She was pleasant to speak with, curious about my world. I happily shared.

The friendly bug man drove us out of the dark colorful place and into the imitation sunlight, across a significant portion of space town, through what I assume were back roads, and up to a structure that actually held cars. It disappeared into the ceiling, disguising its true height.

I had never encountered a parking location with more than one level, so when we approached the entrance, I assumed that the vehicles would be contained to the bottom. But no, the builders had followed the rumored human custom of making structures that climbed toward the sky instead of keeping safely on or under the ground. I'd never seen one in person before. It made me shrink back as we approached, but I told myself to be brave.

A blockade stood at the entrance.

"That is a warning of creating things," Roka told me, fumbling for the word. "Making? Building?"

"Construction?" I guessed.

"Yes, that! It says not to enter."

But the tentacle man was already out of his car, unlocking the gate, and swinging it wide. Roka explained that he had permissions beyond that of most citizens. While he waved us through, followed in his own car, and locked the gate behind us, Roka did her best to explain how policing worked here. I understood most of it, I think.

With the gate secured, the tentacled police officer led the way into the strangest structure I have ever encountered.

It was empty, all seamless gray floors with only a few construction-type machines silent at the far end, and many lines drawn on the ground. Wide sections of window stretched across each wall, though with no glass that I could see. Before I could truly take in the sight, our vehicle approached a ramp and started up it.

Vehicles should not drive at that angle. Or speed. Or duration. I was starting to feel ill by the time we leveled out again. I breathed deeply.

This was the next level — or the one after that? —

where we would switch vehicles for safety reasons. I knew that much of the plan. This level was empty as well, with only a large van parked at the far end. I focused on breathing and settling my innards as we approached.

A red-brown tentacle person wriggled out of the van, wearing the same uniform as the first one, though it was slightly bigger in size. The human that stepped from a different door looked downright ordinary by comparison.

The bug man parked in a corner between a wall and a window, muttering to himself, with the other car right behind us. Everyone got out. We were all quiet except for the blue-gray tentacle man, who greeted his comrades with quiet cheer. I didn't ask Roka what they said. She would tell me what I needed to know. The two of us came to stand next to Dragon and the bug man, while the human pulled her bag from the car and brought up the rear.

"Jacinta will leave for her job from here," Roka told me. "She is an important repair person, and has transportation built into that pack. I will stay with you to translate."

I was extremely grateful. Roka told me firmly that it was her duty, or near enough to it; she'd already given her own people a clear message that she would be gone on official business until the overseers arrived. I wondered how her people had handled the news.

The blue tentacle man stepped forward to introduce his colleagues, who greeted us with polite friendliness that Roka translated for me. The human in particular ("Travis, so glad to meet you") struck me as utterly trustworthy, and I was put just a touch more at ease by the thought that this tall person would be showing me to somewhere safe.

It was just as I was thinking that, and the introductions were moving on to Dragon, whose human translator was still delayed by fidgeting with her pack, that I heard quiet clicks. And a faint zapping sound that caused panic chemicals to flood my brain.

Paralysis guns.

I whirled to see Travis *smiling* at the empty air while

167

people started to drop around me. Our friend the blue tentacle man was first, his vest buzzing visibly from the shot.

"You mud-egg!" I yelled, launching myself at Travis. "We trusted you!" I rammed my armored head into his unarmored groin, clawing and kicking as he went down. The vehicle must have blocked me from view of the invisible attackers. Even with my manicured clawtips, I did damage before my muscles locked in place.

Raging at the invisible bonds, I fell stiffly to the floor beside the wounded traitor and glared my hatred at him. It was all I could do.

Though all sounds were quiet under the heartbeat in my ears, I was distinctly aware of more shouting and motion than a peaceful capture called for. Someone was escaping. I wished them luck with every fiber of my being.

Chapter 25
(Jacinta)

I'd just meant to do a quick scan for cybernetics, purely out of curiosity, to see if gorillas or turtledillos got replacement parts these days. Technically a breach of privacy, and I was prepared to say I'd hit the button on accident if anyone asked. A mechanic's pack can be awkward to handle, you know, especially while walking.

But all thoughts left my head when the screen lit up with tech floating in thin air. Tech that looked suspiciously like weapons.

I rushed to strap my pack on. I needed the jet function *right now—*

The first zap hit Con square in the vest. I dodged to the side and squeezed the thrusters as the scene dissolved into anarchy. The little turtledillo attacked the human cop, Dragon barely got a snarl out before dropping, and startled exclamations told me that both Vittr and Roka had been zapped as well. I was already in the air, blasting toward the window at max speed.

Con shouted "Geronimo!" behind me. It was the same call he'd used in our last game of lightball, after I'd told him choice tidbits from Earth history.

I blasted out onto an empty street, then circled back, passing below the window in time for him to leap into space and grab my ankle. His vest was sparking and he barely made it. I flashed around the first corner I came to while Con held on for dear life.

No hiding spots here, too many pedestrians there...

I really hoped they didn't have cloaked hoverbikes, or some tracking device for the blast residue. I could hear the crackle-fizz of Con's vest from here. If I didn't land soon, one or both of us was likely to get electricity burns.

There! Frillian architecture was always good for secluded crevices. I homed in on a spot between two flying buttresses and a sculpture of coral or whatever. Con dropped from my ankle with a plop. While I maneuvered a landing, he scrambled to take off the vest.

"What just happened?" I demanded.

Con was a mess of waving tentacles and the burble-pop sounds that passed for the fiercest of curses in his own language. He didn't answer me directly. "I can't believe it," he ranted. "After all that talk about personal integrity, and they're both on the take! Of all the traitorous..." He was back to burbling. At least he'd gotten the vest off and shoved it into a corner, where it wouldn't burn either of us. Or the building. Probably.

"So, now what do we do?" I asked. "They won't let us just go about our lives, not when we can report them to whoever's actually trustworthy. I mean, somebody has to be trustworthy; otherwise, they wouldn't have bothered to be secretive. Someone at the top must still be doing their job without canoodling with the criminal element."

He settled his tentacles. "Yes. Possibly fewer people than I *thought* — *thanks* Travis — but there are still plenty of honest ones." He draped a pair of tentacles over his eyes. "It's just a matter of which."

I leaned a shoulder against the stupid flying buttress, sniffing at the smell of the burnt vest. "We might have to wait for the Seers. I mean, they *are* coming, right?"

"That much I'm sure of," Con said adamantly. "I saw the report. It could be a while, though."

Neither of us liked the idea of waiting. But my scanner was no match for proper invisibility tech, and we were outnumbered to a degree that made *me* want to burble some curses too. Laying low was our only option.

But where? Con's buddies couldn't be trusted. I wasn't about to swear that my own coworkers were any better, and my workplace had nowhere to hide anyway. The cops could easily find our homes.

Roka's people might have given us shelter, but as Con pointed out, we were likely about to be framed for any number of things, up to and including kidnapping her and the others. No, we needed an outside party who we could trust to stay away from the cops.

I thought of an idea and wished I hadn't. "Do you remember Crackpot Loyll?"

Con burbled a swear word. "Aw, no."

I'd told Con about the guy already, and he'd admitted to getting the same offer: absurd wealth in exchange for breaking into the Hive's headquarters. Con had turned it down. He'd told me that Loyll's cybernetic mods that day made him suspect that the guy was into recreational body part replacement, which just added to the list of questionable decisions on his part. I personally got the impression that Loyll's original robot parts were from an accident, judging by things he'd said off-handedly, but that didn't change the fact that his common sense was dismal.

Almost as bad as his relationship with the Hive and its various offshoots.

"Loyll definitely won't rat us out," I said. "And I remember where he said he'd be; it's the same spaceport berth as a repair I did last week. Got any better ideas?"

Con dragged a tentacle across his face. "No. Can't believe we're doing this."

I opened my pack and started removing things. "Even better," I said. "We're doing this with you hidden in here, because at least one of us can stay out of sight."

Con burbled at that but climbed into the bag anyway. He barely fit, though he folded up small. I'd seen him fit into more unlikely places before. "Fly safely," he commanded as he zipped it shut, "Or I will destroy your things."

"Duly noted."

I left him a spot to peek out of, then gingerly put the pack on. It was awkward. Con weighed more than the various battery canisters and spare wrenches I'd removed.

171

But the thrusters were rated for much heavier loads than that, so I'd be fine.

"Leaving your vest here," I said over my shoulder as I poked a toe into the inert pile. No more sparks, though the smell of burnt wires made me cough.

Con's voice was muffled. "Good riddance."

I wondered if he meant to leave the job behind with the uniform. But this wasn't the time to ask. Instead, I peeked over the dusty coral statue and decided it was as safe as possible. With my heart beating an action-movie tempo, I jetted out around as many corners as I could find in quick succession.

Civilians pointed after me. No shouts, no zaps. Good so far. Maybe we'd gotten lucky by going to ground so quickly; the bastards assumed I had flown farther and weren't looking here. Well, they'd have no reason to search the spaceport berths for us. My biggest worry was in being recognized as I flew very visibly above the roads.

A mechanic in flight is like an ambulance with its siren going: people make way for us to reach the ailing cyborg or life support system or whatever other critical thing has called us. No one stopped me, but everyone saw.

I took the sparsely-populated roads as much as I could. By the time I reached the residential blocks across from the spaceport, my nerves were singing that our luck couldn't hold. I aimed for a secluded walkway between buildings and landed. No witnesses that I could see. I strolled briskly for a ways before ducking behind a large trash crate and unhooking the pack.

"We're within walking distance," I murmured as I unzipped it for Con to wriggle out. "Let me just change my appearance a little."

While Con played lookout and complained about the smell of the trash ("like Smasher food that's too old to eat, and Waterwill food that's already been eaten"), I bundled away my uniform overshirt and untucked the black T-shirt I wore underneath. That at least covered the belt and harness clips, so it wouldn't be immediately obvious that I was dressed for jetpack use.

I used a bandage to tie my puff of hair into a compressed ponytail. I'd worn worse fashions. Con took a bit of bandage to give himself a headband, which counted as a worse fashion. Worried about time, I pulled out a shock blanket that I kept in case of injured patients and wrapped it around the pack. This would have to do.

It's hard to walk casually when carrying an awkward armful. I did my best, eyes moving constantly while my head faced forward. Con did an absurd swagger that I would have laughed loudly at under different circumstances. We passed humans big and small, Mesmer, and a handful of Roka's people. None gave us a second glance.

We crossed the street and hurried along (casually) to the spaceport. No one stopped us there, or at the auto-pay locker (smelled like feet) where we shoved the pack. The ramp down to the 300-level berths was likewise safe. Our luck couldn't last.

It was lasting. I breathed a sigh of relief when we found the correct berth without incident.

The little gray ship's door slammed open and Loyll rushed out to meet us with such exuberance that I started to worry all over again.

"You changed your mind! Oh, I hoped you would! Come in, come in, I'd offer you snacks, but I don't have a thing you'd find edible." Loyll was just as golden, frog-eyed, and enthusiastic as the last time I'd seen him.

We let ourselves be ushered into the ship, and if Con felt as many misgivings as I did, he hid them well. Loyll had us wait in the airlock while he made sure the outer door shut all the way. Classy. The air smelled like fuel canisters and glue.

I assumed the *inside* of the ship was the best place for secretive conversations, but nope. The door had barely closed before we were being peppered with ideas on how to help him get back the thing he'd lost. And any other thought that crossed his mind.

173

"You're an honest, upstanding sort; I knew that when I met you," Loyll said to Con. "Do you remember checking my license to transport water when I arrived? We had such a conversation! 'I come from an aquatic place; you can do a lot with water.' 'That sounds gross, and I do not wish to pursue it further.'"

Con said he didn't remember, but there was no stopping the guy.

"And Jacinta here knows I'm on the up-and-up." He grinned at me. "Why I've never once asked for an illegal modification! New and unregulated at best. Oh, it will be handy to have both a mechanic and a security officer around since door codes should be enough, but you never know what kind of barriers we might find between us and my belonging, deep in such a criminal den!"

"About that," Con began. It took him some work, but he finally got through to Loyll that we were actually there for a different reason. Even when we made it clear that we couldn't safely show our faces to the station police, Loyll tried to find some way to convince us.

"I'm sure that will all get cleared up by the Seers," he said. "And you'll get such a big promotion for removing my item from the Hive's clutches!"

"Not if we get killed before the Seers arrive," Con said flatly. "And you haven't even told us what exactly this 'item' is."

"It's important, I'll tell you that!" Loyll blustered. "I've gone to great lengths already to try to get it back myself. I even paid some hooligans to cause a distraction while I crept in alone. Of course, they made more of a ruckus than I bargained for, so that didn't turn out well, what with the lockdown and all…"

"Wait, is the lockdown your fault?" Con demanded. "You paid the gang to start that fight?"

With both of us glaring at him, Loyll managed to look slightly guilty. But only slightly. He did his best to slide the conversation back toward his original point. But neither of us was feeling particularly charitable by now.

"Look," Con said. "If you can't even tell us what was stolen, we can't help you."

It was at that moment that the station's loudspeakers played an emergency alert tone. We froze.

An unprofessionally worried voice announced that no one should panic, but we should, in fact, evacuate the station. Quickly. And orderly, of course. But quickly. There was a bomb, you see, with a very short timer.

"You have an hour," the voice said, then stopped. I heard a heartbeat of silence, then shouting pandemonium outside the door.

Loyll smiled. "I guess I can tell you what was stolen now."

Con flailed his tentacles like he wanted to slap the nose off the guy, and I was right there with him.

But we had to be level-headed.

"Con," I said, catching a tentacle as it flew past my head. "All bets are off. If he can shut the bomb down, it's our obligation to go get it."

"Can you?" Con asked, his tentacles bristling while he glared at Loyll.

"*Yes*," he said with certainty. "And if they've activated the timer, there's only one place they would put it."

Chapter 26
(Jacinta)

Loyll was cagey about the details even now, but he did finally spill *some* of the beans. The bomb was a device meant for terraforming entire worlds.

"I'm afraid it will wreak unimaginable havoc on this space station," Loyll said, tapping his knuckles together with distracted clicks. "Even the metal will rust and dissolve. It works through air, you see. The central ventilation hub is the place to set it off. We'd best hurry."

"This is dumb, and I object," Con said. "Anyway, there will be locks on every door leading there. Anything my clearance can't handle will be your job with the tools." He looked my way. "If they've been quick about that framing, my clearance is gone already. Be prepared."

I was as prepared as I could be, given the stupid, stupid circumstances. With all the people employed and bribed by the Hive — security forces! technicians! smuggling ships! — they couldn't think up any better way of escaping the blockade than blowing us all the hell up. Jerks. I hoped the Seers interrogated them with extra tentacles.

Amid a sea of people swarming toward the spaceport berths, Con and I grabbed my pack from the locker. I thought of a single silver lining to this whole mess. If the Seers wanted to face-hug all the people who evacuated, their sweep would cover the Crud Cloud too.

Stranded folks ought to get a ride back to civilization, I thought as I strapped the pack on. *And any raiders who haven't already lit out for greener pastures will be caught. Cold comfort now, but it's something.*

We met Loyll in front of the ship, where he'd brought out his transportation: a dinky two-seater hoverthing.

Con didn't refuse to ride in the cargo bin, but he did complain creatively. It was either that or ride on my lap, swaddled in the shock blanket for minimum recognizability, which was much less dignified.

"Stinks in here," he said as he pulled the hatch shut. "Motor oil and rotten bananas."

"Oh, that's the free sample of banana bread from—" Loyll started to say.

"Don't care. Go." The hatch clicked.

"Going," Loyll sing-songed, sounding much too cheerful. "Try not to step on it. Probably inedible by now."

Before I could ask how long he'd left banana bread in there, we zoomed off into the crowd with my pack on my lap and my grip tight on the seatback in front of me. Good thing there was a handle built into it. I did *not* want to get my fingers crushed between the seat and the cyborg's metal spine.

No one gave us a second look as we fought our way upstream away from the spaceport. Every single person was panicking to some degree. Some leapt over benches and each other in a rush to reach the ships. The general populace had been worried before when the lockdown happened, and unsettled at the prospect of Seers learning their every secret, but now they were flat-out terrified. Desperate for any way to safety.

I wondered if Loyll's little gray cruiser would still be there when he returned. I couldn't bring myself to care either way.

Can't believe he caused the lockdown. Was that terraforming bomb really his originally? Did he bring it onto the station himself, or is that the Hive's fault? It'd be great if he actually explained himself. Maybe we'll get an answer out of him once the thing is shut down. But probably not.

By the time we pulled into the control compound, I was more than ready for some breaking and entering. Loyll parked his hoverthing between an unassuming little side door and the road, not that anyone cared what we were doing. I hit the latch to let Con out of the cargo bin.

He surged out, threatening to throw a moldy packet of what must have once been banana bread at Loyll, who just smiled and ushered him toward the door.

"Time is short," Loyll said.

"So is my lifespan now from having to smell that," Con retorted.

While they bickered, I put away the blanket and strapped my pack into place, giving up on stealth. We wouldn't be fooling anyone on the other end of the security cameras.

Which reminds me, I thought. *This is one of the doors that somebody tried to crack open.* I'd repaired it myself not long ago, though it felt like another era. Back then, I'd believed the security guards who had complained of someone hacking the cameras but failing to hack the lock. They'd blamed young troublemakers.

"Guys," I said as Con activated the brainwave scanner on the door. "There's a good chance the Hive tried to break in just the other day and failed. I had to fix the damage. How would they leave a bomb here now?"

Con peered into the scanner grimly. "Several options come to mind. Either they didn't, and we're in the wrong place, or they got in through a different door, or they murdered the whole compound at once—"

The door slid open on an empty hallway. None of us moved.

"...Or that gossip I heard about most of the staff getting replaced was actually their doing." Con stepped inside. "Let's find out."

I hesitated, then rushed after him. Loyll followed, towing his hoverthing — it just barely fit, and it slowed him down trying not to bump the walls too hard. I knew that it would absolutely get stolen if left outside, but I had to wince at the noise.

As I moved to shush him, I paused. "It's awfully quiet in here," I said, suddenly hyperaware of the lack of voices

179

or office work. Even the chaos outside was muffled.

Con had already moved forward on soft tentacles. "Keep an eye out for murders," he said.

"Not funny," I told him as I followed. The place didn't *smell* like murder. Very clean.

Loyll parked the hoverthing in a corner. "The scoundrels must have evacuated before they announced the danger to all," he said. "Good news for us if they did! A little bit of selfishness on their part means we don't have to fight our way in."

I looked back to ask a skeptical question about his fighting abilities, but Loyll was already hurrying past me with a wrist-mounted scanner showing him the way. Con and I exchanged glances and let him go first.

We passed through several doors and rooms, each more official-looking than the last, with not a soul to be found. Con's clearance got us through every lock but the final one, which I made short work of with my nanocutter. No time to mess around now.

This was the primary control hub: a brightly lit room full of monitors, diagrams, and video feeds, all up and running, all completely abandoned. I couldn't even see anyone moving around on the security screens. The Hive really had infiltrated this place and left.

"It will be at the most central location to spread airflow," Loyll said, moving from one screen to the next. "It's not coming up on my scanner yet, so the room must be shielded."

Con walked to the far side of the room. "Shielded, warded, and bomb-proofed," he said. "This one?" The screen he pointed to showed massive fan blades going full blast.

Loyll rushed over. "Yes, that one!"

"I don't see anything bomblike," Con said, frowning at the screen. I didn't either.

"Let's get inside to look in person," Loyll said, full of confidence. "The scanner will find it once we're past the shields."

We did. It didn't.

The fan made it hard to hear in the echoey metal room, but Loyll had very clearly just told us that the scanner wasn't coming up with anything.

"If it's not here," Con said with masterful restraint, "Where is it?"

Loyll tapped madly at his scanner. "Not here."

"I *said* that."

I checked my watch while he spoke distractedly. Air whirled about my head like a bothersome ghost, which didn't do anything for my stress levels.

"It's a bluff," Loyll declared. "They've realized that they don't need to actually detonate the thing in order to get past the lockdown. Just the threat is enough, especially with agents in the right places! The bosses will have taken all their most valuable assets to a hiding spot, to wait out the arrival of the Seers. Thankfully, I had some time on my hands during that lockdown, and I put trackers on some of their ships. Probably even the right ones."

"How?" Con demanded.

Loyll ignored him, checking a screen from another pocket. "There we go! Look at that; they're all going to the same place. Makes sense; it's close by. The lower ranking members will probably be ordered to disperse." He looked up and displayed a holo image of a nearby sun, with planets and the space station marked as glowing dots. "What is the name of this planet here? It must be newly-contacted. It isn't named on my maps."

I frowned at the image. "The local name for it translates as 'Biggest Rock,'" I told him. "If they're hiding there, we've got problems."

Chapter 27
(Robin)

Hog-tying an invisible alien was a problem, but one that I was determined to solve. No going home to a lifetime of shame for me! Not when I had new friends ready to help. Several of the turtledillos who had crowded into the diner claimed to have seen other "meteors" fall. Two sounded close. They were almost certainly escape pods like mine, and with any luck, they would hold a criminal bug alien as well as my friends. I really hoped Zephyr and Dragon were okay. No way to know without charging out into the storm to look.

"I am fairly sure," Beetle said wryly, crossing her top arms, "That t'crowd of busybodies approached your meteor first because they know I'm a softie about trespassing."

Guilty smiles told me she was right. Sunrise, standing beside her, laughed quietly.

Beetle continued. "Both of those other two hit Sparkthorn land. You folks willing t'risk getting your windows shot out for a good cause?"

A roar of unanimous approval drowned out the rainstorm.

Beetle nodded as if she'd expected nothing less. "Right, then. Back to the truck dance we go. Let's call in all the outliers; they know the way."

So back into the rain we went. I was ushered into Moondark's truck again. She greeted me with a smile and took off hard on the heels of Beetle and Sunrise. I held on and put serious thought into how I would fold myself below window level if the promised shooting started. At least the rain fell consistently, with no dangers from above that I could spot.

The way these folks drove made me glad to be a passenger. I could barely see the ground through the lashing rain, and that was when we stayed on proper roads. We didn't stay there for long. Beetle, leading the pack, jumped the fence first.

Moondark laughed when she took a hard left, hitting the controls to make the hovertruck bounce high enough to clear the simple wooden barrier. Once airborne, we sailed over it, then tipped nose-first down a hill, onto an undulating plain of stringy plants. I grasped the window frame with both hands. I wouldn't fall over, I promised myself, nor would I betray any undignified yelps of startlement. No matter how much the current ride resembled something from the most old-fashioned of roller coasters.

There appeared to be rippling hills under the wild grass, but it was hard to tell. We weren't at much of a vantage point. Other hovercars fanned out on either side, making trails through what was probably crops. Lightning flashed overhead.

"What happens if this truck is hit by lightning?" I asked over the thundering rain.

"Nothing," Moondark shouted back. "As long as t' windows are closed, anyway. It's insulated."

I didn't ask for specifics. I would have liked some since my experience with lightning was limited, and the windows didn't look particularly lightning-proof, but I held my tongue.

"There!" Moondark said, pointing with one arm while she drove with the others. I could just barely make out a round shape on a hilltop under nighttime clouds. Other cars careened toward it, with their headlights joining to make a wash of glaring raindrops. I squinted. Moondark drove faster. I braced my knees against the dashboard and tried to breathe evenly.

When we got closer, I saw that it was indeed one of

the escape pods, one that had come to the kind of landing you might expect from someone who actually knew how to steer it. No trail of destruction; it had landed on the hill and stayed there.

The hatch sat wide open in the rain. Not a great sign. But the rain seemed consistent, at least.

Beetle reached it first, circled the low hill, then parked her hovercar and jumped out. Sunrise went with her while Moondark idled and the rest of the crowd circled around us. Both of the farmers had thrown on what looked like chainmail raincoats that trailed on the ground behind them. Lightning-proofing? I didn't ask, too concerned with what might be inside the pod.

"I don't think they can reach the door," I said to Moondark. "I should get out. Are those coats in case of lightning? I don't suppose you have one with a fighting chance of fitting me?"

Of course not. She gave me the biggest one she had, and I shuffled it on in a hurry. The fact that it was loose enough for large individuals was the only reason I could get my arms through. The extra sleeves drooped at my sides. Hard to tell from inside the truck, but if I crouched, the trailing bit should reach the ground and conduct any strikes away from me. Theoretically.

"Don't forget t'hood," Moondark said as I reached for the door.

"Right, yes." I pulled it up, distracted by the sight of Beetle trying to give Sunrise a boost out in the rain. Other raincoated locals struggled through the grass with the same idea. None of them were going to reach it. Somebody was definitely going to fall down the hill.

"Fashionable!" Moondark told me with the hint of a snicker.

"I'm sure," I said. Good thing that hood was wider than average too; turtledillo necks are longer and their heads smaller than mine. A snug fit. And the waterproof lining was already making me sweat. "All right, let's give it a try."

I opened the door, and rain soaked my legs immediately. The coat barely reached my waist, with the back piece trailing behind. My work pants were meant to withstand various animal messes while on the job, but they weren't built for this. I gritted my teeth and stepped out into the downpour.

The coattail didn't reach the ground. *Dignity comes second to survival*, I decided. With rain bucketing down around me, I dropped to all fours and scrambled up the hill, grabbing handfuls of grass to pull me up. No lightning struck. Everything smelled like dirt and ozone.

As expected, none of the turtledillos had managed to reach the rim of the giant pod. Even I was going to need a leg up. Thankfully, there were more than enough people ready to volunteer.

They boosted. Lightning kept its distance. I leaned against the wet surface while rain splashed into my face, and I stretched to reach the rim. It was a challenge to pull myself up and peek over the edge.

Nothing but a deep puddle of water among all the glowing electronics. Impressive tech, really, to still be working under these conditions. But it couldn't tell me where the passenger/s had gone. Maybe if I knew how to work the controls, but my own crash landing was testament to my lack of skills in that area.

I slid back down. "It's empty," I shouted. "Where's the other one?"

Back into the truck to drip all over Moondark's seats. She just laughed some more, enjoying the adventure. She drove like a maniac in a new direction. Good thing somebody was paying attention to where we were in this rainstorm, because I had no idea. I was busy worrying about whether the invisible ship had picked up the passengers from both pods.

The sky grew a bit lighter ahead. It must have been the edge of the storm. A nice thought, despite the dangers. But the bright area was far enough away that we didn't get to appreciate it. When the caravan slowed again, I squinted at what looked like several other cars parked and waiting. They turned headlights our way and wrecked the visibility.

"Wuh-oh," said Moondark. "Get low."

"Sparkthorns?" I asked, hugging my knees.

"Might lose a window."

"Here we go," I muttered. This was uncomfortable. I tugged the raincoat hood as high as it would go and listened. Outside, I heard shouting that I couldn't make out over the rain.

Was the rain letting up a bit? Maybe. Yes.

I risked a peek over the dashboard, since we hadn't been shot at yet. Rain and headlights still obscured everything, but it wasn't quite as extreme. I spotted the escape pod behind the landowner's cars. It had left a trail down the side of one hill and halfway up the next, rolling much like mine had. Its door was still closed.

Zephyr and Dragon? I thought, afire with worry. I'd been lucky to get away with minor bruises when I landed. That kind of tumble could easily break a neck, especially with two people bouncing around in there. I wanted to rush over and bang on the thing until it opened. But not with trigger-happy locals aiming my way in low visibility.

Beetle and a few others shouted at the turtledillos in the other cars, not making much headway. From what snatches of conversation I caught, the Sparkthorns thought that the crowd was here to steal their glory. This thing had fallen from the sky on *their* land, after all. Beetle's claim that they needed to capture the alien inside for the sake of interstellar commerce wasn't getting her very far. I was going to have to get out.

"Will they shoot me if I stand up?" I asked Moondark.

Before she could answer, the hatch on the escape pod opened and something flashed away. Much too fast to be Zephyr or Dragon. Everybody started shouting. The buglike shape disappeared into the rain.

Moondark gunned the engine in the direction we'd seen it last, while Beetle and the others did the same, and the landowners threatened them all with weapons I couldn't

see. Maybe some of the cars stayed back. This one sure
didn't. Moondark launched us off a hill like a hoverboarder
showing off for her friends, and landed cackling. Other
cars' headlights made it nearly impossible to see.

Then I caught a flash of scrambling bug alien on a
hilltop with sunnier land in the background.

"Over there!" I said, just as the Sparkthorns shot the
engine out from under us.

We both shrieked as the truck spun, grinding down the
hill with tall grass whipping at every window. When it
finally slid to a stop, the rain still pounded and headlights of
other vehicles flashed in all directions. I heard the bangs of
more gunfire.

"It went that way!" Moondark declared, unbuckling
her harness with two hands and thrusting a coil of rope at
me. "Let's get it!"

"We aren't going to get shot?" I asked.

"Nah, they wouldn't hit someone on foot!" she told
me. "That might actually kill a body. Come on!"

I unbuckled my own harness and opened the door
cautiously. The rain was lessening, and the ruckus was out
of sight behind the hill we'd slid down. Proper sunlight
warmed my shoulders. No sign of any invisible ships.

There was, however, a spindly shape fighting through
the tall grass in the distance.

"There!" I shouted to Moondark, and took off.

Woo boy, that grass was hard to run in. It was even
harder for Moondark, with her stubby little turtledillo legs,
but at least she had natural armor to shield her from getting
slapped by the grass. I just had to deal with it. The
chainmail hoodie was no help.

By the time we reached full sunlight — well, I did;
Moondark was still a ways behind me — the smuggler bug
was far ahead. He had reached level ground. (She? They?
It? "It" is insulting. Pronouns are annoying.) Anyways, the
alien was colored in shiny black with pink highlights, and
was more than a match for the double wooden fence that
marked another territory change. All the grass grew on this

side. Bare dirt that hadn't been touched by the rain lay on the other.

I could joke about the grass being greener, I grumbled to myself, *But dang it, I am jealous. That looks so much easier to run on.* Still fighting through the grass, I watched the bug alien leap from one row of fence to the other, then down and away like a shot.

When I got close, the two fences suddenly made sense. A deep irrigation trench ran between them, full to the brim with speeding water. I definitely preferred jumping to wading. Assuming I could jump that far.

Aw, crap on a cracker. I could probably clear that distance. Probably. Nothing to do but try. I pushed the coil of rope high on my shoulder and shoved through the last of the grass.

Clambering onto the first fence was easy enough; it was all wooden poles the diameter of my forearm, very Earth-normal despite the deep purple varnish. Not as slippery as I'd feared.

The smuggler was putting a lot of distance between us, though. I cast a look back at Moondark, doing her best, and several familiar cars still plowing through the rain far behind. Maybe one of those could jump the fence, but I wasn't about to wait and ask.

The channel was almost my full body-length wide. I took a deep breath and leapt for it.

My hands closed on the fence, one heel dragged in the water, but my other foot hit land, and I pulled myself over onto the dirt like my life depended on it.

And really, with the lightning about, it very well might have. I'd worry later about what could have happened if lightning had struck the channel with me in it.

Right now, I had a bug alien to chase. With rope in hand and chainmail jingling, I got to my feet and took off across the dirt.

This is more like it! Where did that spiky jerk get to? There.

I had a moment to appreciate the clear line of sight before the pink-and-black figure dropped out of view.

Swearing about trapdoors and rabbit holes, I did my best to run faster. I was swiftly getting a stitch in my side. This was more running than I was suited to. Faster than the little alien behind me, yay, woo, but I had rubbish endurance compared to friends back on Earth.

As I ran, the ground in front of me gradually opened up to a cliff's edge over a crater filled with blue grassland. I realized with a start that it looked like the Footprint of the Moon. I couldn't see the smuggler base in the middle, though. Or the bug alien.

That mystery was solved as I jogged to a breathless halt at the edge, where the hologram illusion faded from view.

Ah, there it is. And there's ol' Pinkie, already at the bottom. Clever bastards, all of them. I stood there for a while, catching my breath and rethinking my strategy. That was definitely pop-up construction, but the super solid kind meant for hostile environments. A bunch of square gray units all shoved together to make one big complex, with three taller ones along the outside. Two of the big ones had hatches on top. Humanoid-sized doors at the ground level were scarce.

Engines revved behind me. I turned just in time to see Beetle's hover car launch over the fences with Moondark riding on the hood, mad bastard that she was. Other cars followed.

"Woo!" Moondark announced when the car skidded to a stop beside me. "Where'd it go?"

"New plan," I declared as Beetle got out. I pointed into the canyon. "Alien went back to base. No more out here to catch. This is too steep for you guys to climb, right?" At Moondark's nod, I continued. "Not for me. I'll sneak in the back and see if I can flush somebody out for you to catch." I handed her the rope with a flourish.

It was a terrible plan. Moondark loved it, opening her beak in the widest grin her face could manage. "Stellar. We'll meet you at t'other side, where t'road is. Hey Beetle, let's go!" she turned to wave three arms and climb back onto the hood. I assumed there wasn't a free seat inside.

Beetle took some convincing about the wisdom of this not-wise-at-all-somebody-talk-me-out-of-it plan, but couldn't think of anything better. And, as I'd pointed out, there didn't appear to be windows on this side of the building.

"But surely they'll be sending people out any second now," Beetle said while her husband ranted passionately about the audacity of these smugglers to build *there*. Beetle ignored him. "That one knows people are chasing. And t'invisible flying whatsit won't stay near town forever!"

I shucked off my chainmail raincoat, and my own coat as well. "All the more reason for me to hurry," I said. "Look, I'll take a pile of these tumbleweed things to hide under, and they'll never see me. It's a classic plot on my planet. If I can't get one of the baddies outside somehow, I'll start a fire or something. I think I can tell which part is the warehouse I was stuck in before, and that has cutting torches."

Again, nobody had any better ideas. Other cars joined up, some with the windows shot out as promised, though I didn't see any injuries. Moondark seemed pretty upbeat about her own truck. She was happy getting a ride from Beetle and Sunrise with an offhand comment that she'd barter it back later. I made a mental note to get some kind of compensation to these folks, assuming everything worked out.

That part was still up in the air.

"Keep an eye on this for me, will you?" I asked as I gave Beetle my coat. "If I don't make it back, it's yours to do with as you see fit."

Beetle swore to care for it like the treasured offworld relic it was. The spare chainmail raincoat didn't get as much fanfare, but she put both in the car while Sunrise made sure the rest of the drivers knew the plan.

I waved goodbye to my new friends as they sped off along the canyon's rim. Enjoying the sunlight and trying not to think too hard about what I'd signed myself up for, I began gathering shrubs. Luckily for me, they were easy to uproot. I'd had no idea when I suggested it earlier. They didn't even smell bad. I tossed a bunch over the edge, enough to hide behind if I crouched, and started down. I knew full well that they wouldn't do me any good against ship scanners. All I could do was gamble that the one from earlier stayed away for another couple minutes.

Crossing fingers, toes, and hair in the old style, I thought. *Here's hoping this actually works.*

I'd had worse climbs. Nothing happened other than a tradeoff between rain-dampened pants and sweat-dampened underclothes. I'd had worse than that too, but it was still uncomfortable. On the plus side, the shrubs waited for me at the bottom, only having tumbled a little ways. I gathered them in my best impression of a haystack, and scuttled across the open ground, ready to freeze at a moment's notice.

Nothing happened. Nothing continued to happen. I really expected something to happen, but nope. My clothes dried out a little more. My footsteps on the sparse blue grass brought up cinnamon-scented memories of rabbit chasing. I caught a glimpse of dust over the far ridge; the convoy would be arriving at the front entrance soon.

This is such a terrible idea. But I was committed now. Maybe I could get my hands on a paralysis gun; that was an encouraging thought. As a precaution in case of a dark interior, I closed one eye tightly to let it adjust to potential dimness.

I reached a door undetected. Crouching behind my screen of shrubs, I tested the handle. It turned. Quietly, even. I opened it slowly, listening hard, and peeked inside with my dark-adjusted eye ready.

An anticlimactic empty corridor greeted me. I left the tumbleweeds outside — they wouldn't be much camouflage indoors — and slipped into the enemy base, all senses alert for whatever I might find.

This really was a dumb idea. But I'd survived every other dumb idea in my life, and I didn't plan on stopping now.

Chapter 28
(Jacinta)

If the Hive bosses were running off to hide on a recently-contacted planet, then there were two possibilities, and they were both bad. The Hive could be working with the locals openly and would have their support against any forces we sent. That could start a war. Or, option two: they were flying under the radar there but still successfully enough to set up a stronghold they had confidence in. The question was how strong. For all we knew, they had enough backup on that planet to take on all comers.

Was this worth jumping into?

Con thrust a tentacle into Loyll's face. "You need to give us more info. It's off the station. No longer our problem. Now, *why* were you trying to steal a terraforming bomb from crime lords in the first place?"

Loyll wore that innocent smile that I didn't trust. "It was stolen from my family first," he said. "I was the closest, and best suited to getting it back."

Con crossed his tentacles in human-style irritation. "Why not tell the authorities if it's as simple as that?"

"Oh, well," Loyll's smile slid. "They — some of your compatriots — cannot be trusted."

Con rolled his eyes. "Gee, thanks."

I stepped in. "What was your family planning to do with it?"

"Terraform a planet, of course!" Loyll said. "Don't worry, there are no native life forms. We checked. Not like these villains are liable to do." He waved a golden hand toward the doorway. "They stole it from us just so they could do horrible things like this."

Con made a rude noise. "You realize we only have your word on that."

"Well, yes." Loyll blinked. "Why wouldn't that be enough?"

I said, "You caused the lockdowns!" just as Con said, "You started a gang war on purpose!"

"That part didn't go as planned," Loyll said. "The hooligans were just supposed to make a *small* distraction. You can't blame that on me."

"Oh, yes we can!" Con insisted.

"At any rate, that's beside the point," Loyll blustered on. "We can get the terraformer back. I have a personal teleportation device with a limited charge—"

"You WHAT?" Con shouted. "Do you have any idea how illegal that is?"

"Yes," Loyll said primly. "Let me finish."

Con thrashed his tentacles and muttered, but he listened. I crossed my own arms and did the same.

"It can teleport a couple of people at once," Loyll continued. "If they stand close. But it needs a target, which is the only reason I didn't pop into the Hive's vault right away. Wouldn't that have been nice! Anyways, our best bet is to get someone close to the terraformer, with a tracer in hand, so I can zap it (and them, of course) away."

Con and I stared at him in silence while he looked surprised that we weren't immediately agreeing.

"And how do you propose we do that?" Con asked. "When it's probably hidden away with the bosses on that distant planet?"

"Ah! This is the fun part!" Loyll said.

I was willing to bet that he was wrong.

"We pretend to be small-time criminals," Loyll explained, "Approaching the big ones with a business proposition."

"What," I said flatly. Con stood on the bare minimum of tentacles so he could cross the others in visible displeasure.

Loyll kept talking, smiling directly at me. "You would

have the best chance to play the part," he said, "Since any background checks would find a mechanic instead of a cop or — well, me."

I opened my mouth to ask about that, but he was still going.

"Specifically, you're a mechanic they don't know, versus a cop not on their payroll. They'll be suspicious of any shady activity on *his* part since they've already discovered that he can't be bought — and don't I know it!" Loyll added with a grin. "But a mechanic might have unsanctioned devices!"

"How do you know they've never approached me?" I asked.

That brought him up short. "Have they?"

"No," I admitted. "But you shouldn't assume."

"Oh, well, that's fine then." He was off and planning again. "So, here's what we do: you get into the starfield in my smallest ship — I can shut off the identification transmitters — *yes*, I know that's illegal too — and you send them a message. 'Hello there, are you interested in a Seer repellant? Only I can operate it, but I'll share it for a good price. I'd use it on just myself, you know, but I'm sure you'll be up for that reasonable price.'"

I ran a hand over my hair, sighing deeply. None of this was what I'd signed up for. "You have a Seer repellant too?"

"Oh!" Loyll laughed. "No, that part is a lie. But I'm sure you can convince them. Telepathy blockers exist, after all. They work by brainwave detection, at least the ones I've seen." He rambled away on the subject, expression cheerful and metal skin shining under the artificial lights.

I slid a look at Con, hand still in my hair. His tentacles were twisted into pretzels with no direct human analogue, but he looked unimpressed. That was about how I felt too. Underwhelmed, displeased, and gripped by the sinking feeling of *We'll have to actually do this, won't we?*

"Con," I said, interrupting Loyll's explanation about the bogus telepathy blocker. "What are our odds of finding someone trustworthy who can go after them in an official

195

ship? Something with a stealth field?"

He shook his octopus-like head. "Garbage," he declared. "They'd hear about it one way or another, and we're kidding ourselves if we think there are any quality ships still onboard."

I frowned. "Good point."

Loyll reached both hands out in entreaty. "Yes, and if we wait for the Seers to sift through everyone drifting about the space station, the Hive will have hidden themselves away too deep to find. The Seers won't blast into a newly-contacted world's territory without going through diplomacy first. Time is on our enemies' side."

"Yes, it is," I allowed. "And if somebody doesn't get the terraformer back from them, they'll almost certainly use it on innocents or sell it to people who will."

"And that someone must be us!" Loyll said, beaming. "Come, before they get settled into where our hailing frequencies might not reach."

I didn't ask how Loyll knew the right hailing frequency to reach the Hive and without giving us away to anyone else nearby. The answer would definitely be something else illegal. I figured if the criminals asked, I'd be vague and say I bought the information. It was almost the truth. I just followed as Loyll pranced back toward the entrance.

Con fell in beside me. "I'm coming too," he said.

"What?" I asked. "They'll suspect something."

"Only if they see me," he said. "There will be plenty of compartments to hide in."

"I appreciate the backup," I said honestly. "But you don't have to."

"Nope, doing it," he declared. "I'm not going to watch my friend risk life and limb from a distance while I sit like a useless lump. And I'm the one who signed up to serve and protect, despite how little that vow seems to mean nowadays."

"If you're sure," I said.

He nodded. "Those sea squirts are responsible for all of the problems in my life right now. I'm coming."

"Then I'll be glad to have you. Let's go put one over on them together."

We made our way back to the rapidly-emptying spaceport with no one the wiser. While the crowds had thinned, they had also become more desperate and less likely to pay attention to us. No one even looked our way while Loyll opened up his gray cruiser and a small yellow station-hopper that he swore was also his. He transferred a few belongings, then ushered me into the little lemon-looking thing and explained the controls. They were nothing I couldn't handle. Oh, and there was a shield on the hull to prevent a detailed scan of the ship, because of course there was. If Loyll was worried about the Seers learning his own dirty secrets and illegal purchases, he hid it well.

We prepared quickly. With my pack in one luggage compartment and Con in another, a fake Seer repellant at my elbow and Loyll in touch via good old fashioned long-distance collar radio (Loyll had a private frequency for that too), I was ready. I didn't ask about the radio.

I also didn't confirm for myself that Con and I were the only ones on our ship, but as it turned out, I probably should have. My last glimpse of Loyll caught a smile that had changed from jaunty to fierce.

197

Chapter 29
(Dragon)

Dragon not see freeze-guns, but notice problem when unable to move. People shout, fall, chaos. Jetpack engine loud. Fixer jet away to safety, with good tentacle man running after. Shell-man scream in anger, attack human. Both fall behind van — Dragon hear shell-man hurting human, who must be traitor and deserving of hurts. Sounds stop.

Distant jetpack and swearing of injured human only sounds. Dragon strain against invisible cage, wanting to sink teeth into villains with freeze-guns. Want to rip and tear, but can't. Can only stare at floor while sharp hands tip Dragon onto hover-cart like broken chair to be taken away. All others frozen too, except for bad tentacle man talking to air, and human bleeding on floor. Dragon not get good look, but approve of that part. Deserve to bleed.

Captors still invisible, but move hovercart to van. Dragon try to move arm, to grab and crush, but still frozen. Other frozen people crowded in with Dragon: shell-man, skinny purple thing, good bug man. No sign of escaped fixer or tentacle-man.

Van start up. Drive quickly. Leave parking garage for roads, then other roads, then inside other building. Hovercarts moved through doors and hallways before freeze-gun start to wear off.

Dragon wonder if everyone in building is traitor — would good ones yell about frozen people on carts? Pass aliens in uniform clothes who don't look twice. Speaking English, but useless. Dragon ready to be *more* angry, then see ripple in air when pass lights. Carts have hologram covers. People see something else, maybe flower pot or sculpture or food. Not all bad, then. But not helpful now.

Still frozen when reach destination. Another. Metal. Cage. With bars, no hard air to break through. No electricity to ruin and escape. Just strong metal, strong even with power out.

Will see if strong enough, Dragon decide. Mentally snarl and test freeze again. Still frozen. And even more annoying: human with cart zap Dragon again before shoving into cage. Obviously not want most powerful captive to free self. Snarl.

Other frozen people put in cage on other side of room, piled on each other like child's toys. Dragon hear no extra zaps for them. Weird aliens not strong enough to break cages, then. Maybe will smart their way out when unfreeze.

Or maybe Dragon will break everything instead. Want to.

Traitors with carts leave, lock door, walk away. Room silent. Dragon try to move every few seconds. Will be ready when able to.

First to unfreeze is bug-man. Dragon still not trust, despite being captive like others, but bug-man make self busy moving others into comfortable positions. Talk whole time in English with weird accent. Sound mad; good. Maybe not traitor after all.

Purple alien unfreeze next, followed by tiny shell-man. Dragon jealous, but listen hard to be sure that shell-man not hurt by traitor human. Not sound hurt. Angry enough to chew glass, but not hurt. Chatter away in own language. Rattle bars. Dragon would have laughed, but still frozen. Cheered up, though.

Skinny alien calm shell-man, then talk to bug-man about bad people fearing something. Dragon not know who talking about, but if "Seers" arrive soon, then maybe not need to break cage.

Still want to, and probably will anyway. But nice to know good people might come.

Conversation take disturbing turn when bug-man point out things that bad people could do to hide from Seers. Seem to think leaving space station best option. Dragon think this good idea until bug-man add that bad people might damage station so everyone else have to leave too. More ships to hide among.

Purple alien seem to think this will probably happen. Talk about it lots. Shell-man test every bar of cage. Dragon keep trying to move against freeze. Going to break *so* many things.

Chapter 30
(Zephyr)

None of the bars would move, and the floor was too solid to dig through. It seemed possible to me that Roka the translator could slip between the bars, but given that no one was suggesting it, maybe they were too close together for even that narrow body to fit through.

The aliens talked in the same language Robin spoke. I had nothing to do but keep searching for an exit and hoping that Dragon's paralysis would wear off soon. *I wonder if Dragon can break free of his own cage when it does*, I thought. The smugglers and their allies certainly seemed to think he could; I'd heard our jailers zap him a second time when we were being unloaded. Hopefully it wasn't a health risk.

I also hoped that the two new friends who appeared to have escaped were safe somewhere. But I couldn't do anything about it either way, so I focused my attention on the friends in the room.

While I'd been initially excited to realize that our captors had never checked our various pockets for useful devices, I came to realize that these paralysis guns seemed to affect electronics too. Both of the aliens produced handheld communicators that had been reduced to doorstops. The human and her bag of tools were long gone, though most of that would likely have been rendered useless as well if she'd been captured.

Roka did have a handkerchief that she gave me to wipe off the smears of blood on my claws, which I hadn't noticed. She didn't want it back afterwards. I left it in a corner and didn't regret littering. This place smelled like rocks and alien body odor.

Roka and the good bug-man — Vittr, I think it was — seemed to be trying to think of something to do with the broken communicators when a shockingly loud siren tore the air. Red lights pulsed through the room. A voice spoke from loudspeakers, saying something that must have been important, judging by the startled looks on their faces. Before the announcement was over, Vittr was on his feet, trying desperately to reach the lock on the outside of the door with his pointy forearms. Roka talked quickly, but not to me. I didn't interrupt.

A glance across the room showed Dragon still frozen in place, lying on his side like a large scary statue. He probably understood the announcement, but he couldn't explain it to me either.

The siren was still going; that and the red lights made it hard to think. Trying to breathe deeply and think useful thoughts didn't get me much. I watched the alien attack the lock. Before he could so much as dent it, footsteps raced up to the door. Vittr pulled back inside the bars as the door banged open.

Humans and bug people flowed in with carts and paralysis guns. I tried to dodge, maybe hide behind someone else, but they were good shots, and I was soon laid out on the floor again with aliens on top of me. Then I was transferred to a cart. On top of the aliens this time. At least it was a change of pace.

Poor Dragon, I thought as we were shoved out the door. *He never got to break anything. And they're probably zapping him again.* I couldn't hear any zaps over the alarm. All I could make out were footsteps, shouting, and the distant bang of doors. My view was decent, lying on my side; I watched walls flash past, and people of all species run in every direction. It took a masterful effort not to dissolve into a gibbering panic. Not that that would have changed anything, frozen as I was.

We left the narrow hallways for a bigger room. After a few moments, I spotted hovercars; this was another garage.

One where everyone involved seemed to be throwing things haphazardly into vehicles like they only had minutes left to clear the building.

I hadn't thought I could be more worried, but I was wrong.

A door banged open ahead of us, and the driver of the cart sped up to slam the front end into the car's bumper, neatly depositing the pile of frozen captives into the storage area. I wound up wedged in a corner with barely enough space to breathe. Then the door shut behind us, and all was dark.

The alarm continued, somewhat muffled. Engines started. The loudspeaker said something new. People shouted.

The car took off at a speed that piled the lot of us against the rear door. I didn't know where we were going, but at the moment, I was more concerned with whether we would survive the trip there.

Chapter 31
(Dragon)

Bad people carry Dragon from cage to cart, then to vehicle with bad driver, then to cargo hold of bad-smelling spaceship. Still frozen in place, but not zapped again. Hope to move soon.

Shell-man and others put in next part of cargo hold, separated by blank wall buzzing faintly. Hard to tell while frozen, but think wall made of hard air like some back home. Can be made less solid by pressing right buttons. Or breaking right electronics.

Can't wait to try.

Bad people load things into every other compartment. Move fast and sloppy. Dragon hear more than one thing break, but no one stop to fix or clean up mess. Just kick broken bits away and throw more onto pile.

Bad people leaving station in hurry. Good people probably leaving too. Dragon wonder if should worry about safety. Maybe bad people damaged station like bug-man said. But bad people in charge of danger, and wouldn't make station explode with own ships still on it.

Probably. Depend on level of badness.

Dragon hear last box thrown into hold. Footsteps run out of room. Bug people footsteps, talking in click language like cicadas. Hard to tell if bugs worry about explosion.

Hear faint sound of engines, but no jerk of gravity. Maybe ship move like other one, gently. Could be moving at speed of cheetah fart and not know it.

Spine relax slightly. Freeze wearing off! Big parts go first. Dragon put all muscles into fighting to move. Feel it work.

Can turn head now. See nothing in very small cargo space, just light from ceiling, gray metal panels on floor, and buzzing not-walls on three sides. Metal wall behind. Front not-wall made differently: can see through. See only boxes and garbage.

No sign of where find breakable electronics, but Dragon not mind. Going to smash everything until find right spot. Pity no chairs here; chairs good for throwing against walls.

Able to stand. Able to walk. Almost able to make fist. When can, will start to smash. In meantime, limp over to front not-wall and look out at walkway between other chambers. No bug people. Chambers full of crap, some broken. Nothing look interesting: no obvious weapons or food or talkboxes.

Will ignore for now. Start with not-walls.

Fist ready. Dragon make two, beat against chest in old style, and bellow intent to destroy. Echo is annoying. Slam fists into not-wall, make more annoying sounds.

Bang. Bang. Bang.

No electronics there. Not expect it, but worth trying. Move to other walls.

Bang. Bang. Bang.

None there, not even down at bottom. Try metal floor.

Bam! Bam! Bam!

Much better! Metal plates dent easily. Dragon pretend is heads of bad bug-men and beat floor with no mercy. When plates warp out of place, pry up and throw against not-wall. Make good zapping noises. If no breakable electronics in floor, will try to damage front not-wall with too much metal.

Floor under panels uneven, made of empty spaces and more metal. Thicker. Try cutting with edge of panel, but not worth effort. Throw panel and go back to prying up more. Must be something important under one. Maybe by back wall.

Hear footsteps coming. Wonder what took so long.

Grab stack of bent floor plates, stand on last bit of

level floor and wait. When bug people show faces and guns around corner, Dragon roar at them and fling plate like discus.

Good at discus. Able to cut down small trees with sharp ones.

Plate make sound like lightning bolt when hit not-wall, and bugs scatter like mice. Or like normal bugs! When light is turned on and Scary Big Creature is revealed with swatting tool.

Dragon roar again and fling other swatting tools after the first. Make unholy racket of electronic noise. Maybe enough to damage not-wall? Will try.

Bugs too scared to turn it off long enough to use freeze guns.

Dragon bare teeth in angry smile. Throw plates like whirlwind.

Chapter 32
(Zephyr)

I huddled in the far corner, rolled into my tightest protective ball while the Earth monster in the next cell did his best to tear the ship down around us. The good bug alien and the kind interpreter panicked above me, accomplishing nothing.

Then something flashed with a brightness that I could see through closed eyelids, and everyone exclaimed. I huddled tighter, convinced that we were about to be blasted into space.

But no. When the sounds of destruction stopped, a rush of clattering footsteps and the distinctive zap of a paralysis gun filled the silence. The thump I heard must have been Dragon falling over, frozen again.

Before I could decide how I felt about that, other footsteps approached at a measured pace. Smuggler bugs were chattering. Vittr was cussing them out in their own language and being ignored, while Roka was silent nearby. I saw no reason to unroll.

It was only when a voice spoke in my language that I poked my head into the open.

This bug alien was clearly the boss. Shiny bits of metal and gemstones traced intricate patterns over much of her yellow-white exoskeleton, and subtle whorls of blue marked her limbs, leaving only that big-eyed face clear of alterations. She stood with confidence, taller than the others because of natural size and because they angled their bodies to bring their eye levels lower. She wore a belt-harness-thing with several important-looking gadgets on it. She didn't carry a gun. She had underlings for that.

And she didn't waste time on pleasantries.

"You on the floor," she said slowly. "Did you learn enough from the Earthling to keep this creature calm?"

"Um," I said, thoughts spinning. If I said no, the criminals might decide I was worthless and shoot me. If I said yes, I would be lying through my beaktip. They would put me in the cell with Dragon, then he'd wake mad again, and I'd just hide in a riskier corner while he wrecked the ship. And they'd be mad at me.

Let them. Maybe I'd help Dragon break out. I owed these villains nothing.

"Yes," I said, getting to my feet. "Yes, I did." I had a passing thought that Roka the interpreter understood the conversation, and she was likely wondering what I had planned. I put it from my mind.

"Good," the sparkly boss said. "Next question: what became of the survivors of the ship that crashed on your planet?"

"They were—" I thought about it. The last I had seen them, they were in their invisible shuttle, fighting it out with Rumble's crew. I didn't know whether they had won the fight or not.

But if they had, surely they would have contacted their allies by now? Rumble might have killed them. Or, more likely, held them captive for a large government bounty. Rumble was so smart. And he still had the stealth-breaker! These aliens didn't know about it.

I had an idea.

"They're probably locked away in Rumble's basement!" I declared. "And he'll do the same to you too if you're not careful!"

"Who is Rumble?" the boss asked. "And why should I fear him?"

I waxed poetic about the man's most impressive traits, being sure to steer the conversation away from anything useful. Rumble possessed determination and loyal friends, not to mention an inspiring physique and a voice that could convince a person to walk off a cliff. These things I described at length, but not his tools. And I didn't stop talking.

Not until the boss clicked at her underlings, likely telling them to change the ship's direction toward the city area I'd mentioned. Two of them scampered off while I continued, expressing confidence that Rumble the Valiant would persevere against the likes of these offworld ruffians.

The boss directed the remaining ruffians to move me from one cell to the next. This involved a lot of threatening gun-waving while they lowered our force field long enough to grab me. Vittr and Roka obediently kept their distance. I just kept talking. By the time they shoved me in with Dragon, I was off on a tangent about the evils of smuggling, and that was a topic I could expound on at length. The boss walked away. She clearly didn't care to hear it.

Neither did the guard left to watch us, but that one moved out of my line of sight, pretending to be as invisible as the ship.

As the ship is to MOST people, I thought smugly. I brought my rant to a stop. The room was silent.

The aliens in the next cell exchanged words quietly. Dragon didn't move. He looked uncomfortable frozen on the uneven floor, so I tapped over, toeclaws clicking on the warped metal, to see if I could help. I couldn't, given his size, but I stroked the fur on his head and murmured soothing promises of violence toward our enemies.

Eventually, I spotted the first sign of thaw: a slow curl toward a sit-up. I caroled the news to Roka, then had a moment of worry that the guard at the stairs could hear, but thought better of it. Worst case, he would come over and re-freeze Dragon before he thawed fully, but that seemed unlikely since I was supposedly keeping him calm. Hopefully, Dragon would act calm enough not to raise suspicions until he was ready to move. Then I would happily help him throw parts of the floor. He'd certainly ripped out enough to give us plenty of ammo.

He did stay calm. The gorilla regained the ability to

stand without voicing more than an irritated grunt. I called to Roka, explaining through her translations the situation that we were now in. The gorilla nodded much like Robin usually did, then began stretching. I was relieved to find him more patient than I'd expected.

Dragon flexed his fingers, looked at me with an unreadable expression, then picked up a warped floor tile. He gestured toward the force field with it, making a noise that was probably a question.

"Roka, can you ask him to wait a few minutes?" I called. "Rumble should—"

Distant thumps interrupted me, making a curious patter that I suddenly recognized as projectiles hitting the ship. Rumble's weapons! Were they up to piercing this ship's defenses? The location of the strikes seemed to be changing, as if testing for weak spots.

An alien voice called from upstairs. The guard immediately left us, clattering away while the impacts grew louder. I started to worry that the ship might simply explode. It could easily have a combustible fuel tank. A new vibration from under the floor was truly alarming.

Not as alarming as the sound of Dragon roaring from close up. I flinched when he threw the tile with terrifying force, causing sparks to fly in a way they certainly weren't supposed to.

Roka shouted that she and Vittr would try to help overload the circuits on their side. Footsteps and more flickering said they were throwing themselves bodily at the wall. I hoped it didn't hurt.

Dragon roared again and flung broken floor pieces as quickly as he could pick them up. True to my word, I grabbed one myself, dismayed to find it incredibly heavy. When I threw it, the thing didn't reach the force field. I hoped that Dragon was too busy to notice.

I was gauging the angles of Dragon's shots, trying to find a safe place for me to stand closer to the wall, when a two-handed assault from him in sync with another charge next door caused the force field to explode in sparks and electricity. When I unrolled to look, it was gone. Dragon was already running for the stairs.

Roka appeared and yelled something in Robin's language, which caused him to reluctantly come to a halt. I scrambled to join them. By the time I reached the front of the cell, Roka was directing Dragon to rip a large panel off the wall, while Vittr gave suggestions. I was impressed anew with how fast the narrow alien spoke.

Then, when Dragon had done his part and thundered on his way, I was impressed with something else: Roka's shape let her fit into a space that I never would have considered habitable. She crawled right into the gap in the metal wall.

Vittr gestured, speaking quickly with silver elbow joints flashing in the light, giving instructions about something. I wanted to ask what the plan was, but I hesitated to interrupt. It sounded important.

Roka said something while only half her leg showed, then over the sounds of distant battle (and a less distant rampage), I heard a small snap.

The lights went out.

Panicking seemed the thing to do. I hyperventilated and scrambled toward where I remembered the nearest corner to be. By the time I got there, dim red lights were glowing to life from several places in the walls, just barely enough to see the room. Roka crawled back out of the spaceship's innards while Vittr appeared to be congratulating her on a job well done.

She caught a glimpse of my wide-eyed huddle and hurried to explain.

Vittr, she said, knew the inner workings of this type of ship well. It was his people's tech, after all. And his fury at the behavior of these villains matched mine.

The bug man ripped open a box to find something that made him chatter in angry delight. Roka told me they were more of the "flashbangs" that had caused the bright light earlier.

Vittr shouted something cheerful, threw a bag over

one shoulder, then charged toward the stairs with his many legs clicking. Roka urged me to follow. I did my absolute best to match his speed.

We climbed the wide gray staircase, each in our own fashion, and found a trail of destruction left by our large friend. Broken things and unconscious bug people littered the metal floor. There were no weapons to scavenge yet, but I kept my eyes open while we ran.

Violence raged around the next corner. Vittr stopped to peer around it carefully, and I huddled behind him while Roka looked. They whispered briefly. Roka crouched and told me to cover my eyes. Then she shouted something for Dragon to hear.

I squeezed my eyes shut as Vittr threw something. Even with my hands over my face, that flashbang shone with a piercing glow. The enemies exclaimed in surprise. Then in pain when Dragon took advantage of the moment.

Soon the room was quiet, and Dragon's heavy footsteps moved on to the next one. Vittr scurried around the corner. Roka leapt after him, fast on that single leg, and I rushed to join them.

A pair of unconscious bug aliens sprawled on the floor with paralysis guns there for the taking. Vittr already had one, and Roka struggled with the other. It was designed for two hands: one to steady it and one to fire.

"Can I help?" I asked, standing by her side and gesturing.

We worked it out quickly. She would hold the thing, and I would contribute my small fingers to fire it. All that remained was getting into a position with enemies to shoot.

Vittr nodded briskly and moved forward. Roka clutched the gun and hopped after him, keeping an eye on my pace. I tried not to disappoint.

A translated word from Vittr told us that the chamber ahead was the control room. By the sounds of things, the rest of the baddies were holed up in there while Dragon threatened them from the narrow hallway. The ship still vibrated from gunfire against the hull, and I spared a moment to wonder how Rumble was doing.

"Flashbang," Roka told me. I covered my face as she repeated it for Dragon. When the light cleared, I scrambled to take my position with the gun. Vittr fired around the corner.

We edged forward awkwardly just in time to see Dragon throw the limp bug alien he'd been using as a shield. This bowled over the enemies, giving the three of us all the opening we needed to freeze the lot of them. A single panicked voice from inside the control room was a sign we'd done well.

Vittr clambered over the frozen forms of our enemies, disappearing into the room before Dragon could. Zaps filled the air. Dragon roared in what sounded like triumph.

I let go of the gun and started climbing over the mess to join them. Roka beat me there.

By the time I entered the control room, Vittr was poking madly at the controls while Roka and Dragon cleared the frozen enemies out of the way. I sidestepped the stiff form of the gem-bedecked boss who'd been so condescending earlier. I gave serious thought to yelling at her or stealing a gem. I settled for a rude gesture and a solid kick. We had important things to do.

Vittr flicked something that made the viewscreen useful; he was landing the ship in the middle of a decrepit city street. Rumble's people were fanned out around it, still firing. Vittr said something and pointed to what could have been a microphone.

Roka spoke into it. "Please stop shooting!" she said. "We have taken over the ship!"

I leapt forward to add my voice. "Rumble, it's me, Zephyr! It's safe now!"

The gunfire stopped as we landed, silent as ever, then Vittr opened every door he could find. I was still talking into the microphone when a familiar deep voice laughed from the hallway.

"Well done, small fry! Care to split the bounty with us?"

Chapter 33
(Jacinta)

The Hive believed me. By all the odd gods, they actually accepted the cover story about having tech that would hide them from the Seers. At least, they believed it enough to invite me onboard — via careful directions and their much larger ship swallowing mine up like a whale.

Though, possibly, they just wanted me to stop broadcasting the illegal conversation where everyone could hear.

As the bay doors shut behind me, I hoped that everyone had indeed heard. That would make these jerks all the easier to track down when the Seers started checking private memories later. Everything rode on Loyll being right about the bluff. If all my worldly belongings were atomized in the next few minutes and I was down here for nothing, I was going to track Loyll down and disassemble his favorite robotic bits.

I landed the little yellow ship in a crowded launch bay. Other ships and storage crates were everywhere, along with armed Mesmer watching me from all sides. As soon as I shut off the engines, a bedazzled blue leader lit into a round of questioning while her underlings pointed a variety of weapons at me. I gave short answers into the microphone. Good thing Loyll had pointed out the controls for that one; it might have taken me a bit too long to find otherwise, and these weren't the sort of people who liked to wait.

"Very well," the leader finally said. "You may exit slowly."

I took her at her word, making every motion as smooth as if I was repairing a panicky cyborg. They watched me through the windshield as I pressed the hatch release and picked up the small silver box labeled "Seer repellant." They probably couldn't read the words from outside. They'd better not be able to scan past the shielding on it to see the teleporter target inside. Loyll had sworn the target was just as invisible as Con was, nestled inside the luggage compartment by the door. I pretended to be an honest criminal and stepped out to face the waiting ring of weapon barrels.

To my surprise, the ship's large bay door slid open to admit planetary sunlight. I'll never get used to ships with high-quality inertial dampeners.

"Give it," commanded the glittery leader, who was hard to look at in the light. All those spangles on her deep blue exoskeleton were probably meant to look like stars, but to me, they were just irritating.

I held up the box. Somebody snatched it away and opened it. "Be careful," I said. "The mechanisms are delicate." Thankfully the mess of tech inside meant nothing to anyone there.

"Walk," the leader said. The others led the way out of the big ship and into a sunny hangar, where the breeze drifting in made my nose itch. I thought I heard the quiet slap of tentacles as they escorted me away.

The Seers ought to find my memories interesting. Focusing on the unsettling mind-reading to come was a decent way to avoid thinking about the bigger worries, like whether I'd be shot before I got the chance to bare my insecurities to a stranger. Whee.

Busy crowds filled the hangar, and I didn't get much opportunity to sightsee. It looked like a human brand of cheap construction. I frowned but kept my opinion to myself as the quick-stepping Mesmers ushered me between ships, through a doorway, and through a maze of passageways that I did my best to keep track of. One room in particular looked important: I caught a glimpse of what could only be a vault door as we passed. I put a big red star on my mental map for that one.

That's probably where they have the terraformer, I thought. *I wonder if I can get them to confirm it. Stealthily, of course. It'll save us some time when Loyll appears.*

I was just thinking this when my escort parted to usher me into a room. I wondered why none of them went first, then as soon as I passed the door, it shut behind me. The room held only a pair of the Mesmer chest-cushions that passed for chairs, and a table bolted down. Boring gray walls.

Great. So much for seeing the boss right away.

To give Loyll some context as he listened on the collar radio, I called through the door, "So I guess the boss is busy? Gonna see me later? Be careful with that thing, okay? It really is fragile."

No one answered me, though their muttered words and footsteps (both a flurry of clicks) told me that a guard was stationed outside. The majority of the group hustled away, taking the teleporter target with them. I heaved a sigh and tried to be optimistic.

Loyll could pop in at any time, I thought. *Now would make sense, before the target gets taken far away from me to who knows where. But no sign of him yet, so I guess he's waiting a bit. I hope he doesn't have any trouble with the teleporter.*

There were several other things that I hoped right then: that Con would be able to join us when the time came, that there weren't more guards watching than Loyll could handle, that generally everything worked out somehow. My odds weren't great.

Then voices outside clicked urgently, and the door opened again. Guns and bug eyes were aimed at me.

"Human," the tallest green one addressed me, "Were there any others on your ship?"

"No," I said, acting like that was obvious. "Did you see how tiny it is? More couldn't fit."

The pair behind him talked in a fast-paced mix of languages. Between scattered familiar words and the occasional gesture, I got the impression that an intruder lurked in the compound off to the left.

Remembering the way Con had bragged about being able to imitate human shape using the spare jumpsuit from the ship, I smiled. He worked fast. If we survived this, I'd owe him a drink.

"Wait, can you guys see ghosts?" I asked in excitement. "Nobody ever believes me! I swear that ship has been haunted since I got it; the last owner died in the seat."

That got the reaction I was hoping for: alarm that they tried to hide. The tall Mesmer quizzed me on the specifics, which I made up with enthusiasm.

Then a smaller red-orange Mesmer joined them from the righthand corridor with a similar report from a completely different part of the compound.

The leader turned back to me. "How many ghosts did you say the ship contained? Can they multiply?"

I continued making things up while I privately wondered. Con was good, but not that fast. Who was the other one?

Chapter 34
(Robin)

I was having a grand time sneaking about the place. In what had been a dream of mine since childhood, I had found a trash can with a removable base big enough to work as a costume. It didn't even stink much, just a bit of alien food smell.

Tiptoeing through the hallways undetected, I moved from corner to corner whenever the coast was clear. Apparently, this sort of shenanigans didn't pop up much in bug alien media, because absolutely no one looked twice at the trash can, no matter where I parked it.

This was absurd, and foolish, and I could die at any time, but I was *living* for it.

I had so many near misses. They just walked right by me, suspecting nothing.

At one point, I shucked off my disguise in an empty conference room to climb the furniture for a look out a high window, and somebody opened the door behind me. I crouched on top of the bookshelf/whatever, knocking over a bowl of decorative spheres as I whirled to see a pink bug alien looking more goggle-eyed than usual. When he started to say something, I grabbed one of the spheres and winged it at him with all my might.

It was heavier than I'd expected, and it flew really well. Took a chunk out of the door when he ducked. He scrambled back into the hallway and clicked like mad about the intruder.

With a wild leap, I grabbed the trash can and pulled it over my head. My breathing echoed, though I tried to keep it down.

MARA LYNN JOHNSTONE

When several bug baddies came looking for me, they assumed I'd gone out the window. I made a mental note to go in the opposite direction as soon as they left. Which they did, finally. I waited a while longer until I could breathe evenly.

Safe in my trash can, I crept out the door and toward the first likely corner, listening hard. This really was a stupid plan. Why hadn't I thought it through? Surely there were better ways to flush out a bug alien who we could drag in front of high society. I didn't even know how to find the front door from here. The warehouse full of supplies wasn't where I'd thought it had been.

Well, too late now. I could try to hog-tie a captive on my own, but this trash can held no room for two. Maybe I could steal another ship?

Terrible idea, but it had worked before. Sort of. Worth a try, anyway. I had a rough concept of where the hangar waited — theoretically — so I made my way there, worrying as I did that the turtledillo posse was waiting at the front of the compound, concerned about me.

My visibility through the hatch left much to be desired. I wanted to spy on everything here. Bug aliens scuttled by, talking in more than one language and looking busy. Some carried things. Some escorted others who looked important. A couple carried video communicators, and the people on the other end of the conversation weren't always the same species. So far everyone in the base was, though.

I'd just had that thought when something shuffled past my hiding place. The footsteps were so different from the insectile clicks that I peeked out of the hatch before the whatever disappeared around a corner. I got a glimpse of something humanoid in a flight suit, walking in the *most* unnatural way. Bones shouldn't bend like that. Then it was gone. I closed the hatch again to wait a little before moving on. I didn't know what I'd seen, but the back of my brain, where instincts lived, said that I wanted *nothing* to do with it. So I waited.

224

Other unexplained sights peppered my trip through the place. I really wanted to know about some of the items that those criminals were carrying around (this one glowed orange; that one smelled like a spicy flower), and which humans they were talking to on their communicators. The bug aliens themselves ran the range of colors, and I could tell which were high-ranking by the decorations and the body language. Instead of bowing to superiors, they held themselves at different heights in a way that felt very foreign to me. Like walking around with bent knees all the time.

At one point, I held still for something scuttling more quietly than usual. It moved past me like everything else. I didn't press my luck by looking this time. Did they have baby bugs here? Or maybe just small ones? Oh well, I'd either find out or I wouldn't. When it was gone, I resumed my creeping along.

The hangar was pretty close, I thought, when I reached an open doorway with a lot of action inside. Hm. Problem. I listened for an idea of the scene inside, and how likely it would be that they'd spot me easing past the door.

Multiple voices, all in clickspeak. The sound of alien electronics being tapped and typed on. Video screens with projected voices. Everything sounded urgent in there, which only made sense.

Then something outside *exploded*, rocking the floor and making every bug in the room exclaim at once. I barely kept in a startled gasp.

They weren't coming toward the door. Very few footsteps, many voices. I edged sideways to peek inside, extremely obvious if they happened to look.

They didn't. The eight or so bug aliens were all focused on the screen that showed a smoking crater in the outside wall. Good news all around! I put the question of who had done that aside for the moment and glided past the door as smoothly as possible. I made it.

Then I hiked up the trash can and ran, peeking out through a seam. An ideal shadowy corner waited next to the hangar entrance; I could see it as soon as I rounded yet another corner, and I popped into place before the many footsteps inside the hangar reached the door.

Lots of bug aliens moved to and fro. I wondered if I would get a chance to leave this corner without getting caught. Did I have another direction to take, aside from the hangar's main entrance?

I opened the hatch just a crack and looked around. To my surprise, the shadowy corner held a doorway and a broken light. My speedy deduction said *storage room* and *someone clumsy with something heavy*. The scrape on the wall looked like the kind of thing that a person could get a stern talking-to for.

Oh well, not my problem. I edged toward the door a little bit at a time, with no one the wiser.

Fun fact: bug aliens aren't fond of doorknobs. Even the ones with proper fingers instead of praying mantis grabby arms tend to have trouble grasping hard round things. And even the door handles that humans use aren't always the best, at least the horizontal ones. Vertical paddles are the way to go. That way, even the mantis-like types can bump one to the side, and so can a person whose arms are full.

Also, a person whose arms are inside a trash can. The can had just enough of a corner that I could lean against the latch until it clicked open.

Nobody looking? Good.

I crept into the room, which did look like a storage area, complete with dim lighting and stuff everywhere. No bug aliens, though. Dusty air.

Moving quietly, I took off the can and wedged it in front of the door. Then I found the light switch panel and gave it a good press. It was a bigger place than I'd thought; only part was visible from here, with the rest just past a dividing wall. Something made a scrabbling sound when the lights went on.

I froze, one hand reaching back for the trash can and the other in front of me in search of a weapon.

Decision time. Leaving meant probably getting caught

by the bugs in the hangar. Staying could mean getting caught, getting shot, or heck, even getting *eaten* wasn't off the table at this point. For all I knew, a dangerous animal had escaped its crate in here. Most of the boxes on the floor looked like they'd been heaved around at random. Probably to make space for more important things.

I hadn't made a decision, but I found myself easing forward anyway. What the heck. I flattened against the wall and kept moving. One of the boxes had broken open, spilling canned food across the floor. I picked up two cans, feeling more confident now that I was armed. The average human's throwing ability was widely regarded as frightening among the galactic community, something that made me proud for the sake of my baseball-playing, rock-chucking ancestors. Hooray for ball-and-socket shoulder joints. I gripped the cans tightly and looked around this latest corner.

I didn't expect to find a tiny golden robot with spidery legs and many arms, pushing against one of the boxes with all its might. The box was one of many clustered about a round yellow spaceship, which wouldn't be flying anywhere without the help of a forklift to move some of them. But the little guy was clearly trying.

Was that what I'd heard in the hallway earlier? Possibly. Was it in league with the baddies? Probably. Did it look *incredibly desperate* in trying to get at the ship? Yes.

I will die as I lived, I thought. *Making friends.*

"Do you need help?" I whispered.

Chapter 35
(Robin)

He did indeed need help. The little thing spoke with a male-sounding voice, and he didn't take much prompting to give an avalanche of explanation.

"Yes! I can't get into my ship! They shoved it in here like a broken hovercycle; so rude! I was only gone for a few minutes, long enough to get this." He fondled a rocket-shaped whatsit on a hovercart behind him, which I hadn't noticed among the rest of the junk. "Then I came back to find they blocked the doors!"

"Did you ask them to—"

"Oh no, they can't know I'm here," he interrupted, waving those tiny arms emphatically. "They stole this from my family. They won't like me taking it back."

"Ah. I imagine not."

The little guy was still talking. "After all the work we put into claiming an uninhabited planet, and scraping together the funds to customize a terraformer that would rebuild it for us, so we can bring our species back to life! The gengineering ships are ready to go. We'll have a new generation that's actually organic again, instead of digital minds, hidden to escape the purge." He tapped one spidery leg against his own body.

I had questions, but just stood there with my mouth open. The guy clearly had a lot to get off his metallic chest.

"The Lightdrinkers will live again! In seas of delicious bioluminescence! The children will know what it's like to eat, not just recharge!" He threw himself against the box, pushing with all his tiny might. "But the Hive *stole* it, and I got it *back*, and if I can just get the *door* open, I can get away before they destroy us all again!"

"Can I help you with that?" I asked.

"Oh, yes, please." He sagged with relief, scuttling up onto the hovercart to get out of my way. "I tried shooting a hole in the wall with my other ship — it's piloted by my larger shell body, which is about your size; remote control, you know — but that barely made a dent. Took out their communication array, which is something, but not the shields."

"I wondered what that was," I said as I picked my way over the messy floor and set my shoulder against the wooden crate. One good shove moved it away among the rubble. All the rest were still in place. That didn't seem to matter.

"Oh! Thank you, thank you *so* much," the little guy said as he scampered past me to stick one tiny leg into a pinhole that caused a hatch to slide upward. As it finished opening, he dragged the hovercart into the ship and waved me a frantic goodbye. I waved back.

The door closed.

I realized I was in a small enclosed space with something about to take off. I lunged for the hallway entrance, rounding the corner and curling into a ball beside the trash can. It was good that I did.

A quiet whirr was all the warning I got before the ship blasted a gaping hole in the ceiling. Then it zoomed away among the stars, and the building collapsed around me. A beam thudded down inches from my feet. White dust coated everything, making me cough. I reached for my trash can disguise as the door shoved open to admit a bunch of smuggler bugs ready to zap anything that moved.

I was a statue in the dust. Reallllly starting to hate paralysis guns.

They said many things and made many gestures, and I understood none of them. I found myself being dragged by the ankle — wow, the indignity — down several hallways while all I could do was hope I left a messy trail of dust for them to clean up. Finally, they threw me into another room with a fine view of the floor. More sharp words, then a door locked.

"So you're not a ghost," said a human voice.

Someone brushed dust off my clothes and turned me over. A short Latina in reddish work pants and a gray shirt with a wrench logo. I'd never seen her before, which was more than a little strange. The list of humans on the planet was short. But then, this whole criminal compound wasn't supposed to be here, so I guess it wasn't that strange.

While she waited for me to thaw enough for a proper conversation, the stranger told me her side of things. Apparently, her name was Jacinta, and there was a *lot* going on that wasn't supposed to be.

"We're hoping that the terraformer is easy to find and that Loyll can also find *us* after he's got it," she was saying when I started to thaw. "Honestly, the whole thing is more than a little slapdash, but we didn't have a lot of options."

I couldn't quite move my jaw yet when the door opened for a repeat performance. This time they threw in a familiar-looking jumpsuit that flopped like a rag doll.

"Con!" Jacinta said as the door shut, and I strained my eyes sideways to see. Something was climbing out of the suit. Something with tentacles, and a vocabulary full of complaints. Ah. That made a lot more sense.

"Any word from Loyll?" the tentacle alien asked — Con, I assumed.

"No, not a thing," Jacinta said. "Do you know what those explosions were?"

"I know the Hive shot back at something with the ground-to-space guns," Con said. "I heard them talking about it. Otherwise, I dunno. The communication with their ships in space is down too." He looked toward me. "Maybe our new friend broke them. Who's this?"

"I haven't had the chance to ask," Jacinta said. "Looks like she'll be able to tell us soon, though."

An octopuslike face suddenly loomed inches from mine. "Hi there. Can you talk yet?"

With some difficulty, I found that I could. "Yyyyes.

231

And you're not going to like what I saw. Is Loyll a tiny robotic guy? Flies a rounded yellow spaceship? Eager to terraform a world for his people?"

"Um." The pair of them exchanged complicated expressions.

Jacinta spoke up. "Guess I win the bet about his organics-to-cybernetics ratio. Sounds like that whole body was a shell. Where is he?"

"Gone," I said. "Buggered off to space with the terraforming thing." I strained to sit up. "I know that's not what you were hoping to hear."

Con slapped a tentacle against the floor. "No, it's not!" he said. "I can't believe he lied about the teleporter. How are we going to get out of here? Wait, how did you get in?"

I told them about my own ill-formed plan and the fleet of locals outside. As I'd suspected, these guys confirmed that the farmers didn't stand much of a chance against the arsenal that these high-tech criminals had on hand.

"Hopefully they'll see that and keep their distance," I said. "Maybe they can get someone else to help. I have no idea who's close enough right now, though. And the timeline is short to shove one of these guys in front of a camera to prove that it wasn't humanity's fault about all the rabbits."

"Police?" suggested the tentacle guy.

"Doubt it."

"News crews?" asked the human.

"Useless."

"Surely somebody," the human said.

Something else exploded. Then another thing. And another. By the sound of it, bombs were going off in a circle all around the compound. That had to be from a spaceship. But whose?

Chapter 36
(Zephyr)

It was exhilarating, riding into battle at the helm of this sleek warship with unlikely allies by my side. Vittr piloted the craft with a constant stream of grumbles in a language that I did not know, and Roka did not translate. I'm sure it was largely complaints about the immoral villains that besmirched his species' good name. We were on the same page about that. This crime ring had to go *down*.

And of all of us, none were inclined to wait for an official verdict when I knew where the base lay, and every one of us was ready to break shells.

The ship moved with startling speed. Vittr had us there nearly as soon as Rumble's crew shut the door behind themselves. They all bristled with weapons, while Roka planned to use the ship's guns, and Dragon didn't need any.

I stood in the center of the command cabin, calling the shots. Rumble waited in the doorway behind me with a smile that I chose to interpret as fond.

"There it is!" I exclaimed. "Fire!"

Under the dancing fingers of Roka's single hand, the ship launched a missile of some sort that burst in midair. Vittr chattered angrily while he moved the ship closer, and Roka fired again. This shot made an explosion of a different color, but it did no more damage.

"What is it?" I asked. "They didn't have a force field before!"

Over Vittr's chattering, Roka said, "They do now. But Vittr thinks we can find a weak spot. Hold tight."

The ship moved in a circle, firing around the compound, while insectile villains appeared at the doors with weapons to fire back at us. These made more of an impact than Rumble's had, but not by much.

I was wondering why they didn't have anything more impressive when we reached the wall with the gaping crater. A separate hole marked the ceiling nearby.

Rumble laughed. "They've already got problems! Come on, land this thing and let's go make 'em worse." His cronies chorused agreement behind him.

Vittr said something, to which Roka nodded. "We may have allies inside," she said loudly. "We don't know what caused that hole. Only fight those who offer you a battle!" She repeated this to Dragon, who nodded with an audible whuff through his nostrils.

Vittr said something else, which Roka didn't translate until she'd followed his pointed directions to retrieve an orange can of something from what looked like the previous pilot's interrupted lunch. She held it up for all to see, and said simply, "The bad guys inside look like Vittr. Make sure you don't shoot him." She handed it to Vittr, who popped the lid and dumped an unpleasant-looking bright orange sludge over his own head. He complained loudly while he smeared it around — Roka helped get it down his back — then he promptly went back to the controls. A leaf-green bug man with silver joints, liberally smudged with orange. There definitely wouldn't be another of those inside. At least it smelled appetizing; like some form of seafood.

Vittr spoke briefly as he turned the ship toward the crowd of enemies leaving the building from all sides. They carried a variety of weapons now.

Roka shot a few of them (So dramatic! Like an action-adventure!), then they shot our ship, and there was no more question of when to land and resume the battle on foot. It was something of a sudden impact. My shell hit the floor hard.

Everyone complained, but no one admitted to actual injuries. While I scrambled to my feet, it pleased me to see that I was far from the only one to have fallen. I said nothing about it. Doors opened, and Rumble's crew led the charge.

Dragon thundered out after them (they wisely parted to let him pass). Vittr did more things to the controls, opening a hidden compartment with more weapons, including something more suited to Roka's arm. I bravely shouldered the large paralysis gun myself. Vittr grabbed something I didn't recognize, and we joined the fight. A wide empty space lay between the ship and the compound.

Thank you, Dragon.

And thank you, Rumble! He and his crew were doing a marvelous job of keeping the attackers back. I couldn't honestly tell which of their guns were paralysis weapons and which were the more lethal kind, and honestly, I didn't care. This smuggling ring would go down by any means necessary. Vittr plowed a speedy path toward the building, with Roka and myself close behind. Close-ish, in my case. These aliens were fast.

I kept my wits about me as I ran across the grass, with my weapon ready and my eyes darting in all directions. When I neared the building, I saw movement in the distance.

Dozens of trucks hovered at the edge of the canyon, with a veritable crowd of Rockbacks! Maybe they were the ones who had shot the building!

"Roka!" I shouted over the gunfire. "We should join up with—" But as I spoke, they all got back into their trucks, with a struggling bug alien tied up in the back of the biggest one. The bulk of the fleet turned and peeled off toward the distant town, leaving only two vehicles parked by some boulders, as close to out of sight as possible. The drivers observed the battle from afar.

"Never mind!" I told Roka.

She glanced at the dust cloud and nodded. We proceeded toward the enemy stronghold. Vittr was already at the door, crouched to peek in at ground level. He waited for us before slipping inside.

We followed. So did Rumble's crew. The next few

minutes were a wash of turmoil: running and shooting and hiding and pretending we had more of a plan to this than just "wreck everything."

Not that we needed one, really. Dragon, in particular, was great at wrecking everything. He smashed in every door that we passed and broke anything that he decided looked dangerous. The villains fought back, but only the lower-ranking ones without any spangles on their exoskeletons. I started to get concerned that the masterminds were either gone, hidden deep, or about to mount a surprise attack.

I was distracted from these worries by the sound of a familiar voice.

"In here!" Robin yelled from behind a door. "Let us out!" Two other voices joined her, speaking in several languages as the captives pounded on the door.

Dragon was the fastest, but I was closest, and I found that the door didn't need a key from this side. I swung it wide, greeting my friend with a smile, a paralysis gun, and a small army. "You're free!"

"Zephyr!" Robin exclaimed, clearly delighted. She and the other two spilled out of the room — another human and a tentacle person — were those the two we'd met earlier? Impossible to tell. Everything was moving too quickly to be certain, what with the ongoing battle and the shouting and Dragon charging off to wreck something else. Now was not the time for chatting.

"Got any more of those?" Robin asked, pointing at the paralysis gun.

"I think Vittr does," I said, searching for the orange-and-green. There he was, yes, with a couple spare weapons slung around his waist junction, nearly as food-covered as he was.

He didn't mind parting with them, and no one complained.

"This way!" I declared, pointing in the direction Dragon had gone. We went that way in a mad charge that shook the floor. I had never felt so alive.

We made good progress through the compound,

wreaking havoc as we went, fanning out to check every hallway, until one of Rumble's people who'd run ahead dashed back to report what looked like the leaders escaping.

That wouldn't do. We changed our angle of attack and ran for it.

Only a portion of the army remained with me at this point; I couldn't tell at a glance how many had gone a different way, but it was lots. I heard Dragon off to the side, smashing something made of glass, and Robin had stuck close to me, but otherwise, the familiar faces were all down different hallways.

I wished them all well, and focused on *running faster* so I could stop the villains who had caused so much tragedy in my family and community.

We reached a secondary hangar — the first was a lost cause — with only one ship and a ceiling open to the sky. A handful of spangled bug leaders were climbing in. I shouted and fired, and I wasn't the only one, but the ship lay in its own private force field bubble. We could only watch as the last criminal stepped inside, the engines roared to life, and the door slowly shut on our only chance of catching them.

I screamed in rage and threw myself against the force field. I could see them laughing at me through that open door. Other people around me fired weapons, but it did nothing.

Then localized chaos erupted inside the ship, with the villains shouting and moving around in the tight quarters, and the faint sound of yet another gun going off. The villains by the door shoved each other in an effort to leave the ship.

A yellow one sprang out, only to get zapped in the back by a paralysis beam. He clattered to the floor inside the force field while the ruckus in the ship settled into an eerie calm. Those of us outside quieted in confusion.

Then a single bug alien stepped outside, holding a paralysis gun aloft in victory. He was green, with no spangles. His joints were silver, and there was hastily-wiped-off orange coloring in every crevice.

I learned later that Vittr's triumphant shout said "They are bringing bad name to the species NO MORE!"

Cheers shook the room. Vittr bowed theatrically, then stepped back inside to turn off the motor and the force field. We all stampeded over to congratulate him and tie up the villains securely.

They would face the law! At long last.

I couldn't be happier.

At least I thought so, until Rumble gave my cheek a caress and a wink. Suddenly the future looked absolutely grand.

Chapter 37
(Robin)

I took a position at the comm center that I'd recently crept past in a trash can, sitting now on an alien chair that looked more like a weightlifting bench, and I prepared for an exciting phone call. Vittr had already showed me which buttons to press. He was away in search of somewhere to wash off the festive shrimp paste while I called the turtledillo authorities.

"Greetings; what is the nature of your emergenc— Oh!" The dispatcher on the video screen broke off when she saw a human smiling back at her.

I waved. "Hello! Long story, but the camouflaged smuggler's base in the Footprint of the Moon has been neutralized. We could use some help before they all wake up."

"Yes, of course!" she said, regaining her composure. "Roughly how many smugglers have been apprehended? And are they offworlders or Rockbacks?"

I gave her the rundown with my best estimate, which I felt was pretty accurate since I'd seen the room where the baddies were being stored like so many bug-shaped sculptures. Rumble's crew was currently sweeping the compound for any holdouts.

The dispatcher gave me good news in return. "There are already camera drones on the way to you, since we received a report about the battle there from civilians who managed to capture an offworlder."

"Oh, they did it! Hooray!" I sat up straighter. "Was that enough evidence to prove that Earth had nothing to do with the smuggling?"

"Yes," she said. "The offworlder's confession was accepted."

"Wahoo!" I cheered, waving my arms in a most unprofessional manner, but I didn't care. The alliance was saved!

The dispatcher withheld judgement. "We're trying to get in touch with the authorities at the space station," she said. "I understand there's something of a crisis underway there, so we may have a bit of a wait, but I'm sending our forces to you. Please hold."

When the screen turned a swirling blue, I collapsed back onto the chair-bench in relief. We were off the hook. I wouldn't get sent home in shame, to a lifetime of regrets and sadness, and neither would my coworkers. No word yet about the animals in the woods, but I was willing to bet we'd be allowed to catch them soon.

I listened to the action outside while I waited for the dispatcher to return. A snatch of English sounded like the other human telling Dragon that something was safe for him to eat. The deep voice was Rumble's, and the higher one was Zephyr, following him around like a smitten puppy. Somebody fired a paralysis gun, which made me worry, but it was just a single shot with no voices raised, so I relaxed again.

I turned my head in time to watch a pair of Rumble's people drag yet another frozen bug alien toward the holding room. The shot must have been just in case.

The screen chimed, and I sat up to greet the dispatcher with questions about rabbits. Her answers were encouraging.

"We should have an override approved soon for the sovereignty of the forest," she told me. "It's linked to the one allowing the forces to enter the Footprint of the Moon, which should be just minutes away. I'm not sure about the space station authorities— What's that?" She turned to speak with someone offscreen. "I've just been told that we did get in touch with them, and they're changing route."

"Oh good," I said, just as people outside started

shouting. "What's that?" I asked, though the dispatcher couldn't know. I yelled toward the corridor, "Hey, what's happening?" Nobody answered me. Then I remembered the security cameras. "Where is it; that was one of these other screens... Aha!" I left the chair and the worried dispatcher to get a close look at the view outside the compound.

Multiple spaceships had landed, though no one had gotten out yet. Rumble's people were threatening them and demanding that they declare their allegiance. I rushed back to the screen.

"Hey, if that's the space cops, can you relay a message to them that there are probably only two people here who can translate between them and the locals? One's me, and the other is a narrow alien with just one arm and leg. I gotta go in case she's not already out there. Thanks, bye!" I left the screen on because I'd been taught never to hang up on emergency operators, then I ran for it because I didn't trust anyone involved not to get trigger-happy.

Roka stood at the entrance, doing her best to communicate with both groups at once. Her grasp of Rockback was pretty good for someone obviously new at it, but this was a tricky proposition. I jumped into the fray.

"Guys, put the guns down. Hey in there! It's safe to come out, just don't shoot anyone! All the bad guys are in a room thataway."

The tentacle dude joined us and greeted the space cops like old friends, which made everything easier. Eventually, all the twitchy people stood down, and we showed the nice folks with spacecuffs toward the holding cell. They were a mix of humans, tentacle types, and one blobby fellow that I knew better than to stare at. I wanted to; Waterwills were rare in my experience, but this one probably got that a lot.

As I looked away, stepping aside to let them work, I wondered just where Rumble's people had disappeared to all of a sudden. Nobody was paying attention to me anymore, so I went and looked.

Following voices, I reached the side door just in time to see a tender goodbye between Rumble and Zephyr. Lots of caresses with all those arms. Rumble said something quiet that sounded like a promise to meet up later, then he climbed into the seat of an exceptionally spangly hoverbike that wasn't made for him. He had to crouch there with his lower arms grasping the cushion and his upper arms working the controls.

I had just enough time to take in the awkward sight before he blasted off across the landscape with all his cronies behind him. They raised a racket, as well as a dust cloud despite the hover engines. I coughed and waved it away, squinting. Not a space cop in sight. I wondered if they would even care that these ne'er-do-wells had stolen a whole fleet of offworld transportation.

Zephyr waved goodbye into the dust with three hands, the last one shading his eyes. "Those bikes don't turn invisible," he told me. "But they're much better than anything local. Rumble considers them fair payment for helping defend everyone's territory from these evil interlopers."

"Yeah, guess I can't argue with that," I said. "And they can't get into space, so probably no one will hassle him for dangerous tech." I gave Zephyr a sidelong look. "I'm surprised you didn't go with him."

The little accountant gave me an affronted look. "I have authorities to talk to," he said. "I want to see that everything gets taken care of."

"Also fair," I said. The dust cloud thinned, though I could taste the grit in my teeth already. "C'mon, let's make sure the space cops don't leave before talking to the local authorities. They shouldn't be long now."

"Yes, I see the drones." Zephyr pointed out a handful of flying specks approaching from the left while the dust trail led right. "Let's go prepare a meeting." He scampered back inside, and I followed close behind him.

The turtledillo peacekeepers did arrive soon (with vehicles that *didn't* make a dust cloud), followed by news crews (with vehicles that did), and if I thought that was a circus, it was nothing compared to when the Seer ship touched down.

I'd never seen these highfalutin' supercops in person before. They were *weird*. Their ship looked bizarre from the start: made from some kind of liquid metal that moved like dignified black jello. It settled in for a landing without any visible propulsion system, and tendrils of ooze reached out like landing gear to guide it into place. The whole thing glorped onto the ground. Then a door unfolded into a ramp, and the Seers paraded out... and they had faces full of tentacles because of course they did. Telepathic ones.

I happily let the space station cops be liaisons. They probably had more to discuss anyway. I heard a snippet of conversation about reparations that the cops would have to make to gang members of a different species who they had shot earlier, and that sounded like a whole lot of "not my problem."

But then of course, the Seers wanted to interview everyone present, and "interview" meant a telepathic face hug. I got in line between Zephyr and Dragon, doing my level best not to show any nervousness. Keeping Dragon calm was enough of a distraction.

"This should be over soon," I told him. "They just want to see our memories of what the bad bugs did."

Dragon nodded vigorously, shifting from one foot to the other. <Want hurry,> he signed with a grunt. <Many memories to show.> He ground his knuckles into the dirt like he was giving it a noogie.

"Yeah, me too," I agreed.

Zephyr poked me in the back, a gesture that would have made a polite tap on another turtledillo's shell. "Sorry," he said. "Is this process... unpleasant?"

"It shouldn't be," I said. "I've never done it before, but everyone says it's easy."

Zephyr accepted that, standing as tall as he could while the Seers came down the line, and I hoped I hadn't lied to him.

Dragon was eager to go first. I watched as the tall figure in dark flowy robes placed hands on his shoulders and tentacles on his face. They were both still for a long moment — the only motion was the faint patterns on their robe, which moved in hypnotic spirals — then the Seer stepped back and moved on to me.

I put on an excellent act of pretending not to be terrified, if I do say so myself. I knew it was safe, and civilized, and very necessary right now, but some things will upset the human hindbrain no matter what. A bundle of wiggly tentacles coming at you was one of them. I closed my eyes.

At the first touch, a wordless query popped into my head like someone inputting a computer search. My memory banks responded. I was treated to an accelerated replay of all that had happened to me in the last few days relating to the criminal ring that had caused so much trouble. Interesting to watch. I wondered what memories the other people in this lineup had to contribute and what the Seers thought of it all. I got absolutely zero feedback from the connection.

Then it was over, with another wordless thought appearing in my mind, this one of gratitude. The tentacles withdrew. The Seer stepped to the side and bent over Zephyr. My clothes were only a little damp with nervous sweat. I breathed deeply and answered Dragon's questions about tentacles.

Further along the line, the other human sneezed and muttered about allergies to alien plants. It was a lovely sunny day.

After that, it devolved into a whirlwind of activity, most of which I didn't have to handle myself. The Seers took custody of the criminals, vowing to work with the space station's police forces to round up the rest — many of whom had infiltrated the cops' ranks. Sounded like a right mess. But at least the station wasn't damaged.

I said my goodbyes to the civilians who'd gotten mixed up in this before they caught a ride back home. I committed their names to memory in case I ever saw them again.

"It was a pleasure getting locked in a room with you," I said, offering a handshake to my fellow human.

Jacinta laughed. "Likewise!"

Con's tentacleshake was unpleasantly squishy, but I'd had worse. Roka's single hand felt strange in a double-jointed way, and Vittr didn't even try. He just raised his pincer arms and exclaimed, "Hooray for all of us!"

"Hooray!" I cheered. The whole group joined in, even Zephyr, who probably hadn't understood the words. Dragon roared. This meant we had to reassure more than a few onlookers, spacer and local alike, but it was okay.

Then the foursome were hustled off into a ship, and some official-looking turtledillos ushered Zephyr, Dragon, and me toward landbound transportation. I had a fleeting thought that the trip to the space station would be both farther and faster than the one we were about to take in hovercars.

But for the first time in ages, we weren't in a hurry. How nice.

Unfortunately, that was the only nice thing about the trip, since the Rockback cruiser barely fit me, and Dragon had to ride in the jail cell in the back. It didn't take quite as much convincing to get him in there as I expected. He knew this was the first step toward going home.

The next step was making it through the throngs of paparazzi who swarmed us at the capital. This time when Dragon bellowed, Zephyr and I just grinned.

Our escort took advantage of the sudden gap in the crowd to direct us through a door that the news crews didn't dare breach. This building had been made with interspecies diplomacy in mind, so we had plenty of space to stand up. Vertically, anyways. The room was crowded with turtledillos in agrarian shell paint, which turned out to be my friends, the heroic farmer types.

"You live!" declared Beetle. "Well done!"

"Well done to *you*," I replied, "Getting that smuggler to the authorities!"

Moondark raised her beak with pride. "I tied t'raincoat around his head myself."

"Your ruckus made a fine distraction," Beetle told me.

Sunrise came trotting in with my coat, which the couple returned with fanfare. I thanked them and introduced Zephyr and Dragon (who they had politely not asked about yet).

Our talk was interrupted by the arrival of some very high-ranking authority figures, a couple of which were even human. We went over everything again. I managed to ask a few questions in between answering them: was the alliance *really* safe? (Yes, well done.) Were we allowed to catch the animals yet? (Yes, and people were already working on it. A spaceship or two were lending their scanners to the cause.) Fantastic. Was there anywhere I could get a change of clothes? (After the debriefing.)

We talked ourselves hoarse — at least those of us who understood the language; Dragon was offered cushions to rest on, and he took a nap at the side of the noisy room. I was more than a little jealous. But all this history in the making needed my attention.

Finally, the authorities had talked to us enough. They moved on to make decrees and give a press conference or whatever, leaving us civilians with a promise of "reimbursement for any material losses incurred during relevant adventures." Moondark looked particularly happy about that. When I remembered that my wallet and phone had been taken, I was too. A swarm of underlings took over. They made notes about expenses and contact information while human diplomats arrived to wake and escort Dragon away.

He accepted this attention with regal aplomb, making sure to give Zephyr a pat on the head and me an overwhelming hug before he went. My back popped in three places.

When I could breathe again, I said, "Goodbye! I hope you have a nice flight home. Lots of people will want to talk to you there."

The gorilla nodded. <Dragon will write book about adventure,> he said. <Be famous.>

"Fine plan," I agreed.

He followed the diplomats away while Zephyr and I waved. The farmers were leaving out a different door (time for more waving), and official-looking turtledillos announced that there were cars waiting to ferry me home and Zephyr to where he'd left his own car in the rough part of town. They assured him that any damage or loss would be covered. I thought privately that he might take the chance to go visit Rumble already, though it was none of my business if he did.

"Well," Zephyr said briskly, "I guess I'll see you at work at some point!"

"Definitely," I told him. "I'll be around for as long as you folks will have me."

"I daresay that will be a long time if the two of us have anything to say about it," he said, which got a smile from me.

Even if this problem was too big for me alone, I thought, *I didn't have to handle it all by myself.* I'd stressed about breaking my track record of success in things I really threw myself into, but it had never been about my solo efforts. *On Earth or light-years from home, teamwork wins.* I'd remember that next time.

At the polite insistence of the waiting turtledillos, Zephyr led the way to the waiting cars, and I was happy to follow. To home, and rest, and rabbit-catching, and a long future as one of the few select humans on this alien world. I couldn't wait.

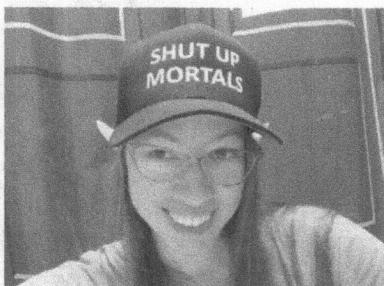

Mara Lynn Johnstone grew up in a house on a hill, of which the top floor was built first. She split her time between climbing trees, drawing fantastical things, reading books, and writing her own. Always interested in fiction, she went on to get a Master's Degree in creative writing, and to acquire a husband, son, and three cats. She has published four books and many short stories. She still writes, draws, reads, and enjoys climbing things. She can be found up trees, in bookstores, lost in thought, and at:

Website: MaraLynnJohnstone.com
Twitter: @MarlynnOfMany
Tumblr: @MarlynnOfMany
Facebook: facebook.com/AuthorMara

Printed in the USA
CPSIA information can be obtained
at www.ICGtesting.com
LVHW031618150924
791134LV00013B/72

9 798218 088071